"I'm glad yo

"It's hard...when it lives inside you. I held Mexico inside for so long. It hurt. It's painful letting it out. But it's far more harmful to keep it in," she added.

"If Jaime finds us—if he comes for you or Babette— I will end him, Pia. I'll make it so you never have to look over your shoulder again. And I owe him for every sleepless night you've ever had. For every day you had to wade through to find yourself again, I will put that son of a bitch in the ground."

She didn't know how to take that. Sam, pure and true, wanting to take a life. Not as a soldier in the name of his country.

Even if that life belonged to her personal demon... *Not Sam*, she thought with a slight shiver.

She would learn this island, in and out. If Jaime came, she would be ready for him.

Dear Reader,

It's often difficult meeting characters in books (or movies) who represent me and my neurodivergent friends, family and colleagues. It's even harder to find a female main character who does so—certainly one without smelling salts or a fainting couch or one who is neither mocked nor misunderstood.

When I read Sherry Thomas's Lady Sherlock series for the first time, I felt wildly excited to learn that Charlotte Holmes is a neurodivergent FMC who has carried a popular series while solving cases, outwitting villains and falling in love with the dashing Lord Ingram.

While it seems that neurodivergent representation is on the rise in the world of publishing, I felt inspired by Lady Charlotte and heroines like her to introduce Pia to the Southern Justice trilogy.

Even before her experiences in human trafficking made her everyday struggles with trauma, depression and anxiety a challenge, Pia has always been different from her peers. She's also built her own business, is a single mother and refuses to cower or back down when the man who made her life a living nightmare returns. She is strong, resilient and worthy of love and the life she has fought to make for herself and her daughter.

Writing a book is never easy, but this one was especially challenging because of some of the subject matter—also because I wanted to give Pia the book she truly deserves. I hope I've succeeded.

Happy reading, as always!

Amber

CROSSING DEADLY TIDES

AMBER LEIGH WILLIAMS

ROMANTIC SUSPENSE

Harlequin®
ROMANTIC SUSPENSE™

Recycling programs for this product may not exist in your area.

ISBN-13: 978-1-335-50280-3

Crossing Deadly Tides

Copyright © 2025 by Amber Leigh Williams

For questions and comments about the quality of this book, please contact us at CustomerService@Harlequin.com.

TM and ® are trademarks of Harlequin Enterprises ULC.

Harlequin Enterprises ULC
22 Adelaide St. West, 41st Floor
Toronto, Ontario M5H 4E3, Canada
www.Harlequin.com

Printed in Lithuania

MIX
Paper | Supporting responsible forestry
FSC® C021394
www.fsc.org

Amber Leigh Williams writes pulse-pounding romantic suspense and sexy small-town romance. When she's not writing, she enjoys traveling and being outdoors with her family and dogs. She is fluent in sarcasm and is known to hoard books like the book dragon she is. An advocate for literacy, she is an ardent supporter of libraries and the constitutional right to read. Learn more at www.amberleighwilliams.com.

Books by Amber Leigh Williams

Harlequin Romantic Suspense

Southern Justice

Escape to the Bayou
Crossing Deadly Tides

The Coltons of Arizona

Colton's Last Resort

Fuego, New Mexico

Coldero Ridge Cowboy
Ollero Creek Conspiracy
Close Range Cattleman

Hunted on the Bay

Visit the Author Profile page
at Harlequin.com for more titles.

For Boo.

Remember that question we asked each other once:
What's your favorite word?

I've found mine. It's *Sissy*.

Thank you for being my first and forever friend.
This one's for you.

Prologue

Pablo Solaro, the man with the shrinking cap of black hair and kohl-black eyes, perused each of them.

"You are Americans."

When Grace spoke up, Sloane hissed, "Don't tell him anything."

Pablo's expression didn't change, but the air around him felt relaxed and self-assured. Amusement flickered across his gaze. "You remember my son, Alejandro?"

Pia reached for Grace's hand when Alejandro moved into view. He smiled, too, but not the pleasing smile he'd aimed at Grace over the last few days. This one was lethal and knowing.

The postgraduation Mexican vacation Pia, Grace and Sloane had embarked on felt ideal only a few short hours ago. Sloane had rented the luxury oceanfront villa on the tip of Isla Mujeres with money earned from the Escarra rum business. Her father, the senator, wouldn't have been pleased with how she'd spent it. Nor would Grace's mother. Both thought the girls had taken a road trip to the Florida Keys.

The getaway had felt like paradise. They'd swum in turquoise waters, explored Mayan ruins, zip-lined and enjoyed the local party scene.

That was how Grace came face-to-face with Alejandro.

Pia and Sloane had watched the couple drink and dance and agreed that their friend was more than deserving of a fling.

Now they knew that Alejandro had been the linchpin—the reason the men had stormed the villa, thrown hoods over their heads and shoved them into waiting cars.

"You son of a bitch," Sloane muttered at him.

Alejandro pointed to her. "This one will be trouble," he told his father.

"She will be separated from the rest if she cannot be compliant," Pablo noted.

Separated? Pia stepped closer to Grace. Her friend squeezed her hand in a viselike grip.

"This one gave herself easily," Alejandro said of Grace.

Grace made a choked noise. "Why are you doing this?" she asked.

"It's just business, *carne fresca*."

Pia knew the words meant *fresh meat*. It was what their kidnappers had called them at the villa. Her stomach pitched.

"This one," Alejandro said, addressing Pia for the first time. "The dark one says she's a virgin."

Grace drew in a breath as Pia flinched. She looked at her friend. "Did you…?" Pia whispered. "To *him*?"

Grace's brown eyes flashed with tears. "I may have. Offhand. I'm sorry, Pia. I didn't know he was—"

"No talking." Pablo didn't raise his voice. He didn't have to. A chill knifed through Pia as he surveyed her. It took everything she had not to shrink back. "She'll fetch a better price than the others."

Sloane advanced, all legs and authority. She towered over both men. "Our families will come looking for us. If you lay a finger on—"

Alejandro silenced her with a backhand.

Sloane went flying.

Pia cried out. Grace surged forward, hands balled into fists. Their kidnappers rushed in, pulling her back by the arms. Sloane sat up, blood forming at the corner of her mouth. She locked eyes with Pia.

Pia reached for her. Someone restrained her, and she heard a scream as the room erupted into chaos. She called for Sloane as she was pulled away.

The door swung shut in her face.

She saw the car—not the van they had arrived in, but an unfamiliar vehicle with a driver ready behind the wheel. He motioned them forward.

Pia dragged her feet. She wouldn't be separated from the others. She called out again for them.

A hand covered her mouth, silencing her.

The man in front of her was tall—as tall as Sloane. His shoulders were wide under a cream-colored shirt unbuttoned at the collar. Dark hair hung long and clean around a chiseled face. His lips pursed in a shushing motion.

It was his eyes that stilled her. Like Alejandro's, they were midnight black, but they glittered. Not with malice or intent, but with something softer and covetous.

"Your name is Pia," he said.

The kidnappers hadn't called them by name. The sound of her own made her head clear. She jerked her chin in a brief nod.

"I am Jaime."

She didn't want to be afraid. She wanted to be strong, like Sloane and Grace. Her chin wobbled and her heart pounded, but she asked, "You're one of them? A Solaro?"

He lowered his face toward hers. She recoiled, though he smelled richly of cologne. His lips curved as he scanned every inch of her face. "I'm the one who's going to save you."

She shook her head but froze mid-motion when his fingers feathered across her cheek. She wanted to tell him not to touch her but couldn't get anything out except, "My friends…"

"If you come with me now—if you're a good girl—I'll make sure of their safety."

She swallowed. Her throat felt bone dry. "You can do that?"

"I can do anything."

"You'll take us home?" she asked hopefully.

His smile broadened as he thumbed the pulse in the hollow of her throat. "I will take you home. Right now."

As he pulled her toward the black car, she looked back at the warehouse, where she could still hear shouting and commotion.

He put a hand on her head, forcing her down into the back seat of the car.

Jaime didn't take her home to New Orleans. He took her to the hacienda. And what followed was a nightmare.

Chapter 1

Twelve years later

The day died like a phoenix, its fire tail plummeting toward the horizon.

Pia Russo stood on the bow of her skiff, a long-handled, three-pronged spear pole clasped in both hands.

The front of the boat glowed white as it bobbed above the restful waters of the pass. The beam cut across the shallow sea floor. Over time, the tide had made the bed gentle and rolling. Under the glare of flounder lights, it looked like the surface of the moon.

At least, that was what her daughter used to say.

Feet planted on the bow platform, Pia rotated her head to the stern where Babette sat, one hand clamped on the tiller, the other holding a science fiction novel. Her face was lit by the book light clamped between the pages and her dark eyes followed the flow of words ravenously.

Eleven, Pia thought with both a pained twang and a sense of wonder. Her baby would be eleven in a month's time.

Lately, Babette talked less about imaginative things. Her mind was encyclopedic, quicker to inform, question and correct every day. She'd skipped another grade level at the beginning of the school year.

Pia wondered if studying elbow to elbow with brooding teenagers from eight to three every weekday was the reason for her daughter's bouts of moodiness. Thank goodness she still sought science fiction and fantasy worlds in quiet moments—and that she still liked to paint. Flamingo Bay, the sliver of a community Pia had chosen on the Gulf of Mexico to raise Babette and help find her feet again, reserved a booth for their resident child artist at the spring arts and crafts festival. People gathered outside, craning their necks to watch her bring her seascapes to life.

An art school in Georgia had recently offered her a scholarship.

Was the reason Babette politely declined because she wasn't ready...or because she sensed Pia's reluctance to let her go?

Pia drew the cold, salty air deep into her lungs. It peeled back the cobwebs.

When she had found the jewel-bright piling house hidden among the white sand dunes a heartbeat away from the crush of the sea outside Flamingo Bay, she'd found her center. The sea had grounded her. She'd been on the brink of motherhood, riding the hard edge of trauma.

She'd stood on the beach, cheeks wet with drying tears, and listened to the treacherous breakers thunder and die as they collided with the shore. Babette's feet had paddled on the underside of her hands, as if eager to outswim the tide. And Pia had felt her mind go quiet for the first time since Mexico.

Babette and the sea. Those were the reasons Pia had rebuilt her life—rebuilt herself.

The girl who had left for Mexico had died there. The hacienda had claimed her. Its walls had been her tomb.

The whish of minute waves made Pia cant her ear toward

the mouth of the pass. A north wind had calmed the Gulf to a whisper. Still, that unceasing pulse called to her. It made the ache in her lower back and the dregs of this morning's upset stomach shrink away. Her doubts and questions scattered, and she focused again on the floor of the pass. "We're drifting away from the wall," she noted.

Babette lifted her attention enough from the pages to course correct. The skiff nosed toward the seawall. "Sorry," Babette replied. "The current."

"It's low tide," Pia noted. "This is a good spot. Can you keep us here?"

"Um." Babette's voice was laced with uncertainty. "I'd have to put it in Reverse and steer backward..."

"Do you think you can?" Pia asked, turning to look at her daughter, more curious than expectant.

Babette closed the book with a snap and set it on the bench next to her. Without a word, she shook back her long fall of black hair. Both hands wrapped around the tiller. She switched gears, bumping the boat into Reverse. Eyeing the distance to the wall, she began to steer.

"A little closer," Pia urged, watching the bottom. She could feel the tide. It slipped and grabbed the hull, making Babette work for it.

She didn't complain. Stubbornly, she inched them closer, shortening the distance to the seawall where their prey would sleep.

Pia didn't have to look back again to know Babette's mouth was set in a line, her eyes arrows of intent. Babette may prefer to live in books or through the world on her canvas, but she was born with sea legs and a will of iron. Warm Gulf tide pools, lagoons and inlets were her habitat as much as they were the sandpipers' and the fiddler crabs'.

"Good," Pia praised, pride flashing. Her breath caught

when she saw an impression in the sand. "Hold it steady," she added, quieter. She tightened her grip on the spear pole.

She timed it, pulse rising with each second. Thrusting the pole downward, she threw her weight behind the points of the gig.

Under its sand blanket, the flounder kicked, fighting the gig's teeth.

"Cut the engine!" Pia called. She went down on her knees to keep from tipping over the side.

Babette turned off the trolling motor before scrambling across the bench seats. "Did you get it?"

The flat fish writhed, weighty with desperation. Pia didn't move, and the boat came to a standstill. The effort not to lose the fish swamped her body with heat. Sweat popped along the collar of her windbreaker. "Bucket?"

"Ready."

Pia waited until the flounder weakened, making sure the prongs had gone all the way through its hide before she fed the length of the pole back through her hands.

"Mom," Babette breathed, her hands coming to rest on Pia's shoulders as the oblong shape of the fish appeared over the gunwale. "It's *huge!*"

The flounder made it over the side without wiggling free and Pia allowed herself the first lick of excitement. "Twenty inches," she estimated, aiming for the bucket Babette had brought forward.

"More!" Babette shrieked.

"Hang on," Pia cautioned, unable to fight a smile. "We need to get him loose."

They worked together. The flounder plopped into the water-filled bucket. Then Pia let the gig fall to the floor of the skiff, the pads of her palms protesting and weariness settling in.

Babette rose to her feet, fists pumping in the air. "We did it!"

Pia caught the glint of childlike glee in Babette's eyes. Her heart soared. Things had been stilted between them since Sam's departure after Christmas. Babette had blamed her preoccupation on her studies, preferring to spend more and more time in her room with books and music or in her studio painting in a cloud of ruminating silence.

Pia had felt her child slipping away. She mourned the playfulness, the impishness and all the childish tendencies that were crinkling and fading like leaves after fall. To glimpse the playfulness again, even for a second, soothed. They'd needed this experience.

Babette clapped her hands. "It's twenty-two inches. It must be. We'll be eating flounder for days!"

"There'll be plenty," Pia said. Flounder piccata over rice was Babette's favorite meal.

"It's even bigger than the one we caught with Sam," Babette chirped. "Remember?"

Sam. Pia's smile tapered off.

The glimmer in Babette's eyes dulled. Her grin slipped. Her face heated, anger spurring underneath. "You do remember?"

Pia nodded. "I remember."

"It's a good memory," Babette insisted.

"I never said it wasn't," Pia replied.

"Then why do you look like that when I talk about him?" Babette charged, pointing to Pia's face.

Pia fought the urge to reach for her cheeks. "Like what?"

"Like someone gigged *you.*"

"Don't be silly," Pia said, shifting the bucket so that it was out of the way. She climbed to the back of the boat, hiding her face in the darkness. "The tide's taking us out. We need to get back into the lagoon."

"If talking about him makes you so upset, why do you wear his ring?"

Pia froze with her hand on the tiller. "What?"

"His ring." Babette gestured to the hand Pia had placed on her knee. "The diamond ring he gave you for Christmas."

Pia looked down. Even in the dark, the solitary diamond glimmered. Her heart picked up pace. The ache behind it seared. "It's just a ring."

"You act like I don't know anything," Babette complained.

"You know a great deal," Pia said, hoisting the tiller motor and dropping the more powerful gas-powered engine's propeller into the water. She yanked the pull start, and the satisfying roar told her they'd make it without paddling.

"Why can't you just come out and say you and Sam are engaged? What's *wrong* with you?"

"Enough, Babette," Pia said, not raising her voice but injecting enough authority into the command to make Babette's questioning nature simmer into the same brimming silence she'd practiced for the last eight weeks.

The Gulf's whisper had grown to a wet hiss. Babette dropped to the platform of the bow, arms knit across her front and mouth puckered in a pronounced frown.

Pia looked away and put the motor in gear. She turned the bow before the Gulf's waves could spray them and accelerated to break its backsliding pull. As the bow lowered and the skiff cut across the channel, she watched Babette turn to sit cross-legged, facing forward, her back ramrod straight.

Regret soured Pia's mouth. She rode the wave of guilt that had been her boon companion since her fight with Sam and the ultimatum he'd left with her.

It's all or nothing.

He'd given her the ring in the bed they'd come to share over the last five years. His blond hair had been sexily rumpled. The bare skin of his perfectly sculpted shoulders had caught the moonlight beaming through the window. He'd offered her his heart. His name. His love, forever. *Be my wife, Pia.*

She had been paralyzed.

…my wife…

Those two words had transported her back to the hacienda. As if she'd never left. Over the years, the trauma hadn't completely subsided. It had lain in wait for quiet moments to flood her dreams or, on the worst days, make her check the locks on the doors compulsively.

But after twelve years, those pockets of terror had lost their razor's edge. They had grown far between. She couldn't hope to be rid of them forever. She knew that. But she'd basked in the certainty that they could no longer control her.

Until…*my wife.*

Jaime Solaro's voice had felt as close as ever.

…kiss·me, my little wife…

…hold still for me, chiquita…

…be a good girl and don't make me hurt you…

Nausea made her stomach roil. She pressed her hand to it, to the secret she held there. For the first time in a long time, Pia wished she were on solid ground. She wished for something loud enough, sure enough, to drown out Jaime's words.

Sam had been patient. And kind. It was his kindness that had endeared him to her. He'd known from the moment they met she had been through something she was trying to forget.

He had taught her to steer a boat, to flounder, the names of the intricate series of inland waterways and how to navigate them. He'd taught her all the best fishing spots and watched Babette while Pia cooked and cleaned. Pia had been content to call him friend…though the silent glimpses he stole of her when he thought she wasn't looking had grown longer. When she'd learned to raise her eyes to meet them, he would look away, caught. But after a while, he hadn't. And something inside her had felt safe enough…hopeful enough, to whisper his name.

No, it hadn't been anything more than friendship until the long, mutual looks had become too much—until they'd made her ache. Softly at first. Then…*oh saints*, eventually she hadn't been able to stand the sweet, keen sting. The anticipation had grown too big, too loud. One night, after Babette fell asleep to the sound of Sam reading, after Pia watched him carry her small form up the stairs to her room, she broke. She'd tucked Babette in and kissed her baby's hair, turned out the light, making sure the window was locked.

She made it to the landing before dragging Sam to her by the collar of his shirt and kissing him senseless. His breath had seized and his body had grown still.

He hadn't claimed her mouth; he'd sipped from her, impossibly tender. And her heart hadn't clenched with fear, as she'd expected. It had raced as anticipation and longing swept her away. She'd never had that. Before Mexico, she'd never had a boy touch her, kiss her. The hacienda had stolen her freedom, her innocence, her agency…

She'd mourned all of those things. But at last, she'd chosen. She'd chosen the man who had waited for her to trust enough, to feel safe enough, to let him in.

Why? she'd asked Sam once.

Why what?

Why did you wait so long for me? she'd wondered, studying the way her fingers fit between his.

I've waited my whole life for you, Pia. A smile warmed the words. *I figured another few years wouldn't kill me.*

The novelty of tripping into love for the first time had been equal parts lovely and alarming. Babette's open and complete admiration of him had only encouraged her.

Babette had badly wished for a father figure. The mother-daughter bond had felt ironclad. Her and Pia's life in the beach house had felt complete. Until Sam, it hadn't occurred to Pia that Babette might want or need something more traditional.

Babette's insistence that Sam play a larger, more defined role in her life grew louder and louder. She hadn't batted an eye when Sam moved in.

For Pia, learning to make space for Sam in her home hadn't been as easy as falling in love with him. Before motherhood, before Mexico, she'd depended on herself. Her father had died when she was young, and her mother never recovered.

Pia hadn't thought to question Luna's long bouts of melancholy when she'd kept to her bed, drunk herself stupid or refused to do anything for herself.

Pia hadn't questioned it until she became a mother, too. She'd felt herself inching close to the same pit of despair Luna had never clawed her way out of, and she'd reached for the self-reliance she had developed as a young girl.

Luna died several months after Pia was rescued from Mexico. She hadn't wanted to live in her mother's bayou house, not with despair beating against the walls of her head.

Finding the place in Flamingo Bay had felt like a turning point. Heavy with third trimester weight and pangs, she bought the beach house—the dream house—and learned, slowly, to live with the quiet.

Pia had returned to her mother's house, Casaluna, with Sloane and Grace to ponder whether the ancient place was worth selling. A torrential flood had swollen the banks of the bayou and Babette had chosen that moment to come into the world.

When contractions started, Pia had had no choice but to drag herself up to her old bed. With Sloane and Grace's help, she'd pushed her daughter into the world.

A week after Babette's birth, she'd returned home to Flamingo Bay. And though Grace and Sloane visited often, Pia had taken on motherhood single-handedly. She'd met Babette's needs while working a full-time job, earning her open water dive certificate and her professional diving and guide certifications, buying a boat, and starting her own business, Salty Mermaid Tours.

Babette had traversed the stages from baby to toddler to child all too quickly. She'd started insisting on independence, too—carrying her own bucket, walking up the dunes without a hand to hold, dog-paddling in the shallows—and Pia had wondered how her mother had stayed in bed, how she'd closed her eyes to her own daughter's milestones, big and small.

When Sam moved in, it had been challenging to accept the fact that she no longer had to change light bulbs or prepare every meal. Admittedly, she'd clung to her responsibilities.

I was yours, Sam said before he left. *But you've never really been mine. Have you, Pia?*

That *was* had been stuck on a loop in her head for weeks. Had that been his way of saying he no longer loved her?

She looked down at her hand, his ring. He'd left it on the dresser when he'd dropped his ultimatum and made it clear he was going back to the Middle East. She'd left it there for days, wondering what to do with the conflict, the hurt, the longing.

The diamond caught a moonbeam. The gleam lasted a split second. It was enough for her mind to flash back to

Christmas when Sam knelt in the tangle of sheets and opened his hand to show her.

Pia let herself return to that moment. Just for a second. She'd seen the ring and the intention in his soft blue eyes, and she'd known what it meant.

Sam was asking her to marry him. And for one unguarded moment, she'd felt...

Babette stood up at the bow, grabbing the taut bowline for support. She pointed, looking back at Pia.

Pia frowned as the beach house came into view. As they approached from the east, the lagoon narrowed into a brackish, narrow channel with still, murky waters. There was a small dock to tie the skiff up to.

The light over it was out.

Pia slowed to idle speed. "It's dark," she warned when Babette squatted to make the leap to the dock. "Don't miss."

Babette jumped, bowline in hand. Pia released a breath when she heard her paint-flecked Converses thump down—one, two—on the dock's composite boards. She cut the engine, reaching out to grab the edge as Babette pulled the line tight and wrapped it around the farthest cleat.

Pia tossed her the rope for the stern when she finished. Through the heavy-lidded sea oats, she could see the lights waiting for them on the balcony. She glanced up at the light pole above them. "Maybe something kicked the breaker."

"Bucket," Babette said, reaching.

Pia picked up Babette's book and passed it to her before she hefted the heavy five-gallon tub. "Set it near the sawhorses, then go up and bathe. I'll clean the fish." Weariness was a weighted blanket around her shoulders. She did her best to shrug it off. There was work to be done before bed. She recognized the pit in her stomach. Hunger. They were still an hour from dinner.

She would need to eat something small between now and then to keep the hunger at bay. Over the last few weeks, she'd been tiptoeing around her stomach's sensitivity. She took turns being so hungry the bite of it was impossible to ignore or the idea of food made bile knot at the base of her throat. It had made the long days aboard the *Salty Mermaid* ferrying marine scientists from the nearby sea lab to wildlife beacons nothing short of hell.

As Babette started to carry the bucket across the dock, something crunched under her feet.

She slowed. Pia went rigid.

"Why is there glass here?" Babette asked. She looked up at the light.

Pia, too, lifted her chin. Her heart dropped. "Wait," she said before Babette could take another step.

"What?" Babette asked as Pia set the spear pole on the dock along with the small airtight box that held her cell phone, keys and wallet. As Pia climbed onto the dock, Babette added, "Mom?"

Pia tried to see through the dark. There was a carport under the house. She could see the silhouette of her truck and the old motorcycle Sam had been tinkering with before he accepted the invitation from a colleague overseas. There was no sign of a strange car in the drive, and it was quiet. Winter had choked out the voices of frogs and night bugs.

The quiet was normal. Any other night, Pia would revel in it. Tonight, however, she felt the tiny hairs on the back of her neck stir. The skin at the small of her back itched.

Pia lifted the points of the gig, still dark with the flounder's blood. "Stay behind me," she whispered, then led the way forward.

Chapter 2

Pia took the steps one at a time. The wind chimes hanging from the eaves of the house didn't greet her, and the stillness felt...eerie. She slowed as she ascended to the balcony.

"Mom, what's wrong?" Babette said behind her.

"Sh." Pia scanned the deck. Several Adirondack chairs faced the rail. Their cushions were in place. A small table before them held the queen conch shell Babette had dug out of the sand after a tropical storm had swept across their swath of coastline.

Smaller shells surrounded it, a colorful medley of unbroken cockles, nautiluses, tulips, cones, whelks, crowns and abalones. Babette could rattle off their scientific designations and name the animal that had made each shell its home.

The bed swing on the far end of the balcony lay untouched. A rain chain dangling near the glass entry door to the house was quiet. The bulbs of the bistro lights that crisscrossed overhead gleamed.

Babette shifted her feet. "You're starting to weird me out."

Pia shook her head. "There's no one here."

"Of course there's no one here," Babette said. "We live more than a mile from town. It's the offseason. And the closest houses are summer rentals."

That was precisely what Pia kept telling herself. But the

itch at the base of her spine had grown into a prickling sensation. She felt eyes…watching.

"I'm starving," Babette complained. "And we both smell like fish. Can we go in?"

Pia looked down at the fist balled around her keys. The one for the balcony door was clamped lethally between her first and middle finger. She released the tightened muscles until she felt her high shoulders lower. Digging deep, she inhaled. Forcing the air out, she tried to deflate the tension that had sunk into every line of her body.

And felt the sensation of the baby moving inside her womb for the first time.

She cradled the space, closed her eyes and softened the rest of the way.

It was the first time she'd felt that bud of life. Relief and wonder coursed through her. Her heart bounded in response.

She must have made some sound because Babette's hand gripped her wrist. "Are you okay?"

Pia heard her daughter's alarm and nodded swiftly. "Yes." She opened her eyes and found Babette's heart-shaped face staring up into hers. The sensation subsided. Pia raised her hand to Babette's cheek. Smiling, she traced the flat ridge of her cheekbone beneath her thumb. "I'm hungry, too."

Babette's dark eyes searched Pia's. "You were sick this morning. I heard you."

"I'm better now," Pia assured her. "You don't have to worry about me, bébé."

The light in Babette's eyes dimmed before she lowered them, her small knob of a chin dropping to her chest. She jerked her shoulders in a shrug. "It's just the two of us here now."

That had once been enough, Pia thought, and felt all the little thrills she'd felt just moments before vanishing. Would it be enough again if Sam chose not to return? Pia didn't lift her hand from her daughter's face, knowing that would break Babette's heart. And, admittedly, her own.

"Do you think he'll come back?"

Pia brushed her fingertips over Babette's curtain bangs. "Of course he will," she said in a whisper, even as doubt circled and preyed on her.

Surely…no matter how upset Sam was with Pia, he would come back for Babette's sake. He'd spent the better part of the last decade showing her how a father should behave—how a real man showed up.

It had been a marvel for Pia to watch. She'd never had that. The foolish young man her mother had fallen in love with met an untimely end. And though her mother had made no secret of the men she brought home to her curtained four-poster bed at Casaluna, none of them had stuck around to act as a stand-in.

Pia unlocked the door. It stuck a bit when she opened it. Peering at the jamb, she noted the loose seal. The beach house may have been newer than dilapidated Casaluna, but its proximity to the sea meant rapid weathering.

She was just happy it wasn't a roof leak. She wasn't keen on climbing a ladder with her constitution so finicky.

Babette washed her hands at the sink before drying them with a towel. Then she opened the refrigerator.

"No soda," Pia told her, propping the spear pole against the wall next to the door. She selected a fillet knife from the butcher block on the counter. "It's after seven. And there's school tomorrow."

Babette let out a well-worn sigh, choosing a bottle of water. "I'm going to shower," she said as she slouched out.

Pia fished a recycled plastic grocery bag from the cabinet underneath the sink, then filled a large bowl with ice. Taking one long look around the living room with its walls of periwinkle, seascapes Babette had done through the years, black-and-white photographs, dry arms of driftwood, and shadow boxes filled with feathers, sand dollars and cuttle-fish bones, Pia made sure everything was as it should be.

Again, the quiet struck her. Except for the faint whisper of running water in the pipes above, the house was silent.

Pia found her favorite photo on the wall. The frame had been decorated with shells. Babette grinned toothily, her eyes squinting against the hard angle of the sun. Next to her, Pia's face was aimed sideways, and Sam's was turned to hers. Their soft smiles said everything.

She swore the place at the base of her left ring finger thrummed beneath the ring band.

She thought of the mess she would make cleaning the fish. Using two fingers, she wiggled the ring from her finger and set it on the window ledge above the sink. Moving to the door again, Pia went back out, doing her best not to think about Sam or where he was or if he thought about her. He thought about Babette, she knew. Worried about her. Missed her.

Does he miss me, too?

"Stop it," she muttered. "Just…stop."

Underneath the house, she found the sawhorses in place. Babette had set the flounder on the plywood that straddled them like a table.

Pia turned on the single bulb above the garage area and went about the process of cleaning the fish.

She had the fillets cleared of scales, skin and bones when she heard the balcony door slam and fast footfalls thumping down the steps. She set the meat in the icy dish and wiped her hands on a tattered rag as Babette clambered to the ground. "Mom, I can't find Slider!"

Pia set the rag aside. "Did you take him out of the terrarium before we left?"

"No," Babette answered. "Please help me find him!"

"Okay," Pia said. "There's no need to panic. I'm sure he's in the house somewhere."

"What if he fell down the stairs?" Babette moaned as Pia picked up the dish. She'd have to come back and clean the mess of blood and scales off the plywood later. "What if he's lost somewhere, hurt?"

Careful not to touch her daughter until she, too, had washed her hands, she put her arm around the slender line of Babette's shoulders. "I'm sure he's fine. Come on. It's too cold for you to be outside without socks or shoes."

They climbed the stairs together. In the kitchen, Pia set the dish on the counter next to the sink, then washed her hands with soap, scrubbing under her nails and between her fingers. She dried them before joining a frantic Babette in her search for her pet turtle.

"He's not in my room," Babette explained.

"Did you check under the bed?"

"Yes."

"The door was open?" Pia asked, pushing her way into Babette's room on the second floor. Her studio was on the third floor, so there was no paint, canvas, or drop cloth in this room. Instead, there were piles of books, others shoved onto shelves. The window blinds were closed and the large terrarium in the corner was empty.

"The door was shut," Babette countered. "And so was the lid."

Pia inspected the top of the terrarium. "This was shut, too?"

"That's what I said. I don't *get it*!"

The lid was sealed. Slider might be fast, but he'd have

trouble climbing to the top of the tank, much less opening the lid and then shutting it before scuttling away.

As Pia crouched to look under the bed skirt, Babette made a frustrated noise. "I told you, I already checked under there."

Pia moved another stack of books aside and found nothing but dust motes, the missing lens of Babette's telescope, and a litany of gel pens. "Did you find any droppings?" she asked, scanning the rug.

"Not one," Babette said, folding her arms over her stomach. An anxious line formed between her eyes. "He's gone. He's really gone this time."

"No," Pia said with a firm shake of her head. "He's just hiding. That's all. You check the study. I'll check the other bedroom."

Babette nodded before rushing from the room in her blue-and-gray Ravenclaw pajamas.

"Come on, Slider," Pia said, entering the bedroom she'd chosen for its proximity to what had once been the nursery. She often found that she still needed Babette close, just one wall away, when she slept. "Where are you?"

She switched on the light, then crouched to check under the queen-size sleigh bed Sam's great-aunt had bequeathed her.

Lyudmyla Filipek had been born in Ukraine and migrated with her family, Sam's grandfather included, to Minnesota during the Second World War. She'd married a captain of the Royal Canadian Air Force and after retirement, the two of them fled the harsh winters in the north for the balmy Gulf Coast.

A widow, Lyudmyla had lived in the closest neighboring beach house. In her own way, she had taken Pia under her wing.

Single girls like us need to stick together, Lyudmyla had said in her thick Eastern European accent, clinking her glass of freshly squeezed lemonade against Pia's on the balcony where they spent the bulk of the afternoon watching the sea change.

At that point, Lyudmyla was in her nineties. Pia and Babette had enjoyed three years of her steadfast companionship before she succumbed to pneumonia after several weeks in a hospital in Jackson, Mississippi.

Sam had been at her bedside. Lyudmyla had waited for him to leave the room to find a nurse before she took Pia's hand in hers. A smile had warmed her thin, white face as she said, *He is my nephew Maks's youngest son and my favorite great-nephew. A photographer. Started out in the army and wrote columns. Newspapers printed them anonymously for the safety of him and his brothers-in-arms. 'The Realities of War: A Soldier in Afghanistan,' they called them. He left the army after his older brother, Alek, a wartime correspondent, disappeared over there. Sam became a war photographer just to find him and bring him back to Maks and his wife, Deirdre. None of them have been the same since Alek disappeared. But Sam is a fine man. A finer one you will not find in this world.*

She'd grinned at Pia, the impish, knowing grin of a matchmaker, and winked. *I told the nurses you are his wife. Otherwise, they would not let you see me.*

Sam had called his great-aunt *Myla*, and he'd been her constant in the last weeks of her life. He hadn't balked at Pia's frequent visits with a toddler in tow. He'd been warm with Babette and her. When it became clear Lyudmyla was losing the battle with her health, Pia had asked Grace to keep Babette so Pia could join Sam in his vigil.

By that time, Lyudmyla had subsided into a sleep doctors warned them she would not return from. Luna had done the same thing in the days leading up to her passing. The sound of the monitors beeping, droning, the smells of hospital, illness and death waiting in the wings, had bombarded Pia.

It was Sam's quiet voice that had soothed her. His presence, too. She hadn't had to wonder why he was Lyudmyla's favorite. He'd shown her.

When Lyudmyla slipped away, he hadn't hidden his grief. She'd seen it working in the muscles of his jaw and flooding his kind eyes.

She hadn't held a man, before or after Mexico. After, she had spent a great deal of time rejecting the idea of intimacy...proximity, even.

Yet she hadn't been able to watch him swim against the tide of sadness alone.

She'd held him, let him lean, let go. And she'd found that the circle of his arms didn't make her panic. It hadn't made her ill. She'd held him and she'd felt one tiny broken piece of her mend.

She'd helped him, his father and mother clean out Lyudmyla's house. Sam had joined Pia and Babette on their long afternoon walks along the beach. He and his father had even helped her carry the heavy sleigh bed up the two flights of stairs into her bedroom.

I'll come back, he'd told her and Babette when it came time for him and his parents to leave—them to the North Shore, him to DC.

Pia gritted her teeth as she searched for Slider in corners, empty gift boxes she'd yet to clear from the chaos of Christmas, and the closet. Sam hadn't said those words this last time.

She knew she could text him, as Babette did with regularity. They had emailed each other frequently when he'd gone to the Middle East in the past. On a job for DC. Or to look for Alek. His brother's disappearance haunted him to this day.

He was never gone for more than six weeks at a time.

It had been eight. And Pia had to admit Babette wasn't the only one growing anxious.

Pia's stomach groaned. Pressing her hand into the ledge of the dresser, she took a moment to swim her way through hunger.

He didn't know about the baby. The one they'd made together.

She needed to tell him. She knew that—*had* known it from the moment the strip turned pink.

But his silence felt damning. And he'd always promised to come back.

Why hadn't he this time?

She couldn't imagine her first conversation with him since he went away, since his proposal, being, *Hey, remember that night on the beach when we did more than snuggle? Well, congratulations, Filipek, you're a daddy!*

She'd let him come home and decompress from the Middle East. Then she would find the right words and tell him.

Hopefully, she wouldn't be showing more than she was now. Her pants were already tight. Her wet suits, too, she'd found out during a dive a week ago. Babette would notice eventually, and Pia knew her texts to the Middle East would convey the news.

She switched on the bathroom light as she stepped in. No sign of a reptile. Pia checked behind the commode.

The big smeared handprint on the mirror made her stop.

She clutched her heart when it hit the downbeat harder than usual. It picked up pace as she remembered the broken light at the dock.

The handprint was bigger than hers. It cloaked the reflection of her face, leaving her shoulders standing headless.

"Mom?"

Pia fumbled for speech. "I'm… I'm here," she called back

through the house. She rounded the jamb as Babette sailed through the door, cell phone in hand.

"It's for you."

"Me?" Pia asked. The phone case glittered. It was Babette's, not hers. She thought of Sam. The relief nearly choked her.

"It's not him," Babette said, reading Pia well.

Pia struggled with disappointment. "Then who…"

"I don't know," she said with a shrug. "I heard it ring and there was this guy on the line with a weird voice who asked to speak with my mother. Did you find Slider?"

Pia shook her head as she took the phone. "We're going to need to check the first floor."

"I knew he fell down the stairs," Babette groaned.

Pia raised the phone to her ear. She waited until Babette raced from the room to continue the search. "Who is this?" she demanded. "Why are you calling my child's cell phone?"

"Buenos dias, chiquita."

The voice was familiar to her.

Ice skated down her spine. At its base, the nerves prickled with intensity. Her heart lurched toward her stomach, and she couldn't breathe.

"I knew I'd find you," Jaime said in an even tone. As if this were a pleasant conversation they'd exchanged every day since she'd escaped the hacienda. "My little wife."

She fled for the window. Yanking back the curtain, she searched the gentle slope of the shell-lined drive, the yard, the reeds, the ink-black water.

"Tell my daughter not to worry about her turtle," Jaime continued. "Papa's on his way."

In the distance, on the narrow, two-lane road falling away at the shoulders, she saw the unblinking eyes of LED headlights. She backed away from the window, ended the call and screamed for Babette.

Chapter 3

"Where are we going?"

"Hurry," Pia said urgently. Her teeth chattered with anxiety and adrenaline. She locked her jaw to make them stop and struggled to think through the fear.

This far south, cold temperatures made iguanas drop from trees. She felt like one of them. The ice seeped into every channel, every molecule, debilitating her. Her limbs felt heavy, her movements halting.

She had to think. They had to get out of the house. She yanked Babette's full wet suit from her closet, dumped out her school backpack, and stuffed it inside.

"Why do I need my wet suit?" Babette asked. "We can't leave now. We haven't found Slider!"

"He's not here."

"What do you mean, he's not here? *What is going on?*"

Pia charged into the hallway. She took the stairs two at a time to the kitchen, switching off lights as she went. "I need you to do exactly as I say."

"Who was on the phone?"

Pia threw open the pantry door, grabbed a box of power bars, water bottles, stuffed them in the bag. Her pulse roared in her ears. Her head was spinning, a tornado of terror. She had one foot in the beach house and the other in the hacienda.

Get Babette out, she ordered herself and zipped the backpack in a jerky motion. "Turn out the lights."

"All of them?" Babette asked wildly.

"All of them," Pia bit off, hooking the strap over her shoulder. When Babette did as she was told, she thrust her coat at her and grabbed her own. "Put this on and your boots. Quickly."

Babette punched her arms through the sleeves, stepping into her rain boots. "Mom, you're really scaring me."

Pia checked the window. The headlights were closer.

She needed a weapon. The spear pole and its three prongs, black with dried blood, centered under her gaze. She grabbed it.

How was she going to get her truck out unseen?

She thought of the skiff. Opening the back door, she grabbed Babette by the shoulder and turned her to face her. "From here, we go quietly. No talking. No questions. Just follow me. No matter what happens, don't make a sound."

Babette's eyes were wide. Her mouth opened but snapped closed when Pia shook her head.

"I'll explain everything later," Pia whispered. She caught Babette's hand in hers and pulled her across the balcony to the stairs.

They crept to the ground. The carport light was off. Pia heard the small sound of brakes shrieking. A flash of headlights cut through the night. "Duck," she breathed as they flooded the yard.

Babette crouched with her near the grille of Pia's truck, her breathing loud as tires crunched over the loose driveway.

"Crawl under," Pia whispered, nudging Babette when her daughter looked at her, bewildered. "Do it," she mouthed.

Babette lowered her head and went down on her stomach to shimmy underneath the chassis. Pia went down on her belly, taking off the backpack. She pushed it and the pole in front of her as she army-crawled to where Babette lay, cheek to the ground. Again, she put her finger to her mouth when Babette's eyes sought hers. She could feel her daughter quaking in fear and wished she could comfort her, but her own hands shook uncontrollably. Working to regulate her breathing, placing one unsteady hand on Babette and the other on the spear, she watched the tires of the oncoming vehicle roll to a stop behind hers, headlights off.

The engine turned off. Doors opened. Four pairs of feet hit the ground. The metallic *chink* of a bullet being chambered was unmistakable.

Babette whimpered.

Pia pressed her cheek to hers, fitting her hand lightly over her mouth. She kissed her temple as the footsteps grew closer. She no longer needed to worry about quieting her lungs. There was no breath to be found in them. Her heart hammered against the ground beneath her.

The men were underneath the house. As they came abreast of Pia's truck, something hissed.

The chassis inched closer to their heads as the tire closest to Babette hissed, too.

They'd slashed the tires.

She felt the tremors going through Babette and kept her hand over her mouth.

Someone spoke, clipped and quiet.

Orders. Pia reached into her distant Spanish, back to Mexico. Memories she didn't want to touch.

Boat. She recognized the word. And *house*.

As two men moved to the stairs and the others walked toward the dock, she waited until their footsteps faded. Then she shimmied out from underneath the truck.

"Mom?" Babette whispered tremulously.

Pia reached for her. "Let's go."

"I can't."

Pia looked over her shoulder for the men. "You have to come with me."

"They'll see us."

"They won't," Pia said, tugging on Babette's fingers. "We need to move. Now."

Babette whimpered again, but she latched onto Pia's hands and pulled herself out from underneath the truck. "Why are they here?"

"Hold this," she whispered, handing her the gig. She spotted the metal snips scattered among Sam's tools near his motorcycle. She grabbed them and approached the men's truck.

"What are you doing?" Babette asked.

Pia located the valve on the driver's-side tire. Using the snips, she cut it in two.

"Mom," Babette mumbled.

Pia did the same to the back left tire. Running out of time, she crept back to Sam's motorcycle. She felt for the ignition and sent up a thanks when she felt the key there.

"We can't take this," Babette said as Pia swung the backpack on and straddled the seat.

"Get on," Pia said, tipping up the kickstand. She took the spear and laid it across her lap. Then she gripped the handlebars.

"Have you ever even driven a motorcycle?"

"Sam taught me." A while ago. But Babette didn't need to know that. "Grab on to me. Feet on the pegs." When Babette did as instructed, Pia took a steadying breath and placed her right foot on the footrest.

She turned the key one click, switched off the headlights fast. The backlight of the speedometer and gas gauge flickered on.

A good sign, she thought. "Please," she ground out. Then she hit the ignition switch.

The motor's purr ripped through the night.

"Mom!" Babette shrieked at the sound of shouting.

"Hang on!" Pia gunned it.

Tires squealed. Gunshots popped. They clanged off the body of her truck. The shells of the drive scattered beneath them. Pia angled the grips to make the turn for the road.

The bike wobbled. Babette screamed.

Fighting for the bike to stay upright, Pia waited until she felt the treads grab asphalt before she ducked over the handlebars. "Stay low!" Babette's front pressed to her back. The bike straightened, steadied, and Pia accelerated further.

The tunnel of palm trees flashed past as they shot through the dark. Pia could see the center line of the road in the moonlight. She followed it, blinded to anything else. The wind rushed at her, forcing her eyes to close. They watered from the cold. She worked to keep them open as her hair streamed back and Babette's sobs cut through the noise.

She slowed to look back once, saw nothing but empty road, then patted Babette's knee. "It's all right!" she called over the wind. "There's no one following us!"

Babette didn't reply. She buried her face in the bag strapped to Pia's back and continued to sob.

"Keep hanging on, bébé," Pia told her before mashing the accelerator again so that the engine whined, and the lights of Flamingo Bay streaked closer.

The town had three stoplights, one diner, a post office, a police station, a church with a steeple, and a town hall. The rest of the main drag was dedicated to a souvenir store, a bait shop, the dive shop and a gas station that carried marine fuel.

It was late enough that the stoplights blinked yellow. As

she neared the police station, she saw that its lights were out. Panic leapt inside her. Would anyone be there to help? Did she have enough time to stop and find out?

Could a small police sheriff and deputy really stack up against Jaime's lethal men? The church steeple's shadow loomed. It moved under the lights lining the street as she drove by, making her jump. Unnerved, she put on her headlights. Not one car was parked in any of the spots downtown. Everyone had gone home for the night. She and Babette were completely alone.

She steered the motorcycle down the slope to the marina. The Salty Mermaid Tours office was situated on the beachfront between the scuba diving school and a kayak rental place. Carefully, she directed the motorcycle into the narrow alley between her office and the school, winding around it to park in the dark, sandy lot behind it.

"Wh-Why are we here?" Babette asked as Pia turned off the ignition.

"I need to grab a few things," she murmured. She waited for Babette to plant her feet and disembark before she stood up, swinging one leg over the seat. "We'll have to be fast again."

"You passed the sheriff's station," Babette said, trailing Pia to the back door.

Pia dug the keys she had shoved in one of the outer pockets of the backpack and struggled to locate the right one in the dark. "I know."

"Those men had guns," Babette said as Pia sank the key into the lock and turned the handle. The security monitor beeped. Pia ushered Babette inside before shutting the door, locking it again and mashing the code into the keypad next to it to keep the alarm from tripping.

"We need to get to the boat," Pia explained. She switched

on the lights and opened the backpack as she went into the locker. "Then we'll contact Sloane. She'll know what to do."

"Why Sloane?" Babette asked, shaking her head. "She's not a police officer."

"She's with the FBI," Pia revealed.

"Oh," Babette said. Her chin wobbled. "You didn't tell me."

There were a lot of things Pia had never told her daughter. *Not now*, she schooled herself, grabbing her thicker wet suit. She put it into the backpack, along with two pairs of booties and fins, masks, regulators, and BCDs, buoyancy control devices. Moving around the room, she added dive weights, a dive computer, knife, light, tank bangers and a compass.

"We're going diving...now?" Babette asked, voice treading lightly. As if she thought her mother had lost her mind.

"It's just in case," Pia said, grabbing another bag and crossing the hall into the kitchen. She opened the cupboard doors and used her arm to sweep the contents into the bag. From the drawer, she grabbed hydration packs and plastic utensils. In the fridge, she found sports drinks and more water. "We won't need all these things."

"Then why are we bringing them?"

Pia used her keys to open the locked door next to her office. Inside, she checked tanks and chose two. "I'm going to need some help to carry all this to the dock."

Babette took the tank Pia handed her.

Pia noted her pallor, her searching gaze and the tears drying on her cheeks. She took a moment. Just a moment, lowering her brow flat against Babette's. Closing her eyes, she whispered, "Breathe."

"Were those men going to—"

"Breathe, bébé," Pia repeated and took her own advice, dragging in a ragged breath and forcing it out. When Babette followed suit, she said, "Again."

Babette took another breath and released it. "I'm scared."

"I know." Pia couldn't tell her how scared she was, too.

"Why is this happening?"

"I'll tell you everything I can," Pia promised. "Right now, we need to get to the dock, load the boat and get out of Flamingo Bay."

"Then you'll call Sloane and the FBI?"

"Yes," Pia said. Pulling back, she gauged her daughter's face. "Are you okay?"

Babette shook her head. "No. But I can carry the tank. And a bag."

"Good." Pia touched her cheek. "I need you to trust me. Can you do that?"

This time, Babette bobbed a nod. Her bottom lip trembled. "I wish Sam was here."

Pia felt herself wish, too. She hefted her tank, then the backpack. On second thought, she grabbed the cashbox from behind the front desk. "Let's go."

Sam Filipek didn't lower into his bunk at Forward Operating Base Delaram. He collapsed into it.

He and his brother's close friend and fellow war correspondent, Stephen Lakhoni, had been traveling across the Registan Desert for a solid week. They'd lived off rations during the day and taken turns sleeping in their vehicle by night. Village to village, they'd questioned and translated, following rumors and chasing ghosts across the arid countryside.

The fatigue went to his bones as he stretched out. He didn't think he had the energy to untie his boots.

Where there were rumors, there were seeds of fact. In his search for his brother Alek, Sam had learned to sift through lies and half-truths like grains of sand. He'd learned Farsi. He could even speak it, brokenly. Stephen was fluent, thanks to refugee parents who had settled in New York when he was two. Between the two of them, they had at last uncovered a skeleton of truth buried in the desert for sixteen years.

Sam thought about the chapel he'd just left and the crude wooden casket at the altar that bore his brother's body. It had been handcrafted by villagers near the site of the massacre that had remained secret for over a decade.

Terrorists had buried the truth. They'd buried his brother with it.

He turned his head to look at the phone beside the bunk. The screen was black, in sleep mode. Pressing his hand to his eyes, he told himself to sleep, too. Just sleep.

Despite the weight of exhaustion, he could no more drop off than he could remove his boots. He lay awake with images burned in his mind. All those bodies…

He knew what war was. He'd fought in war and documented it.

He knew what it meant, and he knew from experience that it often wasn't fair.

But finding Alek's body among those who had been murdered…

It was more than he could handle.

He needed to call his parents. It was midmorning in Afghanistan, which meant that it was near midnight in Minnesota.

He had kept his promise. He would bring Alek back to them as soon as he could find overseas transport for the casket. However, he would need to notify them before the news reached stateside. The papers would pick up the story. So would all the news channels. Alek had been one of the media's own, and his vanishing had made a splash when the war was on.

The US had pulled out of Afghanistan and everyone who

was still searching at that point had stopped. Interest back home had slowed to a trickle.

Stephen had taken the vigil in the chapel after Sam had sat with the casket in the back of the truck for hours while Sam's friend navigated them safely back to base.

The remains would need to be examined to confirm that the body was Alek's. Sam was certain, however. It was a blessing—albeit a small one—that Alek had been buried with the prosthetic leg he'd earned after a bicycle accident when he was five. The serial number had been a match. If that hadn't been enough to clinch Sam's certainty, the slight chip in his left lateral incisor would have been.

Sam stared at the ceiling. The surrounding bunks were empty. There was noise in the corridor—voices, the slap of boots.

It wasn't the noise that kept him awake.

Sam closed his eyes again as the ache went up inside him. God Jesus, he wished he could hear Pia's voice.

But it was midnight in Mississippi as well. And they hadn't spoken. Not since he'd left.

He thought about leaving a text for her. Babette, too. *Back at base. Safe. Coming home.*

Would Pia want him home? She hadn't stopped him from leaving. She never stopped him from leaving. But this time was different. They'd fought. And he'd said it, hadn't he?

It's all or nothing.

It had been eight weeks. No text. No call. Not even an email. He'd left the choice in her hands. Had she fumbled it? Was this her way of saying she didn't want it—him—a life with him?

He didn't think he could take that with everything else and tried to shove the thoughts and emotions in a box, like he'd done since he touched down in Afghanistan.

For the last time, he ruminated. The search was over. He wouldn't have to return to Registan or Delaram again. Not if he didn't want to.

He felt nothing. No relief. Just that ache.

Too tired, he consoled himself. *Too overwhelmed.*

Later, he would sift through what he felt—what he wanted to do in the future. The search for Alek had defined him... until he'd met Pia. He'd left her and Babette to continue the search off and on. But he'd gravitated back to the place his great-aunt Myla had called home—to the place where Pia and her daughter dwelled.

When he thought of home, his mind flew inexorably to them. Ceaselessly, he winged back to Flamingo Bay.

The phone at the bedside chimed.

Sam made himself sit up. He turned his legs over the side of the low-slung bunk, put his boots to the floor. Scrubbing the weariness from his face and the beard he'd grown over the last month, he gathered himself. Then he picked it up.

Babette.

She was still awake? Sam unlocked the screen and toggled the notification.

Her text blazed across the screen.

SOS!!!

Sam stared at the distress code.

He blinked.

The letters didn't change.

Shaking his head, he tapped the window to start a new text. I'm here, bébé. What's up?

He saw the little bubbles that meant somewhere on the other side of the world, she was typing.

New words appeared beneath his.

Someone tried to kill me and mom!

Sam felt himself come to his feet. He read the text over and over.

He hit the call button with his thumb.

Low signal, the screen warned.

He groaned, squeezing the device.

"Filipek."

Sam glanced up and saw the base command officer approaching. Somewhere in the back of his mind, he came to attention like a soldier. Outwardly, he took several steps forward.

"Problem?" the CO asked.

"Yes, sir. I need to make a call."

"Someone back home?" At Sam's nod, he said, "It's late there."

"It's an emergency. My daughter…" He reread Babette's last text. He'd never referred to her as his daughter before. The words had tripped off his tongue easily. He'd thought of her as his own for so long, it felt natural. "There's trouble."

The CO nodded. "With me," he said, and marched out.

Sam followed.

"By the way," the officer said as they wound through military personnel, "a plane will be here tomorrow morning to transport you, Mr. Lakhoni and your brother back to the States."

"That was fast," Sam commented.

"It will be a dignified transfer. Everything a soldier killed in action deserves."

"My brother wasn't a soldier, sir."

"He was a hero," the officer said simply.

Sam inclined his head. "Thank you, sir. My family thanks you."

"In here," the officer said, ducking into an office space. "There's the phone."

"Appreciate it." Sam didn't sit at the desk when the CO closed the door. Lifting the phone from the cradle, he dialed quickly, then rocked from his heels to his toes as the line clicked, connection made and ringing droned in his ear.

It rang and rang.

Babette's voicemail picked up. "Hey, it's me!" she chirped in the recording. "Leave me a message."

"Babette," Sam said when the indicator beeped. "It's Sam. I got your text. My signal here isn't great, but I'll be back stateside tomorrow. I need to know you and your mother are okay. Keep texting if you can't reach me."

He put the phone back in the cradle reluctantly. Then he snatched it back up. He had Pia's number memorized, too. He dialed, willing her to pick up.

"You've reached Salty Mermaid Tours. Please leave your name and number after the tone and we'll get back to you as soon as possible."

"Pia," he said at the beep. "Babette just texted me. She said you two are in trouble. I need you to call me back. Please, call me back and let me know you're all right." He paused, felt the words rise in his throat. *I love you.*

Something tightened around his vocal cords. The surrounding muscles burned. It muted him. He hadn't told her he loved her before he left. It was the first time they'd parted without the words. Remorse sank inside him like a weight. What if he never saw her again? What if his last words to her had been a damn ultimatum? He dropped the phone back into the cradle and took several minutes to gather himself. When he was sure he could speak again, he went through the contacts on his phone until he found the number he needed and dialed it into the receiver on the desk.

Sloane answered after the second ring. "Escarra."

"Sloane, it's me," he said.

"Sam." She paused. "Do you know what time it is?"

"I'm worried about the girls," he blurted.

"Why? Did you hear something?"

He heard something in Sloane voice, a hint of suspicion. A sense of worry bubbled up underneath the fatigue... His voice dropped and he tightened his grip on the phone. "What's going on?"

"I just got confirmation that Jaime Solaro crossed the border from Mexico and is now at large somewhere in the southeast," Sloane told him.

The stripes of the American flag on the wall behind the desk blurred. "You told me Pia's kidnapper was in prison."

"He escaped."

"From maximum security?" he bit off.

"He had someone on the inside."

Sam hissed, pulling the phone away from his mouth. He took two steps to the door, then two steps back in the small space between it and the desk. The walls seemed to shrink. He took deep breaths of air, drawing it in through his teeth, then released it slowly. "When?" he punched out after raising the phone again.

"My sources tell me the breakout took place last Friday. We believe he crossed the border several days ago."

"Several days—" He stopped. "He could be *anywhere* by now."

"We think he's most likely in the New Orleans area," she informed him. "His men hit Grace's apartment."

Sam's blood ran cold. "Is she okay?"

"She got out in time," Sloane assured him. "I'm meeting her tonight at Casaluna."

"Have you heard from Pia?"

"I've been trying to reach her. Have you?"

"No, but I just got an SOS text from Babette," he informed her. "It said, 'Someone tried to kill me and mom.'"

Sloane cursed. "What else? Do you know their location?"

"No," Sam said. "Nothing." He scooped his hand through his hair. It fisted there. "I tried calling her, but I'm still on base and my signal's low."

"I sent agents to Flamingo Bay a few hours ago to stand guard at the beach house."

"I don't think they made it there in time," Sam spit out in frustration. "Look, I can't get on a plane until tomorrow morning. I need you to find my girls. I need you to make sure they're safe."

"In the next few hours, every law enforcement office within a five-hundred-mile radius will have a BOLO on Jaime Solaro. I'll make sure they have Pia's and Babette's photographs."

Sam thought fast. "If Solaro had enough connections to get himself out of maximum-security prison, he's going to have an escape plan. He has a safe house set up for himself somewhere extradition can't touch him. You need to find Pia before he gets there. If you don't, he'll make her disappear again. Babette, too, most likely."

"I'll find them," Sloane swore. "You have my word."

"I'm counting on you," he said with a rasp. He waited until Sloane hung up before doing the same.

He couldn't think about how close New Orleans was to Flamingo Bay. He couldn't think about how he'd left Pia and Babette to fend for themselves while the animal that was Jaime Solaro escaped from whatever hellhole he'd been thrown into.

He thought only about putting his boots on US soil. He needed to find his family before the cartel found them first.

Chapter 4

Screaming.

Pia woke to screaming.

Jaime had left her alone in the bed he'd told her was theirs after she refused to undress for him. He hadn't yelled at her or struck out. Instead, he'd donned the shirt he'd discarded on the bearskin rug at the foot of the bed and said, "Until you're ready..."

Pia was sure she'd never be ready. He'd brought her to the hacienda and proudly shown her closets full of designer dresses and a young maid named Bianca she could call on for anything.

"For you," he told her. "All of it—if you follow one rule. Do not leave this hacienda. For any reason."

He thought she was his wife, and she was too afraid to contradict him. Because while Jaime Solaro seemed kind and even-tempered, she sensed something in him. A darkness he contained with an iron fist under the guise of formality. And she was terrified of what would happen if she did anything to wipe away that polished exterior. That was the only reason she'd let him touch her after the four-course dinner Bianca prepared for them. That was why she had let him kiss her on the balcony before he walked her up the stairs to the bedroom, his hold on her arm not painful but terrifying just the same.

She'd trembled when he tried to slip the straps of her gown off her shoulders. She'd shook so violently his hands had stopped and she had waited, breathless, for him to explode.

Not only had he kept up that facade of respectability. He'd impossibly seemed to understand...or at least pretended to understand. "We'll wait," he'd said, brushing the hair back from her face, "until the time is right."

As soon as the door closed behind him, she'd collapsed in a fit of strangled sobs, unsure whether to be sick or relieved.

She'd told herself she wouldn't sleep, but sleep came for her. She dreamed of Sloane and Grace and what the Solaros were doing to each of them.

The screams she heard when she woke made her launch out of bed and cross the room to the door she had bolted from the inside. She threw it open and ran through the house... down the grand staircase across the marble floor to the spacious kitchen.

The sounds were coming from rooms off the kitchen. A closed door at the end of a dark hall. She tried to turn the handle as the screams turned to crying. She pounded on it. "Grace!" she called, tears blinding her. "Sloane!"

The cries on the other side of the door subsided into plaintive pleas. But it wasn't Grace's or Sloane's voice. It took Pia several seconds to realize that it was the maid—Bianca.

This was her room. And the sounds that broke through her pleading...

Pia stumbled away from the door. Jaime. He was in there.

Her back rammed against the wall behind her. She covered her mouth with both hands. She'd refused him...so he'd gone to Bianca's room.

If she refused him again, would he keep hurting Bianca?

She tried the door once more, unsure how to stop him. Desperate to stop him.

She ran to the kitchen. There were no knives in the butcher block. The pots and pans, even, had been locked in the cupboard.

She'd go for help, she thought wildly. She ran into the wide atrium. Grabbing the handles of the long double doors, she pulled with all her strength.

They refused to yield.

She saw the ceramic vase on the atrium table and picked it up with two hands, ready to hurl it at the closest window.

She froze. There were bars over them. On the outside of the pane, she saw men milling in the motion lights at the front of the hacienda.

Waiting for her to make an escape. Waiting to lock her back in.

She dropped the vase. It shattered at her feet, exploding into shards and dust.

There was no going for help. No escaping this nightmare.

The hacienda was her prison.

Pia jackknifed out of sleep. She felt the scream rising automatically and lifted a hand to her mouth to stop it. Her nails dug into her cheek until she could force it back down.

Next to her, Babette slept soundly. Pia worked to calm her racing heart.

She hadn't had the dream in eight months—and nothing so visceral as this in years.

Chastising herself for falling asleep in the first place, she lowered her hand from her mouth and took a second to reorient herself in the present. The gentle sway of the boat cabin, the electric whirr of the bilge pump…she clung to these sounds of reality and the potent smell of briny sea air. Lifting her arm, she checked her watch: 5:49 a.m.

"Dammit," she muttered, and swung her legs out of the bunk. She pushed herself up to standing and wavered over her feet, taking a step forward to balance.

Pregnancy was hell on even the sturdiest set of sea legs, it seemed. She waited for her equilibrium to adjust, gritting her teeth when it took longer than she would have liked.

In the tiny bathroom off the cabin, she cranked the water on in the small metal sink and lowered her mouth to the stream. She sucked water into it, swirled it around, hoping to rid herself of the acrid taste of terror and sweat. For a minute…two minutes…three…she allowed herself to kneel on the floor in front of the commode, swallowing saliva that pooled in her mouth. Then she breathed diligently through the rolling waves of nausea…she spelled *sesquipedalianism* out loud once, then again backward…

Tender gray fingers of light touched the pane of the small porthole window above her. Those faint tendrils tore at the dark.

Dawn was coming on.

She closed her eyes and imagined it filling her.

The steadiness she gathered around her as a result wasn't as resolute as she would have liked. But she grabbed on to it. It was enough. It had to be.

She checked on Babette in the other bunk before donning her wet suit. She braided her hair as she climbed the steep steps to the boat deck.

The *Salty Mermaid* was a forty-two-foot dive boat. It was large and comfortable enough to support eight divers without overcrowding. The ladder on its stern allowed easy off-and-on access for divers. The deck was shaded, an asset in the summertime when the sun was blistering. The cabin belowdecks was rarely used as a sleeping space. More, it was a safe space for passengers who were suffering from seasickness or who needed to change in or out of wetsuits.

The wind had died. Night still clung to the sky in the west. But those fingers of gray were turning blue in the east. She felt the cold on her face, but not through the wet suit she used often for cold-water dives. It did well to keep her warm and dry.

She climbed to the bridge and studied the monitor.

The trolling motor had kept them anchored at the coordinates she'd set in the wee hours of the morning. Squinting through the windscreen, she saw a few lights blinking onshore as the residents of Pass Christian slowly woke to greet the day.

Pass Christian was fifty-two miles west of Flamingo Bay. Pia had pushed the dive boat through the night. She'd anchored there offshore when her eyes had refused to focus anymore, and she'd had to stumble down the steps to the cabin or slide into an exhausted slump over the wheel.

Pia had pointed the bow west…toward Louisiana. Toward Sloane, who worked out of the Bureau offices in New Orleans. Toward Grace, who lived in the French Quarter in an apartment above Russo's on St. Peter, the pizzeria Pia's uncles, Giovanni and Marco, owned and operated.

Pia had once lived in the apartment, too, with Gio when the scholarship to the private Catholic girls' school a few blocks away came through for her. Luna wasn't well enough to accompany her and set up house in the Big Easy. So Pia had moved in with Gio and his wife, Pauline, above Russo's where she'd lived through the school year, returning to her mother and Casaluna over Christmas and summer break.

The private school girls hadn't liked her very much. They'd called her a charity case. The swamp rat. It didn't matter that she was first in her class. It didn't matter that by regulation, her uniform matched theirs. They'd known who she was and where she came from…*who* she came from. Second-generation Sicilian Americans. The granddaughter of immigrants whose mother drank herself stupid and whose father had died under mysterious circumstances in gator-infested marshlands.

Holy Mother of Mary School had been its own kind of hell until she met Grace. Grace had been accepted there on scholarship as well—she was from the Ninth Ward, and she, too, had been subjected to bullying. Grace had had a smooth way of dismantling bullies with words and had taken Pia under her wing to teach her the same. *Charity case, my wet big toe. Girl, you're the smartest person I've ever met. I'll tell you what. You help me with my calculus, and I'll introduce you to Santana Escarra.*

Santana Escarra, aka Sloane, had made a reputation for herself at the Holy Mother. With strong Cuban heritage and the legs of a track star, she dismantled bullies in equal measure. But Sloane's specialty wasn't words. It was inch-long nails painted bloodred, foul Spanish expletives that made the nuns clutch their Bibles and her uncanny ability to come out on top of any physical altercation. Her wealthy family and her father's senatorial influence had saved her from being kicked out of the Holy Mother altogether.

Grace and Pia befriended Sloane out of necessity. They stayed friends because Sloane had a soft spot for underdogs. But she also had no qualms about inviting them regularly to her parents' Garden District mansion where they bonded over frequent sleepovers, their shared love of hip-hop, paella—which Sloane's abuela made to perfection—and NOLA itself.

From that point on, to Pia, New Orleans was forever associated with the safety and comfort of Grace and Sloane.

Which was why Pia was determined to get Babette there. To the FBI offices and the federal protection Sloane, as an agent, could provide.

As light crept over the undulating surface of the Gulf, Pia looked long in each direction, then checked the radar for approaching vessels. She listened to the coast guard radio frequency. Then she went back down into the cabin.

She made herself eat a satsuma and a protein bar and drank one bottle of water until it was empty. She studied the maps she kept aboard in case the boat's navigation failed, fanning through them until she found the coast of Louisiana.

All those watery channels she could disappear into. Not all of them would support the *Salty Mermaid's* deep keel. Regardless, the possibilities were endless.

She knew better than anyone how easy it was to disappear in the bayous of her home state, by choice or out of necessity.

If she and Babette couldn't safely dock in New Orleans and get to the Bureau offices there, she knew the way to Casaluna. She knew it well. She had the cashbox, too. They could ditch the *Salty Mermaid* and rent an airboat that would take them upstream.

She traced routes on the map with a mechanical pencil as Babette stirred. "Good morning," Pia murmured.

Babette sat up slowly, looked around, then lifted her fists to her eyes to rub the sleep out of them.

She'd done the same thing since she was a baby. She would wake, rub the sleep out of her eyes, then lift her arms to Pia in a silent plea for morning cuddles.

Pia missed those early morning cuddles. As hard as the life of a single mother was, she'd lived for those moments when she could hold her baby in the quiet and rock her. She missed the way Babette had traced the shape of Pia's face with her tiny fingers, how her dark eyes seemed to marvel over the sight of her mother as much as Pia marveled over her.

Pia's heart lurched a little when Babette dropped her arms. Then narrowed her eyes and studied the maps spread across the floor and her mother sitting cross-legged before them. "Are you going to tell me what's going on?" she drawled.

"We're anchored off Pass Christian," Pia said. She followed one of her penciled lines with her finger. "We'll go west-northwest once we set off in half an hour at fifteen knots. We should slip into Lake Borgne early this afternoon. From there, we'll take the Rigolets to Lake Catherine marina and have a taxi take us into the city."

Babette released a sigh. "I didn't mean about where we're going or what we're doing. I meant about last night. Who were those men? What did they want with us?"

Pia blinked at her. She hadn't faced the reality—in all the running and navigation she'd done through the night—of explaining everything to Babette. About Mexico. About Jaime.

Babette's eyes filled with desperate tears. "Would they have shot us?"

"They didn't," Pia said. Later, she would reward herself for speaking the words so clearly.

"But if they had caught us?"

Pia shook her head. "I learned a long time ago that you can't dwell on the what-ifs. You move forward or you get stuck in the past."

"So," Babette said, drawing one knee up to her chest, "those men. They're from your past?"

Pia could no longer hold her gaze. Her eyes fell to the maps. She blinked rapidly to keep them from blurring together as one. "You should get moving. I laid out your wet suit. I'll fix you some breakfast. Then we can head out. We'll meet Sloane—maybe Grace, too, hopefully—at some point this evening."

"I have a right to know what's happening," Babette said.

"Yes, you have every right," Pia agreed, picking up the pencil again. She went back to tracing their backup route through the bayou. The tip broke. She clicked the button several times to lengthen the lead and tried again. "Right now, we need to focus on where we're going and how to get there."

"Then you'll tell me?" Babette asked.

"Yes."

"Everything?"

Pia fought a sigh. "Yes."

Babette shoved her hands through the loose reams of her hair. "Fine." She reached for the wet suit Pia had draped over the foot of the bed. "Why do I have to wear this? I thought we were going to New Orleans."

"It's just a precaution," Pia said evenly. "Once we dock at Saint Catherine, you can change into street clothes."

"A precaution for what?" Babette asked.

Pia shook her head. "Just put it on. Please, Babette." As Babette reluctantly rose to do as instructed, she asked, "Do you need help? I can—"

"I know how to put on a wet suit," Babette replied angrily.

Pia closed her eyes when the bathroom door slammed shut. When she heard the water running, she dropped her head into her hands until her eyes no longer stung.

Unbidden, Bianca's face flooded her consciousness. Dark eyes, blank and staring. A pool of dark blood glistening under her head. The smell of ash and smoke. The groan of the hacienda's second floor above her…

A sob worked its way up Pia's throat again. She made herself look around, remembering where she was and how far from the hacienda she had come.

It was then she saw the cell phone peering out of the blanket on the bunk.

She scrambled to her feet, maps rustling under her as she crossed to the bed.

She picked up the phone and hit the power button.

The screen flashed on. She checked the battery indicator. It was half full.

Pia blew out a tumultuous breath. She thumbed the app on Babette's home screen for calls.

Sam's name in all caps on the most recent call list grabbed her attention. She didn't think about it. She tapped it.

Lifting the phone to her ear, she listened—prayed that it would go through and she would hear him.

Pia.

God. If she could just talk to him for one moment, she would—

Sam's voice came over the line, brusque and professional, his Minnesota accent washing lightly through the words. "You've reached Filipek. Leave a message. I'll call you back."

The tone blared in her ear. Pia felt her mouth open and forced herself to speak. "Sam," she said. Before, with Babette, she'd sounded so strong. Now…

Tears sprang to her eyes. She closed her mouth, dropping her chin to her chest as the words she needed to say tried to shove their way out.

Come home. We need you…

…I need you…

Instead, the sob she'd worked so hard to placate bubbled forth and she ended the call quickly, distressed as it broke free.

The faraway sound of beeping drew her attention back to the phone.

It was back on the home screen. There were no notifications.

She glanced up the steps to the dock. Taking them two at a time, she heard the beeping sharpen, quicken.

She crossed to the bridge and looked at the monitor.

On the radar, she saw the bright orange arrow of an approaching vessel from the east.

Grabbing the binoculars from the console, she followed the deck to the bow. Planting her feet, she fitted the spyglasses to her eyes, adjusting for clarity and panning.

The sky was a pretty peach now. The horizon line split the peach in half, cutting away into dark water. Waves dotted in white kissed the surface as far as the lenses allowed her to see.

The boat's white bow was easy to spot even in the distance, triangled perfectly in front of its curling wake. She couldn't see the faces aboard, but she saw the men standing at the bow. And the flash of lenses trained on the *Salty Mermaid.*

Her pulse jumped. She lowered the glasses. Thinking quickly, she backed away from the bow, then raced to the cabin steps. "Babette, are you dressed?"

"I'm eating," came the voice from below.

Pia looked at the approaching vessel in the distance and measured its speed. "I need you on deck!"

Chapter 5

In trained motions, Pia attached the dive tank to Babette's BCD. She double-checked and adjusted the Velcro strap until the clamp showed resistance. "Lift," she said.

Babette picked up the tank by lifting the BCD. When the tank didn't waver, Pia nodded. "Good." She attached the regulator.

"Mom, I don't want to go down there," Babette said, eyeing the depths at the back of the dive boat.

Pia forced herself to keep her attention on the equipment. She wanted to stand up, look east, make sure they still had time… "Be still," she instructed. "I'm attaching the hose."

"Mom. Please. Don't make me do this."

"It's going to be fine, Babette," Pia said, keeping the words level. She turned on the air tank, twisting the knob all the way, then back a quarter turn. She listened for leaks or blow-outs. Hearing nothing, she felt a small rise in relief. "We're going to be fine."

"I can't!"

Pia looked into her daughter's face. Babette's lips were folded in a thin line. She was pale, her eyes as round as quarters. Reaching up, Pia laid her hands over her cheeks. "Listen to me," she said, fighting to keep the thread out of her voice that would signal uncertainty. "You are a certified diver. You've done this over a dozen times."

"This is different!" Babette's voice broke.

"It's not," Pia told her. She kissed her forehead just underneath her neoprene hood, took a moment to hug her around the shoulders, before she started moving again, checking the air in the tank. "Take two sips for me."

Babette did so. Then, as she'd been trained to do, lifted her thumb to show that the air was on.

"Good girl," Pia said, then helped fix Babette's mask in place. "I'm going to teach you a trick, okay?" She crouched to work the fins over her feet. "Think of the longest word you know."

The skin of Babette's forehead wrinkled in confusion.

"The longest word," Pia repeated. "Got it?"

Babette nodded after a moment.

"Now spell it." Pia secured Babette's chest buckle, cummerbund and stomach buckle in practiced movements. "Spell it once forward, slowly. Focus on the next letter. Only on the next letter until you get to the end."

Babette watched Pia ready her own gear. Then she lifted her thumb again.

"Done?" At Babette's nod, she checked her tank, her lines, the gauge, attached the BCD. "Now do it again. But this time, backward." As Babette did so, she got into her gear, fitting her mask, fins and hood into place. She took a few sips of air, as Babette had done. Then she reached for the long pole of the flounder gig she had laid close by. "When you're done, do it again. This time with the next longest word you know. Then the next. Keep going until you feel calm again. Don't stop until you do. Not even when we dive. Once we're down, I'll only ask you not to let go of my hand. Okay?"

Babette nodded slowly. She didn't hesitate to step up to the dive platform when Pia motioned for her to do so.

Pia looked around. She could just see the approaching boat's tower over the bow of the *Salty Mermaid. Now*, she thought urgently. They had to dive now if they were going to get away unseen.

"Take two more sips of air," Pia told Babette. She placed her air source in her mouth, breathed once. Twice. "Hold the regulator and your mask in place. Look toward the horizon." When Babette obeyed, Pia fit her regulator into place, grabbed Babette's arm and counted the rest off with three taps.

They stepped forward over the water and fell as one into the rolling sea.

"Sam."

The sound of Pia's voice made Sam clutch the phone to his ear tighter. He didn't breathe, waiting to hear more.

The automated voice of his answering service followed. "To replay this message, press one. To delete—"

He cursed. Then he pressed one quickly and lifted the phone to his ear again.

A few seconds of silence. Then, again, "Sam." This time, a moment before the message ended, he heard the muffled sound of a cry.

"Jesus," Sam hissed through his teeth as the automated voice went through the message options again.

"Was it Babette?"

Sam felt a strong hand brace against his shoulder. The warm, weathered undertones of his father's voice should have soothed him, but they couldn't touch the desperation he felt as deep as his bones. "It was Pia."

The hand bore down, squeezing. His father had working-man's hands. He tended to forget their strength. "Did she say where they were?"

Sam shook his head. He made himself turn.

Maks Filipek's rugged face was limned with shadows and fatigue that could only be brought on by grief and worry. He didn't wear age gently, like crepe. He wore it like erosion. The weathering of his face was saved by his Slavic blue eyes that always carried kindness, high cheekbones and a straight nose. He and Sam's mother, Deirdre, had been waiting at Dover Air Force Base in Delaware when the plane carrying Alek's body had touched down.

"She didn't say," Sam said emptily.

"They'll find them," Maks told him, lowering his brow. "The FBI."

Sam thought of the box he'd brought his brother back to base in and the remains he'd help wrap and place inside. He'd been too late—sixteen years too late—to find Alek.

He wouldn't be late again.

Sam opened his mouth and forced the words out. "I need to go."

Maks nodded. "I know."

"I'm sorry," Sam said. "You need me. Mom needs me. But—"

"Your mother and I have each other." It was amazing how that steely, barbed-wire voice could wrap itself so warmly around the people Maks loved. "Once the coroner's office certifies that it is him and his cause of death, we'll take Alek home. In the meantime, we will plan the memorial. The burial. We will have family and plenty of visitors to keep ourselves occupied."

"Dad," Sam groaned with a shake of his head. "You've both been waiting for this. For Alek. And closure…"

"We have Alek," Maks explained. "You made sure of

that. As for closure, you know that sort of thing takes time. We lost Alek a long time ago. Pia and Babette are still here."

"I need them," Sam said. "I need to know they're okay."

"So you'll go," Maks said with a nod. "And you won't worry about your mom and me. Because when you help the FBI find them, we're going to need to lay eyes on them, too. We'll be together, all of us, for Babette's birthday."

"I don't know how long—"

"Sam," Maks interrupted, taking his son's face in both hands. "Go. Find our girls. Bring them home."

Sam let out a breath, trying to release some of the pressure in his chest. It hadn't stopped building since Sloane had called him again to say that the beach house was deserted and Babette and Pia had left in a hurry. His motorcycle had been found at the Salty Mermaid office in Flamingo Bay and the dive boat, cashbox and some equipment from the office were gone. "I love you," he said in a rush, folding his arms around Maks.

"I love you, too." Maks returned the embrace just as hard, slapping him on the back.

The keel of the approaching vessel cut through the water, slowing as it came abreast of the *Salty Mermaid*.

It wasn't coast guard. Or marine police. Nor was it search-and-rescue.

Underneath, Pia held Babette with one hand and the spear pole with the other as the drone of the engine died. They'd swum away at a safe distance, but she could imagine what was happening above the water.

Ropes would be thrown across the gunnel and tied. Men would go aboard the *Mermaid* to search.

They'd search the bridge. The cabin. The hold.

Pia gripped the spear tighter and told herself that they'd

left no trace. There was no diver's flag. If the men thought to search underwater and had the equipment and know-how to do so, she had a head start and the means to defend herself and Babette.

Still, she counted the beats of her heart as the minutes stretched and the boats bobbed as one. Babette didn't move, but stayed in place, kicking lightly with her flippers. Pia held on to another flash of pride, wondering if the spelling trick had helped her.

Droning kicked in again. The search boat's propeller turned. As she watched, it pulled away from the *Mermaid*.

The noise kicked into high gear and the boat sped away, fast, trailed by its own prop wash.

Babette's kicking strengthened as she moved her arms to swim to the surface.

Pia held tight, her eyes on the frothy trail left by the search vessel. When Babette turned her head, meeting Pia's eyes through the mask, Pia gave a slight shake of her head.

Wait.

The sound of the engine died away slowly, leaving the lulling hush of water.

Just as Pia was about to give Babette a nod that it was okay to surface, the *Mermaid's* hull exploded, engulfed in a torrent of flame.

Chapter 6

Sam pulled up to the beach house and put the truck in Park. He cut the engine and stepped out.

It was late afternoon. He'd stepped off the plane from Delaware only an hour ago and had rented the truck from the airport.

Sloane had warned him not to go to the house. *Active crime scene*, she'd said.

He didn't know where else to start.

Ducking under the police tape, he scanned the tires of Pia's truck. The rubber was flat against the ground. Punctured.

All that was left of the motorcycle were the oil stains it had left behind and the tools strewn helter-skelter across the ground.

Pia had left them that way, all this time?

Had she expected him to come back and start exactly where he had left off?

He ignored the frisson of hope. The sight of blood made him still.

The fish's remains rotted, the smell strong. They'd been left with the fillet knife on the board across the sawhorses. Flounder, he thought, studying them.

He walked across the lawn to the sea oats and the dock.

The skiff was still tied off there. Broken shards of glass caught the light. He examined the light overhead.

Sloane had told him over the phone they'd found a bullet casing. Jaime's men had shot the light out and left fingerprints all over the mirror in the main bathroom. Those fingerprints were being analyzed in a lab somewhere.

He walked back to the house and up the stairs. Using his key, he made entry.

The place had been tossed. The couch was on its back, chairs from the dining room table had been broken, the kitchen ransacked...

Sam shook his head. At least they hadn't set fire to it.

Fire had killed the hacienda in Mexico, he recalled from the stories Pia had told him after some time together.

He knew Jaime Solaro's face from photographs he'd found online. He'd seen the hacienda before and after the fire. He'd studied pictures of Pia after she had returned to the States.

Ghosts had lived in those eyes. Ghosts she'd only just started to chase off when she came to the hospital to see Myla, where Sam met the woman his great-aunt had been so keen to introduce him to.

The furniture could be replaced, he told himself, even as violence hummed in his knotted fists.

This had been Pia's sanctuary. It had been the only home Babette had ever known. It had become his.

They had lived here. Laughed here. Made memories here.

Sam had found his ready-made family at the table in the corner over fish fillets and hush puppies. As he climbed the stairs and peered into the first bedroom, he cursed viciously.

What it had meant to follow Pia up the stairs and into her room for the first time...into her bed... Now the mattress was destroyed, the frame listing to one side, and her sheets were tossed and torn.

He veered into the bathroom and saw the handprint Sloane had described where it had been left undisturbed by the crime scene technicians.

In Babette's room, he saw her books ripped to pieces, her single bed upside-down and the terrarium shattered on the floor.

He went through the various rooms again, trying to find Slider among the ruins.

The turtle had made himself scarce.

Fighting the chill and his own wrath, he roamed the first level. The photographs he'd taken had been ripped from the walls. He picked one up off the floor and stared helplessly at the woman in the wide-brimmed beach hat stretched out on the sand, sleeping toddler beside her.

It was the first photograph he'd taken of the two of them— his favorite. The glass had been shattered. He turned it over and extricated the photo from the matting. Tucking it in his jacket, he set the empty frame on the counter.

Something glinted on the windowsill.

He stepped closer.

In a crossbeam of sunlight, a diamond glimmered.

He could suddenly see Pia washing her hands in the sink, back straight, hands lathering each other up under the fall of water from the tap.

She'd taken off the ring to clean the fish.

He'd seen her do that with the mood ring Babette had given her on her birthday years ago.

This was the engagement ring—the one he'd tried to give her. The one he hadn't seen her wear or even hold.

He reached out, picked up the ring and watched the band flash.

Pia had been wearing his ring the night she and Babette disappeared.

He closed his hand around it, felt it bite into his palm.

He'd found Alek and lost the woman he loved and the child he'd started thinking of as his own.

If he didn't find them, he would find Jaime Solaro. And he would kill him.

"The boat washed ashore here in Pass Christian. What was left of it."

The pieces of the fiberglass hull weren't sunny yellow like the *Salty Mermaid*'s. They were charred. There was nothing left to identify it. "How do you know it's Pia's boat?"

"Part of the hull identification number was found," Sloane Escarra said grimly as she stood next to Sam in the boatyard, along with a small crowd of law enforcement officials. She wore dark sunglasses and didn't look at him. But he could feel the anguish pouring off her. "They're a match. We also found what appears to be pajamas in Babette's size."

He turned to stare at her.

She cleared her throat. "Ravenclaw. Right?"

"Goddammit," he bit off, startling several of the onlookers.

"I'm sorry, Sam," Sloane said grievously.

Sorry? He paced away from her, then back. It took a while for him to say what he needed to say. "There's no sign of remains."

"No," she replied slowly.

Before she could go on, he held up a hand. "I'm not going to believe they were on that boat when it blew. Not until I see hard evidence."

Just as he hadn't been willing to believe Alek had died in a massacre. Until he saw his body for himself several days ago. Just because he wanted…wished…hell, *needed* something to happen didn't mean it would.

Just because he wished they were safe didn't make either Pia or Babette so.

It didn't make them alive, either.

He hung his head and shook it forcefully. "I can't, Sloane."

Sloane's throat moved in a swallow. "Sam...if they're not dead, they're either adrift or they're in Solaro hands. Those are the only two scenarios we have left to consider. I've got coast guard and search-and-rescue on the lookout for them offshore, but we've got a front moving in before noon, which means they'll need to be called off until conditions clear—"

"Did you find the tanks?" Sam cut Sloane off as a thought occurred to him.

"What?"

"The air tanks," he said again, trying to keep the fury... the overwhelming tide of disbelief out of his voice. "Two tanks were taken from the Salty Mermaid's equipment room in Flamingo Bay."

"Aren't air tanks flammable?" she asked.

"They could explode," he considered. "But Pia's were made of aluminum."

"So?"

"Tanks made from composite materials and steel are much more flammable than more common tanks made from aluminum."

She stared at him for a full ten seconds. "You're trying to tell me that Pia knew she had to get her and Babette off the boat? And instead of the more obvious course of action, which was running it aground on the beach and making a run for it on foot, you think she had enough time to get both her and Babette suited up and equipped in their scuba gear before diving and—what? Swimming to shore once the coast was clear?"

"Have you ever played chess with Pia?" he wondered.

"Why is that relevant?"

"She always wins," he answered, "because she's never not thinking twelve steps ahead of everybody else. It'd be frustrating if it wasn't so damn sexy—"

"Focus."

"I am focused," he said, taking a step toward her. "Which is why I know they're still alive. If she and Babette were underwater when the Solaros searched the *Mermaid*, taking any scuba gear with them, Jaime's drawing the same conclusions you are. He'll assume they're adrift or dead. Meanwhile, she and Babette swam ashore and escaped, untraceable."

"I want to believe you," Sloane explained, "but…"

"Did you find the tanks?" he asked again, searching for the patience he needed and nearly coming up short.

"No," she answered finally.

He thought about it, then nodded. "That's why Babette's no longer answering her phone and Pia hasn't tried contacting me through it again. Even if either of them had thought to take it with them, the dive would have killed it."

"Where are you going?" Sloane asked as he walked back to the parking lot where he had left the rental truck.

"I'm going to keep looking for them!" he called back.

"What if you're wrong, Sam? I'm devastated too, but…" She trailed off.

He turned to walk backward so he could address the question. "I can feel in my gut they're out there," he told her. "You get confirmation they were on the *Mermaid*, you let me know. Otherwise…"

As he pivoted back to the parking lot, she asked, "Where are you going to look? I've had men stationed at Casaluna in the event she or Jaime make an appearance there. I've got agents at Grace's place on St. Peter and Russo's Pizzeria. Where else could they have gone?"

"I'm going to find out," he muttered in answer.

"Hey, Sam."

He stopped, took a long breath and flipped back around to face her.

Sloane had crossed her arms over her front. She stood straight, the lower half of her angular face drawn into a long frown. "I was sorry to hear about your brother."

He looked away. Made himself look at her again. He nodded. "I'm sorry, too. How's Grace?"

"She's safe," Sloane replied. "I can't say much else, but she's okay."

"I'm glad."

"We think the Solaros tracked Grace through a mobile device," Sloane said carefully. "You remember Javier Rivera?"

He tried to recall the name. "Isn't that Jaime's brother?"

"Half brother," she distinguished. "He was the reason Grace, Pia and me got out of Mexico. He worked with Mexican police on the inside of the Solaro cartel. Once he realized what they were doing with us, he went against orders. He rescued Grace first, killing her handler, Alejandro Solaro. Grace and Javier then came for me. I'd already escaped once. I went to the hacienda where Jaime was holding Pia. He caught me and punished me."

A broken leg, Sam recalled. Once the girls reached the embassy, Sloane had been badly ill.

"After that, they put me under heavy guard," Sloane explained. "But since the Solaros thought Javier was one of their own, he called them off and got me to his car."

"Then you went to the hacienda," Sam mumbled.

She nodded. "By the time we arrived, it had been set on fire from inside. You know the rest."

Sam knew Javier, Grace and Sloane had arrived at the hacienda just in time to pull Pia from the flames.

Too many close calls. It was a miracle the four of them had pulled it off.

"Javier lives in New Mexico now," Sloane told him. "He works on a cattle ranch there. But when word got out that Jaime had escaped, he flew to New Orleans. To Grace."

"Why?" Sam asked, brow knit.

Sloane sighed. "Javier and Grace's relationship is too complicated for me to explain. I'll just say he warned her about Jaime before the Solaros could hit her apartment. He kept her safe and she him, because nobody knows New Orleans like our Gracie. But after Jaime and his men found them again, we uncovered the strong likelihood that Jaime used Javier's cell phone to trace them. Whenever he made a phone call, the Solaros could pinpoint their position."

"You think they're able to do the same thing with Pia and Babette?" Sam surmised.

She nodded. "My phone is protected. But if the Solaros found the *Salty Mermaid*, it might have been because they dialed Babette's cell phone and she picked up."

It took Sam several long moments to digest this.

"I hope you're right," Sloane went on. "I hope Pia and Babette are still out there—somewhere Jaime can't touch them. He came too close to Grace and nearly killed Javier."

"I'll find them," he said. "You worry about catching Jaime. Because if he lays a finger on either of them first, I swear to God, Sloane—I'll kill that son of a bitch."

She raised a high-arched brow. "Get in line, Papa Bear."

"Mom?"

Pia startled and gripped the steering wheel tighter. It was pitch black out, the only light the beam from the old truck's headlights. The cab smelled musty, like she was the first one who had driven it in years. She glanced over her shoulder. Babette's face was just visible in the glow of the instrument panel as she sat up in the backseat. "Hey. You slept for a while."

"Can I sit up there with you?" Babette asked, her voice raspy.

She hadn't spoken since they'd watched the *Salty Mermaid* explode. Not when Pia had frantically questioned her after they swam to shore. She'd started to think Babette's ears had been damaged by the noise of the explosion. Then she'd seen the glassy look in her eyes.

Her goal from the moment she'd held Babette in her arms was to shield her from trauma. Pia hadn't wanted Babette to experience anything approaching what she, Sloane, and Grace had during or after Mexico.

She'd recognized the look in Babette's eyes on the beach and she hated Jaime Solaro all the more for putting her child through this.

There was no one on the road in front of her and no headlights in the rearview mirrors. She patted the seat next to her.

Babette unbuckled and climbed over the center console. Once she settled in the passenger seat, she latched her seatbelt and stared at the road ahead.

Her eyes were troubled and cavernous, limned by weariness. She looked far older than she should.

Pia's pulse thumped dully. She tasted guilt. Had she really thought they were safe? Why had she let her guard down? She should have taken more precautions. She'd considered changing her name when she learned that Jaime Solaro was still alive. Sure, he'd been in jail at the time, but on some level she'd known.

She'd known he would never give up his claim to her.

Making sure her voice wouldn't wobble, Pia asked, "Are you okay?"

Babette continued to stare at the road for awhile, her expression inscrutable. Finally, she said, "I want to know what's going on."

"After we get where we're going."

"Mom." Babette didn't raise her voice. The fight had gone out of her over the last two days. "Just tell me. Please."

Pia gathered a long breath. She checked the mirrors again. The backcountry road was still blessedly deserted. She checked the fuel gauge. They were down to a quarter of a tank. If they didn't reach their destination soon, they'd be stuck on the side of the highway. There were no gas stations this deep in the country. "Okay," she said cautiously.

Babette looked at her. "Who are the men who keep looking for us?"

"They're members and associates of the Solaro family," she explained.

"What do they want with us?" Babette asked. "Why did they blow up your boat?"

"Because," Pia said, wishing they didn't have to do this now—wishing they *never* had to do this, "when we graduated high school, Grace, Sloane, and I went to Mexico. It was supposed to be fun. We'd been in Catholic school where there were a lot of rules and regulations. Now we were free and we wanted to celebrate. We called it our free girls' vacation. And it was for a little while."

"Something bad happened," Babette guessed.

"Yes," Pia confirmed. She left out Grace's flirtation with Alejandro, how he'd lured her and the rest of them into trusting him…how he'd learned where they were staying. "One night, several men broke into our vacation house. They rounded us up and put us in their van then drove us to a warehouse. There, we were separated. I didn't know at the time where the others were taken. A man named Jaime Solaro took me to his house on the coast."

"Why?" Babette asked. "What did he do to you there?"

There were some details Pia couldn't speak of with her daughter. At least, not until she was older. Maybe not even then. Working past the knot in her throat, Pia swallowed hard and answered, "He hurt me, bébé."

Babette's silence was grave. She sank into it for a while. Then she asked, "Why didn't you leave?"

"I tried," she pointed out. "The house was like a prison. There were guards and bars over the windows."

"Why would he hurt you?" Babette asked. "You didn't do anything to him."

Pia licked her lips. There was a part of the world she wished she never had to expose Babette to. But she would need to know about it in order to protect herself eventually. "There are some men who enjoy hurting women. It's almost like a sickness."

"He was sick?"

"On some level, I think he must have been," Pia said.

"How did you get out?"

"With luck," Pia told her, "and because Grace and Sloane saved me."

"That was very brave of them."

"It was."

"Were they hurt, too?"

"Yes," Pia said grimly.

"Is the man who hurt you still alive? Was he one of the men who tried to take us from the beach house?"

"Those men belong to him," Pia explained.

"So he sent them here to find you. What happens when they do?"

"They won't," Pia determined.

"But if they do…"

Pia shook her head. "They won't, bébé. I'll make sure of it."

"I don't want him to hurt you again," Babette told her.

Pia reached for her hand. She grasped it. "That's not going to happen. I won't let it. I'm not the same person I was then. I'm stronger now, and I know how the Solaros think."

Babette considered this. "I think you would have had to be pretty strong then to get away from him the first time."

A small smile touched Pia's lips. She squeezed Babette's hand. "Thank you."

"Can I ask you another question?" Babette asked.

"Anything," Pia told her.

"Why have you been sick lately?"

Pia heard the waver of worry in Babette voice and strengthened her smile. "I was going to tell Sam so maybe the two of us could tell you together. But since he's not here… I'm going to have a baby."

The silence was taut. Pia's pulse quickened. Should she have waited? What if Babette wasn't ready for this? What if she didn't want it?

"I'm going to be a big sister?" Babette asked tentatively.

"You are," Pia said and blinked because tears lashed at her eyes, blurring the view of the road.

Babette said nothing more. She simply leaned over the console and placed her head on Pia's shoulder.

Pia released a tumultuous breath. "You're not mad?"

"I'm going to be a sister," Babette said again, reverently this time.

Pia hadn't thought it possible, but she laughed and pressed her cheek to the crown of Babette's head. "You're going to be a wonderful sister."

"Sam has to come back now," Babette whispered. "We're going to be a family."

Pia's smile wavered. She swallowed caution, unable to ruin this moment for her daughter.

She wished Sam was there so they could have shared this moment together.

Where are you, Sam? she thought wildly as miles stretched further into the countryside and she and Babette felt more alone than ever.

Sam kept driving long after nightfall. He drove until exhaustion forced him to stop on the side of the road and rest his eyes for a while. Then he drove through the next day, too.

He covered New Orleans, the parish surrounding Casaluna, places along the coast, because he couldn't see Pia straying far from the waters she took comfort in.

That only left one thousand six hundred and eighty miles across five states. Not to mention the thirty-three rivers that ran to the Gulf, offering a handy inland route to anyone escaping the danger and uncertainty of open water.

He thought about playing chess versus Pia—about trying to think ahead of her…

…and realized he was out of his depth.

If she was smart enough to outwit what remained of the Solaro cartel, he didn't have a chance of finding her.

Unless she wanted him to find her.

A last ditch, wild-goose-chase kind of feeling made him hit the highway. The coast fell away, the rural countryside rearing up in its place.

The amazing thing about Louisiana was that even in February, there was a healthy carpet of green on the shoulders of the road. It was the opposite of Minnesota's frozen lakes and barren winter landscape.

He'd fallen in love with the South, thanks to summers he'd spent as a kid on Smuggler's Island with its sticky heat and endless hours under the sun, toes buried in white sand. Happy, lost hours hunting for Jean Lafitte's missing treasure with Alek and the Dunagan brothers in tow.

There were other treasures there, he'd discovered as he grew older. While life took him abroad, first to war, then to search for his lost brother, he kept coming back for long afternoons on Myla's balcony with sweating glasses of lemonade and talk of life in the old country...the hidden world that lived in untouched tide pools he'd grown to love captured through the lens of his Nikon...a child running through sparkling surf, laughing, while her mother chased her in a buff-colored sundress...

He'd known, watching Pia and Babette, he'd never live in Minnesota again.

Weeks after Myla died, he left for the Middle East again on assignment. When he'd tried to tell Pia he would come back, she'd smiled mutedly, unconvinced and understanding.

He'd thought of little else but her and Babette over the following weeks. He hadn't found even the barest trace of Alek during that trip, and he'd been frustrated and disheartened. When he returned to Flamingo Bay, he'd found them again on the beach almost exactly as he left them. The girl with her bucket of wet sand. The mother with her hair braided down her back.

He'd watched them at a distance, how their heads leaned close to each other, Pia speaking in gentle ministrations he couldn't hear over the wind. Watching them had helped bring him back—body, heart, soul.

Then Babette had glanced up. She'd stood, pointing in his direction. Pia's head had turned as Babette started sprinting toward him.

He'd started running, too, scooping her up with a spin so that she cackled wildly. When he stopped, she'd laid her small warm head on his shoulder, her little fingers twining into the hair above his ear.

He'd felt his head align over his heart. He'd felt his world snap back into place.

Pia had caught up, finally.

He'd grinned at her.

She shook her head a little. *She...said your name.*

What?

She said "Sam," Pia had said, breathless.

Has she been talking since I left? he'd asked, knowing Babette had yet to speak at that point.

No, she had said simply.

His indrawn breath had been sharp and involuntary. *She said my name.*

Yes, Pia had said. Offering him one of her rare smiles, she'd laid a hand over his on Babette's back. *Walk with us?*

It was all he'd wished for while he wandered the desert, looking for the lost. Feeling completely and utterly lost. *Absolutely*, he'd replied.

On either side of the highway, the expansive fields turned to woods. The trees thickened, and he made the turnoff for the old hunting cabin. He'd convinced Pia to come there with him once. She hadn't taken to hunting as seamlessly as she had to fishing, but she'd been enchanted by the sight of hummingbirds in the rioting bottlebrush outside their bedroom window.

The tires bumped onto an uneven track. The rough-hewn sign nailed to a tree hung lopsidedly, labeling the land *Property of the Filipeks.*

Myla's husband had leased out the cabin and hunting land

when he was alive. Myla had offered it to Alek, as he had been fond of hunting.

With Alek's body recovered, Sam supposed it would come to him. The idea didn't settle well. This was Alek's place. As the trees crowded either side of the truck and branches skimmed across the windshield, he was forced to slow.

The tire ruts on either side of the road were overgrown. Dust flew up behind him as twilight gathered and he pushed the rental to the end of the rough drive. It opened into a small clearing where the simple bunkhouse had been erected. The bottlebrush tree had grown, as had everything else. It, too, was that Louisiana winter green. He'd opened the driver's window for some fresh air, and the smell of the woods enveloped him.

He didn't see a vehicle. There was no sign of habitation or visitation. It looked abandoned, as it had been for the better part of three years.

Sam slumped in the driver's seat, grinding the shifter into Park. He left the engine idling and wondered what the hell he was supposed to do now.

The metallic *ch-chink* of a rifle cocking made him raise his hands. He cast his eyes to the side mirror and saw the barrel pointed at him through the open window.

A hard voice joined in, biting words out through the teeth. "Get. Out. Of. The. Truck."

"Easy," he cautioned.

"Out!"

"Okay, all right," he said, popping the handle. The door opened. He shoved it wide and, keeping his hands up, stepped out of the truck. "Look, don't shoot me. I'm just here looking for someone."

There was a pause. Then, "Sam?"

His heart skipped a beat. The voice no longer sounded

firm or rough. He lifted his chin and under the brim of his ball cap, he followed baggy camo pants up an oversize sweatshirt. He saw the long thick plait over her shoulder, then sun-kissed cheeks.

His gaze came to rest on her nightshade eyes. The rifle in her hands lowered. Even without it, she was quietly devastating.

His hands hung in the air, suspended. "Pia."

Chapter 7

He looked like a castaway. It made him appear different to her, in some way. It wasn't just the untrimmed hair growing without shape over his collar. Or the golden beard that had grown thick over his square jaw. He looked thinner, his high cheekbones more pronounced.

If she didn't know any better, she'd say he felt nearly as beaten as she did.

So much shone in the eyes underneath his army ball cap as he lowered his hands. "Good God, Pia," he breathed.

"How…" She blinked and swallowed. "How are you here? How did you find us?"

He shook his head, looking. Just looking at her, his eyes darting over every inch of her face. "Sloane found your boat," he rasped. A torrent of grief rolled over his expression. "She thinks you're dead."

But he hadn't?

He had kept looking for them, she realized.

She wanted to close the gap between them. She wanted his arms around her. Not gently. She didn't want or need Sam gentle. She needed all the unwashed longing she saw in his face and all that it entailed.

An ache lanced through her, piercing. She had so much to tell him—so much to say. Too much.

"Sam?"

They turned in unison to face the cabin. Babette, dressed in a hunter-orange T-shirt and cargo pants that had had to be rolled at the waist and cuffs, beamed brightly at the sight of him. "Sam!"

Sam moved toward her as she rushed down the steps. He met her halfway across the scruffy winter grass, catching her mid-leap.

Pia watched them, the rightness of them. His head tipped against hers, his hand on top of her hair, her head on his large shoulder and her arms folded around his neck. Babette's feet hung over the ground for a minute, then two.

Pia remembered the beach and Sam's first homecoming. She hadn't believed she would ever see him again. She'd stopped waiting for Babette to start talking, too, letting her daughter take the milestones as they came. Then that name—*Sam*—and her running on short legs toward his figure in the distance. He'd swept her up and cradled her to him. On some level, Pia had known their lives would never be the same. She'd isolated herself and her baby from the world. And yet they'd been found.

Babette's feet touched down again, but Sam didn't let her go. He clutched her face. "How are you?" he asked, scanning.

"I'm okay," Babette assured him. "I lost my phone."

"That's all right," he soothed. "What matters is that you're okay."

Babette laid her head on his chest, face falling. He gathered her in again, rocking in small motions as her form lifted and fell on a cascade of silent sobs.

Sam's eyes met Pia's. Fear gleamed there, but relief crushed it. He offered her a wavering smile.

She felt two things at once. First, her heart melting. She

had lost it to him, she knew—a long time ago. And that same effervescent sensation in her belly that was the baby moving.

She needed to tell Sam about the baby.

Pia made herself look away, focusing on the rifle. She put the safety on and tried to assert herself.

"You're not wearing shoes," Sam realized. He ran his hands over Babette's arms. "Go inside and get warm."

"Are you staying?" she asked hopefully.

"I won't leave you," he told her. "You have my word."

Her face was red from crying, but her smile brightened everything. Turning from him, she went back to the porch and into the cabin.

"She's taller," Sam said, sliding his hands into his pockets as he watched her go.

Pia nodded, though his back was to her. "How did you find us?" she asked again.

"I've been looking for you for days," he explained as he faced her.

"When did you get back?" she asked.

"After the text from Babette saying you were in trouble."

"She texted you," she realized.

"You tried to call."

She thought of her one-word message. "I found her phone on the boat, and I didn't think. I just—"

He nodded away the rest. "I was in the air at that point. On my way back to you."

She looked at him, unable for a moment to get anything past the knot in her throat. He looked as if he'd lived ten years in the desert instead of eight weeks.

Sam walked toward her. He took the rifle from her hands gently. Head down, he muttered, "I saw the boat, Pia."

She bit her lip, seeing again the cloud of flame on the

surface of the water and the black smoke funneling toward the sky.

"I won't lie to you. For a minute there, I thought…"

She nodded. "It's what I wanted them to think. The Solaros."

"You did well," he said in a choked voice. "Too well. We need to let Sloane know you're alive."

"There's no phone here," she reminded him.

"I'll call her," Sam said. He took another half step forward, and she smelled him—summer rain and all things safe. Longing swept her like a tsunami. "But tell me first. When Jaime came to the house…did he hurt you?"

"No. I'm not sure he was there at all. He called me right before his men arrived that night. Babette and I hid, then got away when they weren't looking."

"They slashed your truck tires," he noted. "So you took the motorcycle?"

"I slashed theirs, too," she said with an unfelt half smile.

His laugh was silent. "You're incredible." His fingertips skimmed across her hair, then her cheek, barely there. She wished he would *touch* her. Really touch her. "You protected Babette. Kept her safe. You've done an amazing job, Pia. Not even the FBI knows where you are. I thought I was grasping at straws coming here."

"You found us," she said in a whisper.

He nodded slowly. "I'm here now. You don't have to do this alone anymore."

A noise welled out of her, unbidden. Later, she thought. Later, she'd tell him how scary it had all been—how afraid she'd felt for Babette. For the baby.

"How much have you told her?"

She took a long breath. "Most everything," she admitted.

"Not the worst of it. But she knows now who the Solaros are. Who Jaime is."

He stilled. "Not that he's her—"

"No," she refused quickly. "Of course not." She didn't think she'd ever be able to tell Babette that. "I was afraid she'd figure it out for herself. But I think she's still absorbing what I told her—what happened to me, Grace and Sloane." And despite the years of healing, the telling had been excruciating.

He touched her arm. Even through the sweatshirt, she itched for more. She wanted the burn of what she felt for him. Something tangible to wrap herself up in and forget. She was ready to collapse. Into him. Into herself.

"Are you hungry?" he asked. "I brought supplies."

From the cabin, Babette's voice lifted through the screen door. "You brought food?"

He chuckled. The sound caught in his throat. "Food, clothes, soap, toiletries, some over-the-counter medicines if you need it, an inhaler…"

Pia felt her eyes flood. She blinked rapidly. "Oh, Sam," she breathed. Babette hadn't had a touch of asthma since a battle with bronchitis when she was five. That he'd thought about it touched her deeply.

"Are there Doritos?" Babette beseeched from the house. "Please tell me there're Doritos!"

Sam opened the passenger door. The brown paper bags on the seat and floorboard overflowed. He grabbed one, set it on the ground, then another.

"You brought a lot of food," Pia observed. "We found some things in the cabin's freezer, but the pickings are slim."

"I've got some canned soups and veggies," he pointed

out. "Nothing perishable. But it'll get us by until we can get Sloane and her team here."

"Babette didn't speak after the explosion," Pia said. "For a whole day. She's going to be damaged by all this. The long-term effects of shock and trauma…"

Sam stopped and turned to her. He braced his hands on her shoulders. "We'll meet them when they come. We'll get her help. Whatever she needs. She's not alone like you were in the beginning. She has us."

Pia fell silent, searching him with her nightshade eyes. She'd lived in that valley of silence, surrendered herself to it, before he'd met her. She'd had to pull herself out of it. A nineteen-year-old mother, scared and alone.

"You've done nothing wrong," he assured her.

She tried to look away. "You're right. Sloane needs to know we're okay. Is Grace…?"

"She's fine."

Pia closed her eyes in relief. "Thank the saints."

"She and Sloane will be glad to know you and Babette are safe, too."

"We'll go into protective custody."

"Yes."

She nodded, accepting. "I wouldn't have been able to protect her on my own much longer. We're about out of food. The truck barely made it here. I pulled it around back, out of sight, so it would look like the cabin was empty."

Again, thinking twelve steps ahead of anyone else. He fought a proud grin. "Where did you get the truck?"

"It was sitting at an empty beach house in Pass Christian," she said cautiously. "And it was unlocked."

"Were the keys in it?"

She shook her head. "No. I…" She scooped a hand back

through her hair, restless. "Sloane showed me once how to hot-wire a vehicle so I…"

"You hot-wired a truck," he said. *Jesus Christ*. He heard himself laughing and wanted to tell her, again, how incredible she was. He moved in.

She inhaled sharply and drew back.

He stopped. The curse blew out of him in a whisper. He needed to feel her against him. He needed it like air. But Christmas loomed large and the line they'd drawn between them returned in full force. "Pia—"

"I need to tell you something," she said in a rush.

He fought for control. It would be easy to let it go—to say it didn't matter. Nothing mattered but knowing they were safe. Nothing mattered more than being with them, here and now. "Should I sit down?"

"Maybe," she considered.

He sobered. "What is it?"

She hesitated. "A week after you left, I… I started feeling funny. Tired. So tired I almost couldn't see straight. I started to get sick."

He froze. "You're sick?" Again, he reached for her.

"It's not what you're thinking," she said, stepping back again cagily. She shook her head. "It's not like that."

"You're not sick?" he asked, confused.

"No. Yes. Not in that way." She heaved a frustrated sigh. "I went to the doctor. She had me take a test."

"A test for what?" he asked.

Her mouth fumbled. Her voice dropped. "A pregnancy test, Sam."

"Preg—" He stopped as realization shot through the dark, echoing endlessly. He felt like he was falling. The earth shrugged beneath him. "You're pregnant?"

She swallowed. "Yes."

"With my…"

Anger forked across her brow in thin lines of warning. "You really need to ask me that?"

"I'm sorry," he blurted. He reached for his head. "I'm sorry." He eyed her middle. He'd thought her face had looked fuller. Was that a bump under her sweatshirt? "A week after…" He did that math quickly in his head. Dammit, he could count. Even when his mind was all over the place. "You went to the doctor a *week* after I left?"

She nodded calmly. She was maddeningly calm. "Yes."

"Pia, I've been gone for two months."

She nodded again. "I know."

She hadn't told him.

He stepped away from her now. He planted his hands on his waist, dug in for a long, cleansing breath. "You could have told me."

"I know," she said once more.

"You *know*?"

"Yes."

He saw her waiting—for him to explode. She'd steeled herself for his anger. And that pissed him off. "You didn't want to tell me?" he challenged.

"You left," she stated. "I didn't know if…"

"You didn't know what? You didn't think I'd come back? You didn't know if I'd want our *child*?"

She stood her ground, jutting her chin forward. When her lower lip trembled, she bit down on it.

He nearly crumbled then. God, he was weak. Angry at her. Weak for her. Frustrated beyond belief because he was suspended between the two like a fish flopping in a net. He cursed bitterly. "I came back."

"Yes," she admitted.

"I would have," he explained, "whether or not Jaime came for you."

She grew silent at that.

"I would have answered the phone," he went on. "I practically waited by the damn thing. I wanted you to call."

"You were angry when you left."

"I was heartbroken, Pia!" he told her. "It was hurt and, yes, that manifested as anger. Maybe that was wrong. But you refused to marry me—after seven years. And it broke my heart."

Her eyes were busy on his face. They looked glassy.

He fought for breath. "I never said I wouldn't come back. I'm not that man. And you know I'm not the kind of man who'd turn his back on his children."

She grabbed her elbows, rocking back on her heels.

He glanced toward the cabin. "Does Babette know?"

Pia nodded. "I told her yesterday."

That was fine. That was right, he thought. Babette was going to be a big sister. And he was going to be a...

He steadied himself, studied her. He could see the fatigue. The slight sheen of sickness and the pallor around her mouth that signaled it. Pia was Sicilian. She was a goddess of the high water, kissed by the sun as certainly and lovingly as the ocean's edge every evening. Her skin was normally golden bronze. "Are you okay?"

"What?" she asked, startled.

"You. Are you all right? Are you healthy?"

Her brows came together. "Yes."

"Don't lie to me."

"I'm not," she claimed. "The doctor says both the baby and I are doing well. I'm just tired, still. And..."

"And what?" he pushed when she trailed off.

"Nauseous," she admitted. "Being on the boat was a struggle."

"Are you able to keep things down?"

"I eat," she told him. "My stomach complains about it. But I keep enough down to maintain my weight."

She'd gone through morning sickness, and he hadn't been there. That was on him. "I shouldn't have left."

"You said it was a good lead," she reminded him. "You said it was important."

It had been a good lead. The best Stephen had uncovered in the last decade. But Pia and the baby... Babette. Jaime, the bastard.

This was his family. It wasn't a family the way he'd wanted it to be. He'd want Pia to say yes. He wanted her to be his wife. He wanted Babette to take his name. And, Sam realized, he wanted a baby with Pia. He'd watched her raise one child. He'd be there from the beginning this time to help her raise this one.

She'd already gone through too much of this alone. He had been needed here over the last eight weeks and he had been absent.

He turned away from her and leaned against the truck. Pressing his head against the hood, he waited for the ground to stop moving.

"Sam?"

"Hmm?"

Her touch feathered across the ridge of his shoulder blade. "Are you okay?"

He released a ragged breath. Then he lifted his head and faced her.

Unable to fight the impulse a moment longer, he pulled her to him. Her mouth dropped. He took it and kissed her with every ounce of who he was.

Her hands clutched his elbows for balance. Then fluttered up to his jaw. They linked around his shoulders before her nails skimmed across the scalp on the back of his head, light and titillating.

It pulled a sound from deep in his chest. She drew it out as certainly as waves uncovered wreckage after a storm. She had wrecked him. And, God help him, he loved her. She was the bubble of air that broke the top of the water when surfacing. He'd felt empty. Not anymore.

Overwhelmed, he pressed his brow to hers. His hands shook, and he clutched her waist.

She pulled herself away, cupping her hand over her mouth. Her eyes closed, but not before he glimpsed what was there. An answer. The one he craved from her. "I thought...you were angry," she whispered, shaking her head.

"I'm furious," he groaned at her. He was furious with himself for needing someone who couldn't figure out whether she needed him.

"I wanted to tell you..." she explained. "I thought about calling you. But it felt wrong. The call could've dropped, or we would have had a poor connection. And after Christmas... I didn't know the right words to say."

He wanted more from her. But that would be pushing. She was scared and tired. He'd pushed her too far already, all to satisfy the needy voice inside him that said *Her. Her, please. Now. Always.*

He leaned in to kiss her temple. He lingered over the warmth of her skin, the smell of her hair. "That's enough," he decided.

"I..."

"It's enough for now," he assured her, then made himself move away. "Let's get these things in before Babette comes foraging for junk food."

Chapter 8

Sam took the night watch. Over dinner, he and Pia had agreed that he would wake her at 3:00 a.m. and take over since it was apparent he hadn't slept in over twenty-four hours.

He let her sleep until five, knowing once the light hit the windows, she'd be awake with the proverbial rooster.

As he crept through the silent house, he rubbed his hands together. It had been cold in the rocking chair on the porch. He cupped them and brought them to his mouth to warm them with his breath.

In the kitchen, he shoveled down a few bites of food, then fixed a plate and set it in the microwave to keep warm. He calculated how many hours they had until Sloane's team arrived around 9:00 a.m. to escort them into protective custody.

There was one bedroom with two full beds. Sam removed his boots at the door, then slipped inside. He checked the safety on the rifle before leaning it against the wall. Then he went to the bed that held Babette.

She was buried up to her eyes in the comforter. He laid his hand on her back, felt it rise and fall away before he moved to the other bed.

He didn't want to wake Pia for the watch and would have kept at it if he'd been able to see straight. For a while, he'd relied solely on his hearing. When he began to nod off, he'd had to call it.

He removed his jacket and laid it on the chair next to the bed. Then he took off the long-sleeve T-shirt he wore underneath, leaving his black undershirt in place. He unbuttoned his jeans and shucked them, leaving the long johns he'd found in the closet before the watch.

He slid under the covers of Pia's bed, careful not to tug on the flat sheet and send her tearing out of sleep.

She hadn't slept much since leaving Flamingo Bay. He wondered when the last time was that she'd slept this soundly.

He wondered how many nightmares she'd had since Jaime called her to tell her he was coming for her and Babette.

Drawn by her warmth, he made sure his hands were at room temperature before touching her. Her back was to him. She faced the door to the bedroom. She wore a tank top. In the dim light from the den, he saw the watery blue tattoo that kissed the top of her spine. He'd ridden that wave, explored it with his hands, his mouth, all the way to the small of her back.

She also had a tiny jewel-toned jellyfish behind the curve of her right ear and an eel that coiled around her left thigh. A sand dollar lived in the hollow of her ankle so that she took the sea with her even when she had to leave Flamingo Bay.

At night, in the desert, she'd been the thing missing from him. He'd felt her like a phantom limb that never stopped to think it shouldn't ache anymore because the real thing wasn't there.

He found his nose in her thick black hair she'd uncoiled from her braid. His hand went to her waist, feeling bare skin. The tank top had rucked over her abdomen as she slept.

Turning his lips to the point of her shoulder, he felt her stir.

"...time is it?" she asked sleepily.

He chose not to answer. Her waist didn't curve inward anymore. It bloomed out, slightly. His pulse quickened.

"Sam?" she whispered.

He followed her waist around to the mound at the center of her belly.

A baby, he thought again, his sleep-starved brain radiating both wonder and disbelief at the notion. The joy of it, even under the circumstances. He claimed that joy, resting his hand there, then tracing it, drawing circles around her womb.

They'd made this.

Her hand seized his.

"Sorry," he murmured, and stopped.

"No." She pressed his palm against the outer curve of her belly. "Do you feel that?"

He waited. "No."

She sighed, a small sound in the dark. "It's a little feeling. A stir just big enough for me to feel."

"How often?" he wondered.

"A little more each day," she revealed. "At first, I didn't notice it. But once I realized…"

"Is it too early to know the sex?" he asked.

"I was scheduled to find out next week."

"How far along are you?"

"Fifteen weeks," she replied.

He did more math, struggling as the gears of his mind stuck, warped with fatigue.

She did it for him. "I think it happened before Thanksgiving. That night you and I took the blanket out on the beach after Babette went to bed."

He remembered how Pia had risen over him, around him, her head tipped back, white with moonglow, her hips torquing under his hands to meet his in fast, heady motions…

As tired as he was, Sam felt his body tighten in response. The vision of her made him need.

He'd thought of asking her then. As they lay together, letting the cool breeze chase heat from their skin, he'd wanted to propose to her there on the spot.

But he'd left the ring up at the house. And he'd already planned for Christmas. Pia and Babette took such glee from Christmas. He'd thought waiting to pop the question that night after the surprises of the day would be perfect. So he'd wrapped the blanket tighter around her and waited until she was ready to make the trek back to the house.

She pushed herself up on an elbow. "There's light at the windows."

He frowned. "Yeah."

"You let me sleep in."

"It's 5:00 a.m.," he pointed out, careful to keep his voice low. "Not ten."

She busied herself getting out of bed. She pulled on a sweater, then shoved her feet into her boots. Grabbing the jacket he'd used from the chair, she punched her arms through the sleeves.

He rolled onto his back and braced a hand under his head, tracing her silhouette in the dark with eyes that felt gritty. "I left you a plate in the microwave."

She looked at him as her fingers braided her hair in fast, twining motions. "Did you?"

He lifted his chin. "Eat," he instructed. His lids forced him to close them.

"You should've woken me sooner."

"When was the last time you slept that long?" he asked. "Or that well?"

Tellingly, she didn't answer. He heard her zip the coat.

The mattress gave next to his hip. A second later, her lips brushed over his. "It's your turn," she whispered.

The paintbrush end of her plait tickled the space above the collar of his shirt. He reached for her.

She wasn't there anymore. "Sleep, Sam," she told him from far away.

The screen door creaked. Pia watched Babette walk out onto the porch behind two steaming ceramic mugs. "Careful," she cautioned, lifting her hands to receive the one offered.

"I filled them too high," Babette said with a slight wince. "But I added the honey that Sam brought."

"Thank you," Pia said. She blew across the surface of the herbal tea as Babette lowered to the rocker next to hers. The heat of the mug sank clean through her hands. "You're up early."

"I couldn't sleep anymore," Babette said quietly.

Pia frowned. Had her nightmares become Babette's, too?

Saints, she hoped not. Telling Babette the truth had riddled Pia with doubt she could no more shake than the feeling that had followed her from Flamingo Bay—the feeling that they were still being watched.

She scanned the trees as she had for the last hour. Seeing nothing beyond evergreen branches fanning in the wind, she asked, "Would you like me to fix you something to eat?"

"I had some of that ham." Babette lifted her shoulder. "It was okay." At Pia's knowing look, the corner of her mouth lifted in a smile. "Okay, it wasn't great. But it wasn't bad either. Who knew you could get ham in a can?"

Pia found she could laugh. "Let me know when you try the Vienna sausage."

Babette's nose wrinkled. "No thanks."

Pia thought ruefully of the flounder piccata they'd never

gotten around to making. She tried to remember their last well-rounded meal. "How're you feeling?"

"Sloane's coming to get us today, right?" Babette asked. Pia nodded.

"And what then?" Babette asked, her uncertainty blinking to life again.

Pia bit the inside of her lip. That was yes to whether Babette's dreams mirrored her own. "A safe house. Somewhere the bad guys can't touch us."

"For how long?" Babette wondered.

"Until the Solaros are caught," Pia replied.

"But that guy—the one who abducted you. Hi-may?"

"Jaime," Pia said with nod.

"He escaped from prison," Babette pointed out. "Won't he just do it again? Won't he keep trying to catch you?"

"It took him twelve years to escape. I highly doubt he can do it again." But she could understand where Babette was coming from. Would Pia ever stop looking over her shoulder, knowing Jaime had walked out of maximum security once?

What if the FBI didn't catch him? Would they be forced to live the rest of their lives away from their house in Flamingo Bay?

Pia took a testing sip of tea. It didn't scald, so she swallowed another.

"You told Sam about the baby."

Pia met Babette's searching gaze. "Yes."

"Good," Babette said with a faint grin. "He said he wouldn't leave again, but if there's a baby, he has even more reason to stay."

"You're reason enough," Pia assured her. "He said what he said because you're enough. You've always been enough."

"Then why did he have to go away again after Christmas?" Babette asked.

Pia tilted her head. "You know why. He promised his parents he would find out what happened to his brother. He made that promise long before he met you or me. And Sam never breaks a promise."

Babette went quiet again. She drank her tea, but a contemplative crease rode the bridge of her nose. She lowered her voice. "I looked at his camera."

"You what?" Pia asked.

"His Nikon," Babette said. "He brought it with him. There was a doe and a fawn in the woods outside the back door. I wanted to take their picture so I could use it to sketch them later. I grabbed his camera from the bag on the table."

"I'm sure he won't mind," Pia considered.

"He might," Babette said ominously. "When he finds out I looked at his camera roll."

Pia's stomach clutched. Sam would have cleared the photos from the Middle East before coming to find them. *Right?* "What did you see?"

Babette didn't look at her. She brought the mug to her mouth with both hands. With her head low and her legs tucked into the chair with her, she suddenly looked smaller than she had seemed in ages.

Pia set the tea on the arm of the chair and reached for Babette's arm. "Bébé?"

"I think he found his brother," Babette said in a whispered rush. "Alek."

"Why do you say that?"

"Because there were pictures of…what do you call them— remains?"

Pia closed her eyes. *No.* Hadn't Babette been through enough over the last few days?

Now this?

"Once I realized it was someone dead, I stopped looking," Babette admitted. "But the remains were in a box. Like a coffin but plain. There was an American flag spread across them."

Pia tightened her grip on Babette's arm. "You weren't meant to see those things."

Babette kept her eyes low as she jerked a shoulder. "It's okay. I'm okay. It's just… What if that was Sam's brother? What if that's the way he found him? He must feel really sad."

Pia swallowed, thinking of the man inside sleeping. He'd looked beaten, she remembered. Was this why? Had he found Alek at last in that condition?

If so, why hadn't he told her?

She'd told him about the baby, she reminded herself. And he'd already been tired when he arrived at the cabin. He'd seen the boat and, she was sure, some part of him had thought she and Babette hadn't escaped. He'd been so relieved to find them alive and safe. Perhaps he hadn't thought of what had transpired in the desert…

Pia nodded in decision. "You don't have to tell him you snooped through his photographs." When Babette lifted her head in surprise, she added, "If it was Alek, he'll tell us. There'll be a memorial, I'm sure. And a burial. The Filipeks will need to lay him to rest."

"But how can Sam be there if he disappears with us?" Babette asked. "He will go with us, won't he? When Sloane takes us to the safe house?"

Pia shook her head, uncertain. Even if Sam wanted to go with them, would he be allowed to? "I… I don't…"

The sound of an engine echoed through the trees.

Pia climbed to her feet. When Babette spoke, she held up her hand for silence and watched the narrow, rutted lane that wound into the trees ahead.

Chapter 9

"Sloane said she wouldn't be here until later," Babette whispered behind Pia.

The engine grew louder. Pia heard tires moving over rough terrain, in and out of puddles, slowly. "Go get Sam."

"Mom—"

"Now, Babette," Pia said, grabbing the rifle from the porch rail.

Babette sprinted to the screen door. It slammed shut behind her and bounced against the frame.

Pia thought of Sam's phone. It hadn't rung. Sloane had promised to call when she and her team were thirty minutes away to give them time to prepare for the transfer.

The door opened again, and Sam stepped out, pulling a shirt over his head. His jeans were unbuttoned still, his boots untied. He eyed the path through the trees, easing the screen closed. "Don't," he said when Babette tried to open it again. "And back away from the door. Go to the back of the house and don't stand in front of any windows."

Pia glimpsed the pistol in his left hand. It was flat against his thigh, hidden from Babette's view. His first finger hovered, ready, just outside the trigger guard.

She knew it was his 9mm Beretta, the same sidearm he'd been equipped with as a soldier in the 101st. He'd told her once if he had to carry a gun as a civilian, it'd be something he was familiar with. Something he'd been trained with that had once felt like an extension of himself.

She saw the soldier in his eyes now, in his stance. Her readiness rose to meet it even as her heart banged away at her eardrums.

"Pia," he said as the sound of the vehicle grew louder. He kept the Beretta low but placed it in a two-handed hold. "Get behind me."

"I have the rifle."

"Get behind me."

She gave in. Positioning herself between his back and the door, she craned her neck to see two LED headlights appear through the brush.

Sam cursed as the front of the SUV came into view. He backed up a step, planting his feet. "It's not the FBI."

"How do you know?" she asked, eyeing the tinted windshield. "Sloane could've come alone."

"I don't think so," he said. He raised the Beretta and squeezed off a round into the trees.

The report bounced off the trunks. It ricocheted off everything.

The SUV stopped.

"Go in the house," he bit off.

"I'm not leaving," Pia said, and cocked the rifle to show it.

He didn't move. His stillness unnerved her. It reminded her of the stingrays that buried themselves in the sand and the people walking around them, unaware of the barbs on their tails with complex venom.

Outside the driver's window, Pia caught a muzzle flash.

Sam opened fire, crowding her against the door.

Pia stepped out, lifted the barrel, and lowered her cheek to the stock. She waited the split second it took for the crosshairs to center over the driver's-side windshield to pull the trigger.

The rifle kicked against her shoulder. She watched the windshield splinter on impact, absorbing it.

"Get down!" Sam shouted. He pivoted and threw his body over hers.

She heard the rapid fire of a submachine gun. Bullets bounced off the logs of the cabin. Her rifle fell away, clattering to the ground as Sam pulled her to the floor. His hand planted against the crown of her head, forcing it low.

He was exposed. "We need to get inside!" she said.

The door opened. Sam cursed when Babette, crouched low, reached for them.

Pia grabbed her hand and scrambled across the threshold. She wrapped her arms around Babette. The door slammed shut behind Sam. Sweat rolled down his face as his eyes met hers. They were flat and angry. "Get her to the truck."

"What about you?" she asked even as she brought Babette to her feet.

"I'm right behind you," he said as he peered through the closest window. He ducked as it shattered. "They're on foot."

Pia clutched Babette's hand as she raced to the back door. Sam had pulled his truck around back with the Bronco Pia had stolen. She knew he'd left the keys in it. Before the start of her morning watch, she'd checked to make sure. "Stay low," she told Babette, looking both ways as they left the cabin. "Go straight to Sam's truck and lie down on the back seat!"

As Babette flew to the truck's cab, Pia went to the back and opened the tonneau cover, revealing the modest cache of weapons she'd secured from the cabin's gun cabinet.

She felt the cold metal handle of the flounder gig she'd placed there and grappled for something else. She eyed the

.30-30 Winchester near it and grabbed it and an ammo box. Juggling the rifle and the rounds, she loaded as she went around the driver's door, thankful that Sloane had spent weeks teaching her target practice at Casaluna. Despite the quavering in her hands and the way they jerked at the sounds of gunfire, she did it by rote.

In her peripheral, she caught the dart of a figure at the side of the house. She spotted the gunman, weapon raised, and lifted the rifle. She squeezed off a round.

The gunman cried out and flattened himself against the grass.

She shouldered open the driver's door of the truck, keeping both eyes trained on either side of the cabin. How many men were in the SUV? How many weapons?

She and Sam wouldn't be able to hold them off forever if the Solaros surrounded the cabin.

The back door burst open and Sam leaped out, shouldering a pack. "Start the truck," he said, sprinting toward the vehicle.

She boosted herself into the driver's seat, reached for the keys in the ignition, but another movement stopped her. "Sam!" she called, pointing to the corner of the house.

"Down!" he shouted. In a sideways swing, he aimed and fired.

The driver's window exploded. Glass sprayed Pia's hair. From her sprawl on the floorboard of the back seat, Babette screamed.

Pia wanted to reach for her, but she needed to get the truck in gear. She groped for the ignition again, felt the key with its rental tag. She twisted it to the right.

The engine turned over.

She mashed the brake and ground the shifter.

The passenger door opened. Sam dived in, shut it. "Go!" he said.

Pia hit the gas.

A man leaped out in front of the truck. She didn't touch the brake even as he raised his weapon to fire. Gripping the steering wheel in both hands, she mashed the accelerator to the floor.

The gunman tried swiveling out of the truck's path. The right fender clipped him. He fell.

The truck bucked as he went under the tire. Sam gripped the distress bar over his head but said nothing as she kept going.

"They're blocking the road," she pointed out.

"Take the hunting trail through the woods. It'll come out into the deer food plot. From there, we can follow the stream to the highway."

"It rained when we got here." She steered the truck toward the break in the pines. "The trail may be boggy."

"The truck's four-wheel drive. We'll make it." He turned, the back of his fingers skimming over her hair. She admired how steady his hands were. She could feel the quaking in her bones.

Sam planted his hand on the back of her headrest and turned to look into the back seat. "Babette. You okay?"

"I'm scared!"

"It's all right," he soothed. "We're all right now."

"Are they following us?" she asked plaintively.

Pia checked the side mirror as they cut through the shade of the forest canopy. "No," she said.

"They'd be stupid to come through here without a four-by-four," Sam added helpfully.

The trail widened, just as he'd said, into a field. The

grass was high. It hadn't been seeded for deer in years. Sam gripped the shifter and yanked it into 4H.

Pia felt the tires lock in.

"We should be good," he said. "Don't slow down. Just keep going in the same direction. See the break in the trees? That leads to the stream, and the stream intersects with the highway. You're doing fine." For a second, his hand covered hers over the wheel.

The words didn't waver, but he was panting. The adrenaline still beat at her from the inside. She tried not to think about how she would feel when it left her.

His expression twisted, pained, as he pressed his free hand into his right hip.

"What's wrong?" she demanded. When he didn't answer, she saw sweat still pouring from his hairline. "Sam!"

"Nothing," he said between his teeth. "It's just a graze."

"You're hit?" she said, reaching for him.

"It's fine, Pia," he argued. "I'm all right. Forgot how much it burns, is all."

The truck bounced in and out of a rut. She put both hands back on the wheel to steady it. "Did you bring a first aid kit?"

"Under the seat in the back," he groaned.

"Babette, check under the seat," Pia called back to her.

"Don't worry about me." He checked the mirror. "Just keep driving."

Pia peered out her mirror, too. She couldn't see anything through the tunnel of trees. "How did they find us?"

"Sloane said something about the Solaros being able to track people through their phones. She thinks that's how they found Grace before Sloane got her to safety."

"But…we lost Babette's phone in the explosion."

"Yeah," Sam said grimly.

She took one look at his angry face. "They're tracking yours, too?"

"I called Sloane last night," he reminded her. "I told her exactly where to find you."

"Did you bring the phone?"

"It was in the bedroom," he pointed out. "I couldn't get to it in time."

Her lips trembled. She firmed them together before asking, "What if Sloane was wrong? What if they have some other way of tracking us? What if, wherever we run, they find us?"

He looked at her long over the space of the cab. "We'll be ready."

Chapter 10

"*Matches,*" *Bianca revealed triumphantly.*

"*That's it?*" *Pia asked. They spoke in undertones so as not to arouse suspicion among the men Jaime had left to watch her while he was away from the hacienda. "There's nothing else?*"

"*Nothing.*" *Bianca's posture collapsed, so that she looked small. She covered the matchsticks in her hand with the other and held them tight to her chest. "Unless Jaime carries his gun with him into the house.*"

Pia shook her head. "I looked while he was sleeping." She shuddered to think of the bed they had shared for several nights now—of his hands on her. The weight of him. The hands he sometimes clasped around her throat.

Pia had let him have her. After listening to Bianca's screams the second night, she hadn't refused him again. She'd known if she did, the bruises on Bianca would be fresh again in the morning.

On the morning of the fourth day, Pia had lain in bed, too demoralized to face the day until Bianca arrived with a breakfast tray. She'd gently stacked the pillows so that Pia could sit up, then she'd brought a cup of tea to her lips. The liquid had spilled down Pia's chin. Bianca had patted it away with a linen cloth. She'd drawn Pia a bath, then ripped the bedsheets off the mattress.

"We'll burn these," she'd said before carrying them away.

A fragile bond was born between them from the moment she let Pia light the match and together they had watched the sheets burn in the fireplace grate.

It had grown. Pia had learned that Bianca, too, had been abducted by the Solaros and then taken from the cartel's human trafficking ring. "Did he say you were his wife, too?" Pia had asked her.

"At first. Before he found out I wasn't a virgin."

"Was he angry?"

"He dragged me out of the bed," Bianca had said quietly after a long silence. "The one you share with him now. He threw me down the stairs."

"I'm sorry."

"I thought he would kill me," Bianca admitted. "I thought I would die in this house. There are rumors about it. Women go in, they say. But they do not come out. We are not the first of Jaime Solaro's wives."

Pia learned other things that seemed too grim to contemplate. For instance, Jaime's claim on her wasn't something his father, Pablo, had granted. By abducting women from the cartel, Jaime had stolen from Pablo. The already tenuous relationship that existed between father and son was on the verge of implosion.

She'd noticed Jaime's behavior unraveling little by little. He came home often with burning eyes and restless feet. He smoked one cigarette after another, pacing and muttering under his breath.

At dinner, Bianca had dropped a fork on the floor. He'd launched out of his chair to attack her.

Pia hadn't thought. She'd stood, too, grabbing his arm before he could swing.

He'd backhanded her so hard she'd fallen onto the table, upending the dishes.

She'd thought of hiding from him instead of following him up the stairs afterward. But she'd thought of what he would do to Bianca—or what he would certainly do to her when he found her.

The next morning, after Jaime left, Pia asked Bianca to find them both a weapon.

She placed her hands around Bianca's, prying them open so she could see the matches again. She thought of the locked doors. The guards. The bars over the windows.

If they set fire to the hacienda, would she and Bianca be able to escape? Or would the fire consume them both?

There was one thing Pia did know. She and Bianca may not be Jaime's first wives, but they would certainly be his last.

"Mom?"

Pia woke with a start. Heat licked her skin. For a split second, she felt the breath of flames. In her lap, her hands were basketed just as they had been around Bianca's.

Someone touched her. "Mom, are you okay?"

She reached for the hand on her shoulder like a lifeline and made herself blink. Her surroundings cleared. She realized she was in the passenger seat of Sam's rental truck. The driver's seat was empty, but the engine idled.

Babette was behind her. She'd been sleeping under Sam's coat, stretched across the back seat, when Pia allowed herself to doze off.

She patted Babette's hand. "Fine," she said. "Just a bad dream."

Babette's palm moved in soothing circles over the surface of her hoodie. "There's some water back here. Do you want it?"

Pia shook her head. Then she felt the heat in her face. She nodded. "Yes. Please."

Babette extended the water bottle over the console. "Sam went to talk to the ferryman."

"Ferryman." It took Pia a second to reorient herself.

They hadn't known where to go after the standoff at the cabin. She had driven for a long time to ensure they weren't followed.

Eventually, she'd pulled off to see to the bullet graze on Sam's hip, disinfecting and bandaging it with the supplies she found in Sam's first aid kit.

They hadn't felt safe enough to stop at a motel for the night. As Sam had driven, he'd told her about Smuggler's Island.

It was a barrier island in a chain off the coast of Mississippi, lesser known than the more popular summer attractions like Ship Island. While the state of Mississippi laid legal claim to the shifting sands of its islands, Smuggler's Island had once been owned exclusively by the Dunagan family. Harvey Dunagan had been a lightkeeper at Smuggler's Island Lighthouse since the late seventies. The lighthouse had been automated for decades, but upkeep was still needed on it and the island's remaining structures.

Harvey Dunagan had been friends with Lyudmyla and her husband and, by turn, Sam's father, and mother. He'd had a wife, Mabel, and two sons. They had invited the Filipeks to vacation on Smuggler's Island in the summers of Sam's youth.

It wasn't the first time she'd heard Sam speak of his summers in Mississippi. As a sanctuary, Smuggler's Island sounded perfect—at least for the time being.

And Pia longed for the rhythm of the sea. Despite what had happened to the *Salty Mermaid*, she felt more certain of herself surrounded by waves than she did on dry land.

She drank half the water in the bottle. When Babette passed her a cereal bar she'd scrounged from Sam's pack, Pia ate it. "Did you get some sleep?" she asked her daughter.

"A little," Babette weighed. "A bed would have been better. And a pillow."

She heard the wistful notes in Babette's voice and badly wanted to hug her. "If the ferryman lets us cross, you'll have both tonight."

Oh, Saints, please let us cross. Her hips, back and neck ached from sleeping upright and a headache nibbled incessantly at her temple.

Where else would they go? Would the men at the hunting cabin have tried to follow them, or did they lie in wait to ambush Sloane and the FBI?

Sam had said Sloane's phone was encrypted, untraceable. But what if he was wrong? Pia had wrestled with whether it would be wise to find a pay phone so she could place a call to Sloane and make sure she was all right.

The driver's door opened and a blast of cool air kissed Pia's cheeks.

Sam climbed behind the wheel, looking every bit the man who'd driven through the night. His eyes, however, danced toward hers. "We're on the ten o'clock ferry."

"Will they search the truck?" she asked, thinking of the weapons cache in the back.

"No," he said with a shake of his head. "The ferryman. I know him. His name's Clem. He was close with the Dunagan boys—to Boyd Dunagan in particular. They were partners."

She caught the meaning behind *partners*. "Isn't Boyd the one who died?"

Sam nodded, the light in his eyes dimming. "His mom, Mabel, died of cancer and Harvey retired. While Hoyt went off to California for work, Boyd couldn't let his family's history on the island go. So he took Harvey's place. For a couple of years, he worked as lightkeeper while Clem ferried people back and forth from the mainland.

"Then Hurricane Katrina happened. There were scientists camped out on the island doing research. Boyd told Clem to ferry them inland, thinking he had enough time to board up and shut everything down. The storm's projected path shifted enough that the east winds and surf slammed into Mississippi. It cleaved the island in two."

"Did they find him?" Pia wondered.

Sam shook his head. "Harvey, Clem and Hoyt searched for weeks. My dad, Alek and I joined them for a time. The lighthouse was still intact, despite flood damage. Most of the fort had been buried in sand, though it was still there. But we never found Boyd or his boat."

Babette propped her cheek on Sam's shoulder. "That's so sad. He was your friend."

That hadn't been the last time Sam had gone looking for a loved one. Pia watched his face closely.

"It was sad," he admitted, tilting his head against Babette's. "Clem stayed on as ferryman once the island opened back to visitors. And Harvey came back to the lighthouse. He's been there ever since."

Pia wondered if the lightkeeper had ever stopped looking for his boy on the horizon.

She knew survivor's guilt was a real thing. Bianca's face flashed before her eyes again and she had to breathe deep until the phantom heat of shame and regret that flooded her cheeks again in reaction eased.

Had Harvey come home because of survivor's guilt? Had Clem stayed on as ferryman because of it?

Sam's hand came to rest on her cheek.

"You're clammy," he noted.

Her eyes closed, and the headache behind them quieted when his thumb passed over her top lip. His touch was a balm. "Bad dream."

"Pia." He whispered it.

"I'm fine," she said, and made it stick. "How long is the ferry ride?"

"Normally, it doesn't take more than half an hour," he pointed out. "But the wind's strong out of the south. So it may take close to forty instead. Can you handle it?"

"Of course I can."

"You said you've been seasick," he reminded her.

"Only when the Gulf's rocking. I ate a bite just now, not a big meal, and I'm hydrated. That should help. It also helps that the weather's cool, not balmy."

"We've got time to swing by the store and pick up some Dramamine. Maybe some prenatal vitamins."

"I'm not sure I can take Dramamine while pregnant," she replied. They'd already chanced a stop at a rural gas station for fuel and provisions since they'd had to abandon most of the food back at the hunting cabin. While waiting behind a trucker at the checkout counter, the small box television mounted above the glass cigarette display had flashed her picture, then Jaime's, on-screen. The sound had been muted, but the subtitles across the bottom of the screen had flashed the words… CONSIDERED ARMED AND DANGEROUS. CALL THE NUMBER ON THE SCREEN TO REPORT ANY INFORMATION…

Sam had left a one-hundred-dollar bill on the edge of the

checkout counter and they'd walked out before anyone could make the connection between the woman on-screen and Pia.

"We'll research it and send Clem if need be," Sam muttered as rain pattered lightly on the windshield. "He does a supply run once a week. We're lucky he still motors to town on Tuesdays."

"Can he get more Doritos?" Babette ventured.

Pia felt her lips curve and watched Sam follow suit. He chuckled. "I don't think that'll be an issue," he answered.

The sound of his laughter swept over Pia. The deep-flowing wave of it took her breath away. Her pulse quickened.

She didn't know she reached for his hand until her fingers laced over the back of his. His laughter died.

She chanced a glance at him. He'd gone back to staring through the windshield as the wipers squeaked and batted at the rain, seeing but not seeing the docks, the white ferry moored there, the smattering of gulls winging overhead.

At the cabin, during the shootout, his eyes had looked so hard. Cold flint.

Soldier's eyes. It didn't matter that he'd spent over a decade out of uniform. The reality of combat had never left him.

The blue of his eyes was no longer hard, she found. With his elbow on the driver's windowsill and the knuckle of his first finger rubbing the seam of his lips, she saw hints of a smile there. More, she found light.

Sam was a soldier, one who'd served his country well. But there was still such light in him. She'd known that from the beginning. It was the same light she'd seen in Lyudmyla—the same light she felt when she held Babette to her or watched her smile.

Those lights had guided her out of the dark.

For a while, she'd wondered why Sam had sought her when her light had died in the hacienda.

As the years put much-needed space between her and the memories, her light had rekindled. When she felt it wake, when she'd felt it grow, she'd known happiness. For the first time, she'd known what contentment tasted like.

Jaime's return had brought the fear and pain and darkness back. If the last few days had taught her anything, it was that healing could be erased. As a by-product, her light felt, once again, fragile.

Jaime would keep coming. They would have to run. Again.

Would she have this baby on the run?

If Jaime found her, would he let her keep it?

Would he hurt Babette as he had hurt her?

If he found them, he would kill Sam, no question. Would he make him suffer first?

Jaime would take Sam's light and Babette's as he had taken hers. He'd break them.

The island may be safe for now. But the Solaros would find it. Jaime would find them.

"I like this song," Babette said, reaching across the center console to turn the knob on the radio.

"Billie Eilish?" Sam said after a moment's listening. "What happened to T. Swift and Imagine Dragons?"

Babette looped her arm through his, then the other through Pia's so the three of them were linked. "I still listen to them. But Billie's my new fave. And Halsey."

"What else did you get into while I was away?" he asked. "Any tattoos I should know about? Do you have a belly button ring?"

Babette's laughter soared. It was music. "Mom's been letting me handle the trolling motor when we take the skiff out."

"Is that right?"

"I painted you."

"Me?"

"Yeah," Babette admitted. She quieted. "I wanted to remember you on the beach with your camera. I painted you crouching down over a tide pool, framing a shot through the lens."

"You wanted to remember," he echoed.

Babette made a noise. "I showed Mom. I think it made her cry."

Pia couldn't avoid Sam's look this time. "It's very good," she said as an excuse. Babette had captured him perfectly. Pia hadn't been prepared for the tousled gleam of his hair or the skillfully rendered line of his shoulders, the absent smile that came over him when he framed a shot he liked.

"Neither of you trusted me to come back," he realized.

"I hoped you would," Babette said. Her fingers plucked the sleeve of his shirt. "I wished you would find him— Alek—so you wouldn't have to go away again. It worked, didn't it? You found him."

Sam seemed immobilized for a moment. "How did you know that?"

Babette lowered her gaze. Pia took a breath, untangling her fingers from Sam's so she could tuck a lock of hair behind Babette's ear. "She found the photos on your camera roll at the cabin," she answered.

Horror struck him. His jaw locked.

Pia caressed the line of Babette's shoulders. "Don't be upset with her. She was taking pictures of deer."

"I'm not upset," he said. Still, he brought his curled fist to his mouth. "I should've taken the memory card out and stored it. I wasn't thinking—"

"Why didn't you tell us you found him?" Babette asked. "You've been looking for him for so long."

Pia choked back her own questions. Was there a reason he didn't want her to know he'd found Alek—that his job in the Middle East was done? That he'd completed his mission, fulfilled his parents' wishes that Alek be brought home?

Why hadn't he confided in her? Were things still so broken between them he couldn't tell her what it had been like? He couldn't let go of his grief with her as he had so easily after Lyudmyla had passed when the two of them were practically strangers?

"You shouldn't have seen that," he said with a shake of his head. "Babette, I'm sorry."

"What happened to him?" Babette wanted to know.

Emotions worked over Sam's face. They colored it, the pink stain of anger or shame rushing up his throat to his cheeks.

"You can tell me," Babette implored.

He reached for humor. It didn't ring true. "Because you listen to Billie and Halsey now?"

"No," she replied. "Because I'm smart, and I know how the world works now."

"Not now, bébé." He dropped a kiss to the crown of her head.

Pia wished she'd seen what Babette had seen. It was hard knowing the depth of its impact without knowing exactly what had been on that camera roll. Sam owed Pia an explanation, if only to help Babette process it.

And the questions still burned on the back of her tongue.

She spotted the ferryman, Clem, in his bright orange beanie and sat up straighter, reaching for the pistol between the seat and the console. "Your friend's ready to load the ferry."

Babette retreated to the back seat as Sam put the truck in gear. He lifted his hand from the wheel in a wave as the tires bumped across the ramp.

Clem didn't raise his hand in return. He didn't smile either. Pia's grip on the pistol tightened in her lap when she saw the man's rough-hewn features under steel-wool eyes. His long face dripped with rain.

"He doesn't look very nice," Babette muttered apprehensively.

"Neither do manta rays," Sam said. "But they're harmless, too." They had the ferry to themselves as February was far outside tourist season and the island was closed to public curiosity until the third week of March. Sam chose a spot near the rail at the front of the boat. He stood on the emergency brake until it engaged, then killed the engine and unclipped his seat belt. "You don't need to worry about Clem."

"Are you sure?" Pia probed.

He glanced at the pistol in her lap. "He's an old friend. And he has no reason to hurt us."

"What if he's seen the bulletins?" she asked. "What if he's seen my face—recognizes it?"

"I'll explain," Sam said readily.

"Neither he nor Harvey will turn us in?" she asked.

"I trust them, Pia. If I can't trust them, I can't trust anyone."

She hesitated. Then she nodded and unlocked her door.

"It's cold and wet out there," he warned.

"I need some air," she admitted, and left the warmth of the cab so that the chill wind could slap her in the face.

The smell of the sea filled her. She embraced it, going straight to the rail. Wrapping her hands around it, she fought the urge to lean out over the water and scoop her hands through it as it lapped against the ferry's hull, deadly and playful all at once. The birds called to her. The sounds of water lulled.

Home, she thought, as the sun strengthened through a shred of cloud cover and warmed her face briefly before it disappeared and rain spit at her cheeks.

She heard the whirr of the ramp. Ignoring that prickling sensation at the base of her neck, she strengthened her hold on the rail.

If they were sailing to freedom, why did the ferry feel like a trap?

Sam trusted the islanders. That was fine. But Pia couldn't let her guard down. Not for a second.

She tucked the pistol into the front pocket of her hoodie, searching for the island in the distance.

Chapter 11

Sam hadn't returned to Smuggler's Island since the search for Boyd Dunagan. After Katrina, it had no longer felt like the island of his youth. In truth, it had felt more like a sandy wasteland, and a hopeless one at that.

He should have come back, he thought as he and Babette found their way to the bridge where Clem stood, his weather-beaten hands fixed on the ferry's helm. Harvey had been grieving his wife and his son, too. Sam should've checked on him, as he'd checked in on Myla regularly in Flamingo Bay after her husband passed.

He, Boyd, Alek and Hoyt had been as good as brothers. Harvey had saved his life once, snatching him out of the arms of the Gulf.

These waters had nearly taken Sam the same way they'd taken Boyd. He had woken on the beach at the west end of Smuggler's, coughing and vomiting water, and heard Alek cry out in relief. When his eyes stopped watering, he'd seen the tears tracking down his brother's face and realized how close he'd come to never waking up.

Alek had never ventured back to Smuggler's Island after that trip. To Sam's knowledge, he'd never sunk his toes in white sand again.

Sam couldn't ignore Pia's questions about Alek for long.

He wrestled with the truth about Alek—with excuses. There hadn't been time to tell her—he'd been too relieved to find them. Too shocked about the baby. Too focused on keeping watch and ensuring they were safe.

There was truth in all that. But there was another. How could he tell her—confide in her—when he was still wrestling with what was inside him and what he now knew about the manner of Alek's death?

He could no more bring that ugliness to her door than he could stand to look at it himself.

That Babette had seen Alek's body…what was left of it… It sickened Sam.

He squeezed her shoulder as he opened the door to the bridge and ushered her in ahead of him. "Clem."

Clem peered at them. He tipped his chin, the pocket under his lip where he kept a wad of Copenhagen jutting out slightly. He frowned at Babette. "No passengers on the bridge."

Sam stood behind her, regardless, fixed. "This is Babette. She just wanted a look."

Clem cast a glance from her to Sam before turning back around to face the front. "She yours?"

"Yes," Sam said, and felt Babette's tension ease. "How've you been?"

Clem jerked a shoulder. "Same old, as they say."

Sam wondered if "same old" meant more bad than good. Boyd had been more to Clem than a friend. They'd been partners in all but name since the state of Mississippi hadn't recognized gay marriage and hadn't been the least bit friendly toward the idea leading up to Boyd's death.

"And Harvey?" Sam asked. "How's he getting on?"

"Had a spot of pneumonia."

Sam frowned. "I hate to hear that."

"Doing better now."

"Good," Sam said, relieved.

"How long y'all plannin' on staying?"

Six words altogether, Sam counted. It was a good day for Clem. "I've wanted to bring the girls out to Smuggler's for a while. We'll stay a week if we can."

"Weather's piss poor for visitin'." He flicked a look at Babette. His face hardened. "'pologies."

"It's okay," Babette said. She slipped from Sam's hold and walked to stand beside the ferryman. "I can see it. The island!" She pointed. "Is that it?"

Clem glanced at her in surprise. "Eagle eyes."

"Do you live there all year?" she asked, curiosity winning out against Clem's curtness.

"Don't got anywhere else."

"What's it like?" she asked.

"Uh…hot in the summer. Hell in winter." He cursed at himself for cursing. Then cursed again. "'pologies."

She gazed at his rough hands, then at the helm. "Can I try?"

"Try what?" he asked. The question barked somewhat.

She lifted a hesitant hand to the helm. "I've always wanted to see what it was like—to bring a ship into port."

"This ain't no ship. It's a ferry."

"Please," she said, and threw a small smile at him to increase the odds.

Sam folded his lips together, amused. It was like watching a rainbow bridge the gap between storm clouds.

Clem scowled at her for a solid seven seconds. When the smile didn't break, he did. "Guess there's no harm in it."

"That's the way," Sam murmured, crossing his arms. He leaned back against the frame of the door and watched the man reluctantly show the girl how to steer the ferryboat.

Movement out of the corner of his eye made him turn

his head. He stilled. Pia stood near the bow, hair streaming out behind her.

Her face was white as a sheet. Her knuckles had paled to match it as her hands clutched the rail in a death grip.

He couldn't leave Babette here with Clem. Neither the girl nor the ferryman would want to be left alone with each other. So he watched, helpless, as Pia rode the waves of motion sickness on her own.

It was rough seeing her this way. Pia was bayou, born and bred. Even before she'd bought a vessel of her own, she'd had no problem with sea legs or seasickness.

He didn't know how to help her. He carried the bulk of responsibility for putting her in this position. He should've stopped what they were doing on the beach before Thanksgiving when he understood where it was going. Neither of them had thought about protection.

He hadn't thought. He'd let his needs take hold, lying back and letting her ride, letting her take hers, relishing the glide of her body, her curves to his planes, her skin to his.

He'd chased it with her—the magic that happened when they came together. The light they made.

She was on the run again—with a child inside her, again. It was difficult to revel in the joy of knowing what they'd made when he knew what she must feel.

They hadn't talked about having more children. Babette had been their sole focus. While motherhood was something she did well and delighted in, he didn't know if she wanted another baby.

When she found out, what had she thought? Before Jaime escaped, had she felt the same delight? Or had she felt only apprehension and anxiety?

He reached into his pocket and let the tip of his fingers brush the warm band inside it. He didn't know why he kept the ring on his person. It was lucky he had, or it would have been lost in the hunting cabin.

If he tried giving it to her again, would it look like he was meeting his obligation to her and their baby? Or would she see him? What he wanted? What he hadn't *stopped* wanting since this started?

He loved her. If Jaime Solaro would disappear…if he would crawl into a hole and die, Sam could tell her. He could offer her the ring and himself again. Then, maybe, they'd live out the rest of their lives on the Gulf with Babette and their baby. A genuine family.

The horn blared. Sam jumped, and he saw Pia do the same. Babette giggled and toggled the horn again in three blasts.

"All right," Clem admonished, batting her hand out of the way. "Don't overdo it."

Sam caught the discreet glance Clem sent him that had *help* written all over it. He held out his hand. "The captain will need to dock soon," he told Babette. "Let's leave him to his work."

Babette's hand slid into his easily. "Thank you," she called back to Clem as Sam opened the door for her.

"I drowned there off that beach."

Pia tore her gaze off the line of sand as the ferry completed its docking measures at Smuggler's Island Marina and caught Sam staring off to the right. He lifted a finger to the lighthouse in the near distance and the trees surrounding it. There, the beach curved out of sight. Lifting her hand to shade her eyes, she squinted. "How?"

"There's another island," he explained. "Another light tower on the other side in disrepair. The channel between is rough water."

"How rough?" she asked.

He made a face. "Rip current. And not the kind you can escape from if you know how."

She tried to see him as a child here. Towheaded Sam with sun-kissed cheeks, slim shoulders, a youthful smile and an eye for adventure. "You tried to swim across."

"I was the youngest of all the boys. I had more to prove. I was a strong swimmer, overconfident. When Boyd dared me to swim across, he did so because he thought I wouldn't be stupid enough to try it."

"But you did," she surmised. "And you couldn't escape the rip."

"Harvey was close by on his fishing boat. The boys waved him down, and he was able to pull me out and bring me ashore. Alek said I was blue in the face. He was sure I was dead. Harvey performed CPR and, after a while, brought me around. It was the only time in my life I saw my brother sob."

"How old were you?"

"Babette's age."

She loosened a breath. "And your parents kept bringing you back here?"

"Dad did," he said, crossing his arms over the rail. He lowered his shoulders over them. "Mom and Alek lost their taste for the beach after that. She asked me not to come back. But when the snow in Minnesota came, all Alek and my friends could think about was hitting the slopes. All I wanted was heat and waves and shore. Eventually, Dad stopped coming, too, and I'd camp out at Myla's in Flamingo Bay for weeks at a time between semesters in college. Drowning didn't scare me off like it should have."

"You know now, though," she pointed out. "Not to swim through rip currents."

He cast her a rueful smile. "You live and learn."

Didn't she just. She tucked the urge away to smooth the

lines from his brow with the flat of her hand. "I can see you here."

"You can?"

She nodded as she turned her gaze down the island's bend again. "Four boys, you the littlest of them all… Did you wear overalls, by chance?"

"And little else."

The image brought her a smile. It felt good, letting the folds of apprehension ease from the corners.

"This is where I learned to swim and fish," he said. "Surf. Dive. All of it."

Pia thought about Flamingo Bay. How, in a way, it was more than the place she called home. "This was your baptism."

"Yeah," he agreed with a slight nod. "That's exactly it."

Again, Pia measured the sand dunes, the boardwalk that snaked through tossing sea oats and palm fronds. "It's who you are."

"A big part of it. We'll come back," he told her. "When this is over. We'll come back to the island and enjoy it the way it's meant to be enjoyed."

She felt the smile drift away like grains of sand. *When*, he said. Not *if*. Desperately, she wished she could be as optimistic as him.

He took her hand and straightened when the ferry engine stopped churning and the deck under their feet shuddered. "Let's go ashore. I'll introduce you to Harvey."

"The man who saved your life."

"Yes. Then we'll see about settling in. Tomorrow, you'll want a tour."

He knew her so well. Her heart tripped over its own beat. "Where's Babette?"

"In the truck where it's warm."

The sea breeze and rain hadn't let up. But the warmth of

the truck cab had felt claustrophobic, and she'd known her seasickness would be worse if she closed herself inside. "Is there a road to the lighthouse?"

"An unpaved one. We'll follow Clem in."

"He lives at the lighthouse, too?"

"His quarters are next door to it, where my family and I used to stay," Sam explained. "Dinners were always communal between us and the Dunagans. Mabel kept chickens for eggs, and they grew their own vegetables."

What it must have been like, raising a family here. Two adults, two children all alone on their island. The remoteness of it struck Pia as idyllic where the isolation might seem like a nightmare to others. "What do you catch around here?"

"Just about anything," he said. "There's a grassy flat where we used to get perch and bass. There's redfish offshore and snapper when it's in season. The channel's deep. If you've got a good trolling motor or wheelman, you can hook anything there from triggerfish to amberjack. On the northeast corner of the island, the boys and I went spearfishing once. Hoyt hooked a nice grouper, but the blood in the water drew in a bull shark. We swam ashore so fast it was like we had propellers of our own."

"I'd like to take Babette fishing," Pia mused. "She and I never got to enjoy the flounder we caught."

"I'll see that you do." He reached up and smoothed the hair the wind kept batting into her face. Tucking it behind her ear, he traced the shell of it. "I hate that you're cold."

The heat of his gaze sank in. She gathered it because she was cooler than she'd like. And because she missed it—his heat. "I'm stronger than I look, Sam."

"Don't I know it." His eyes strayed to her mouth and the longing in them nearly sliced her in two. Her own coiled, sinuous, around her navel, down her thighs.

"Ready to come ashore?" Clem called from the dock.

Sam looked around and gave him a thumbs-up. "I'll drive. Why don't you hide that pistol away with the rest of the fire-arms?"

She felt the weight of the gun and frowned. "Why?"

"Harvey was marines before he settled down into his role of family man and lightkeeper," he said. "He'll know you're packin'."

"Are there no guns allowed here?" she asked.

"He'll be the first to tell you it's your God-given right to own one," Sam said. "But we're arriving unannounced and asking for room and board for the foreseeable future. If he knows about the weapons, he's bound to ask questions, and rightfully so. The island may belong to the state of Mississippi. But it's his. It was my baptism, but it's been his life-blood for fifty years."

She nodded reluctantly. "Okay."

He cupped the back of her neck. "Thank you." Then he lowered his head to hers.

His mouth washed hot across her lips. She opened, seeking.

He made a sound, one of surprise and hunger. The tip of his tongue teased her lower lip, and the light skim of his teeth followed in an encore.

The ache for him raged. All the parts of her that felt sensitized by hormones tingled. Her breasts turned to pins and needles, the sensation almost painful.

She'd wanted him, especially in bed at the cabin when he had traced the shape of her growing belly with his hands. She'd wanted him with an intensity she couldn't fathom.

Her arms went around his waist, gathering him in—the strong, familiar lines of him.

He was leaner, she felt. Hungrier and harder. She thought again of the soldier at the cabin, flat calm and lethal.

She thought she'd known him, all of him from the healed scar tissue beneath his ear from a firefight in Afghanistan to his left ring finger, which hung slightly off center at the first joint thanks to a childhood accident. She'd known him down to the triad of freckles on his lower back.

She'd found secrets in him over the last few days. Anger. Layers she hadn't trod or had been too scared or shy to probe before.

She wanted all of it now. Every inch.

There wasn't one part of Sam she didn't want or love, she discovered. It scared her how much and how far the longing for him went.

"Why didn't you tell me about Alek?" she whispered.

"I couldn't."

"Why?" she asked. "I've told you everything. Even the things I wanted to forget." The things she'd never wanted him to know. Things she'd thought for sure would make him turn away.

He'd stayed. Through the nights she'd fought nightmares and others, the early ones, when intimacy hadn't been something she'd been able to surrender herself to completely. He hadn't pushed her through those nights or walked out like she thought he would.

He'd stayed, held her and let her weep for all the scattered pieces of her soul.

After everything, how could he not bring himself to confide in her? "Is it because I wouldn't take your ring?" she blurted. "Because I hurt you so badly?"

He shook his head. Muscles moved under the frame of his jaw, and she knew he mashed his teeth behind his lips. A nerve in his temple pulsed.

"I need to at least know what Babette saw," she told him.

"He was broken," he said finally, shoveling the words

out. His voice dropped to a whisper. "Pia, his hands were missing."

The cold snaked in again, sneaky and thorough.

"His remains were in such a state…if it hadn't been for the serial number on his prosthetic leg, Stephen and I wouldn't have been able to identify him. I would have denied those remains were his altogether. I can't imagine his suffering. He knew what pain was. But Pia, they *hurt* him. Then they covered it up by burying him with other detainees because they knew exactly who he was. And they knew the price for torturing and killing a war correspondent."

"They didn't count on you," she pointed out. "Or Stephen. They thought what they did would be buried forever. But it wasn't. He's home now. That must count for something."

He didn't respond.

She probed gently. "Do you know who they were—the men who killed him?"

"Some. There was a village nearby. The extremists had a small base of operations there. A training camp, a prison."

"How did Alek wind up in a place like that?"

"I think he meant to," he said. "There was a guide he used and another. A driver. We think we found the body of the guide near Alek's and were told the driver most likely gave them over to the extremists. They put a price on every American's head. They would have paid well, even for a man who wasn't a soldier. Like me. If they wanted someone, they should've gone after someone like me who was trained in warfare, who knew how to fight."

"Men like those don't care about right or wrong," she said vehemently. "They don't give a thought to the rules of engagement or what's fair in the eyes of the law. They see humanity as a weakness." She couldn't stand for him to suffer a moment longer. She pulled him into her arms.

He went willingly. It took his body a moment to ease. She felt his ribs rise in an indrawn breath.

"I'm glad you told me," she said. "It's hard…when it lives inside you. I held Mexico inside for so long. It hurt. It's painful letting it out. But it's far more harmful to keep it in."

His face was in her hair, and their feet moved together in an absent sway. "I told Sloane," he murmured. "I'll tell you now. If Jaime finds us—if he comes for you or Babette—I will end him, Pia. I'll make it so you never have to look over your shoulder again. And I owe him for every sleepless night you've ever had. For every day you had to wade through to find yourself again, I will put that son of bitch in the ground."

She didn't know how to take that. Sam, pure and true, wanting to take a life. Not as a soldier in the name of his country.

Even if that life belonged to her personal demon… *Not Sam*, she thought with a slight shiver.

She would learn this island, in and out. If Jaime came, she would be ready for him.

Harvey Dunagan looked his age. With a flat cap of thick shock-white hair and a Dutch beard in the same shade, he squinted at the sight of Sam enough to make the lines of his face run together. "Well, slap my shamrock and call me a leprechaun," he bellowed.

Sam didn't say a word. Instead, he threw his arms around the man. As Harvey returned the embrace heartily, laughing in disbelief, Sam took comfort in the unreserved strength. As a kid, Harvey and his father had seemed Herculean. It was life-affirming, seeing them carry that forward.

Harvey pulled back, his cheeks flushed from the wind. He patted him hard on the cheek. "You rascal. Sneaking up on an old man in the dead of winter."

"I would've called," Sam weighed, "but…"

Harvey waved away the rest. "As far as surprises go, this one takes the cake. How are you, son?"

"Well enough," Sam answered. "How about you?"

"Fit and fancy."

Sam glanced back at the way they'd come. "Rumor is you've had it rough these last few months."

Harvey made a face. "Clem's been running his mouth again." His gaze moved to Pia and Babette behind Sam. Instantaneous warmth flooded his expression and his lips curved. "You brought company."

Sam turned to them, gesturing them forward when they hesitated. "Harvey, I'd like you to meet Pia."

"We meet at last," Harvey said, beaming, as he grasped Pia's hands in his. "I'm still in touch with my friends in Minnesota. Maks and Deirdre have nothing but wonderful things to say about you, darlin'."

"I feel the same way about them," Pia said. "I hope you won't mind us showing up like this."

"Not at all," he dismissed, and put a hand out for Babette. "And you must be Babette."

Babette tucked herself against Sam's side and studied Harvey discerningly. "I thought you'd look more like a pirate."

Harvey burst into laughter. It rolled into a harsh cough, but the pleasure never washed away. "I'm guessing you keep Sam here on his toes."

"They both do," Sam admitted, meeting Pia's gaze when she sought him.

"Come on in," Harvey said, motioning for them to come closer to the lighthouse. "Let's get out of the wind."

It smelled the same—like the smoky dregs of a fireplace and that ever-present salty residue that permeated the landscape. The rug in the den had faded almost to white and the small porthole windows looked smudged around the edges, but the Dunagan living quarters had changed little with the years.

"It's a bit cramped," Harvey warned Pia and Babette. "But we make do."

Sam knew Harvey lived alone. He had grandkids. Their round, smiling faces beamed out of framed photographs arranged on the sideboard. Hoyt and his wife, Romilee, brought them back to the island once or twice a year. The old man hadn't remarried after his wife passed. He barely got back to the mainland, content with his solitary status on Smuggler's Island. However, he and Mabel Dunagan had raised two boys on the island. They'd been a family of four who'd made the most of their lives alone here.

"You have a lovely home," Pia said, taking in the white-paneled walls offset by brick and blue-and-red-striped cushions.

Harvey gathered up an empty coffee mug and breakfast plate from the coffee table and carted them to the narrow galley kitchen. "Thank you."

Babette peered up the stairs. "Is the lantern up there?"

"It is," Harvey said. "Have you visited a lighthouse before?"

Babette shook her head. "I've painted them, but I've never been inside one."

Harvey beamed. "You'll need a tour, then."

Sam felt guilty, knowing how hard Harvey worked in the offseason to maintain the lighthouse and care for the island. "You don't have to go to any trouble."

"No trouble at all," Harvey dismissed. "I'm happy to do it. When's Clem taking you back to the mainland?"

"We were hoping we could stay for a few nights, if that's all right," Sam ventured.

Harvey practically glowed at the news. "I wouldn't have it any other way."

Chapter 12

Pia dreamed again that night. She saw Sloane so clearly, she tried to reach out and touch her.

I've come to get you out. I don't know where Grace is. But I can get you out.

There was something wrong, Pia knew. She could see it in Sloane's shaking hands and the half-moon shadows under her eyes. *You're hurt.*

They drugged me. It's what they do when the girls fight them.

There are others? Pia asked.

There are dozens. Maybe a hundred or more.

How did you get into the hacienda? There's no way out.

We can get out over the balcony. I found a way to climb down from there. There're guards out front. They don't think you'd be stupid enough to scale down the back side of the cliff.

Pia stopped. *We can't leave!*

What are you talking about? Sloane's eyes were crater-large. One pupil looked larger than the other, slightly. Her hair was a mess, her face slick with perspiration.

There was no way she could climb down a building, much less a cliff wall. Not in this condition. *Bianca. We have to take Bianca with us.*

Who's Bianca?

Pia didn't explain. Instead, she raced into the corridor, calling Bianca's name.

Sloane had found the way out. They wouldn't have to light a match. They wouldn't have to brave the fire. They could escape the hacienda together.

She'd rather plummet over the cliff edge to the rocks and ocean below rather than stay here another moment.

She reached the door to Bianca's room and pounded. *Bianca! Sloane's here. She came to get us—*

The door snatched open. The face that greeted her wasn't Bianca's.

It was Jaime's.

When he lunged, it was for Sloane's throat.

"I don't think your girl slept."

Sam stood with his back to the room, coffee in between his hands, as he watched Pia roam the curve of the western shore in the dawn's tender light.

Harvey Dunagan moved to the long line of windows that made up the long wall of his comfortably furnished den. He wore a plaid shirt, unbuttoned over a beleaguered gray marines T-shirt. There was a small paunch over his center, but he stood rod-backed and stern.

To look at Harvey was to know a hardened veteran. It was easy to miss the twinkle in his eye and the readiness of his smile, even if the family tragedies he'd faced had dimmed some of it.

"She doesn't," Sam admitted. "Not usually."

"Is the bed not comfortable?"

"It's great," Sam assured him. He raised a hand to Harvey's back. He'd put Sam and Pia in Hoyt's old room and Babette in the one with the connected bathroom—Boyd's. Both had been redone. Nothing of the boys remained except memories neither Babette nor Pia could see. "Thank you for letting us bunk in the lighthouse."

"Clem's not one for housekeeping," Harvey mused. "And he's hard around the edges."

"I think he's kind of cuddly." At Harvey's knowing look, Sam laughed a little. "Like a lionfish."

"He earned his spines. What keeps Pia from sleep?"

Sam knew exactly who chased Pia out of her nightmares. And it burned him. "She's expecting," he heard himself say instead.

Harvey's eyes bore into Sam. "Is this your way of telling me you're going to be a daddy?"

Daddy. Sam's stomach flipped at the word. "I already am."

"The little girl."

"Babette," Sam reminded him. "She's mine in all the ways that matter."

"What is biology when we build truer things like love and family?" Harvey challenged.

"I learned that here," Sam thought out loud. "Hoyt and Boyd were my brothers every bit as much as Alek."

"Boyd thought the same of you," Harvey told him. "Hoyt still does." He clapped a hand over the back of Sam's head and brought him in for a hard hug. "Congratulations."

Sam let himself be held. Little Sam flickered back to life in for the briefest of moments. He closed his eyes. "Thanks."

"So, is there a wedding in the future?"

Sam made a noise. "I'd like there to be. But Pia's—"

"Not traditional," Harvey assumed, "like us."

Sam settled for agreeing because it was simpler.

"I'm happy for you. Is that why you came—to tell me?"

Sam chastised himself for lying. "Yes."

"Tonight, then, we'll have a fish fry to celebrate," Harvey told him. "Do your girls eat fish?"

"They're regular fisherwomen," Sam said with not a small measure of pride.

"Fantastic. I'll talk to Clem, see what we can rustle up before the day's end. Meanwhile, after breakfast, we'll see about that tour of the island."

"While I'm here," Sam said, "I'd like to help with your lightkeeper duties."

"There's plenty of upkeep," Harvey considered. "But you're guests."

Sam couldn't let this go. "Let me help you. It's important to me."

Harvey inclined his head. "So you can stop wrestling over whether you want to tell me what kind of trouble you're into?"

Sam froze. "Trouble?"

Harvey's gaze was hazel, changeable, and wise. "I've seen enough to know when it's coming." He raised his hand when Sam opened his mouth. "You've come here either to escape from it or heal from it. It doesn't matter which. When the time's right, though, you'll need to confide in me. You know I'll help."

Sam didn't know what to say. Emotions caught in his throat.

"I think I hear the little one puttering around upstairs," Harvey pointed out. "Go check on her. I'll watch Pia."

Sam didn't need to hesitate. "Thank you," he said, and headed upstairs.

"If you want to watch the sunrise, you'll have a better view on the other side of the island."

Pia jolted. She turned to find Harvey crossing the sand to where she stood on the tide line, just shy of letting the waves kiss her toes. When she'd left the lighthouse's living quarters, she'd been sure everyone else was still asleep. "I like to watch night break."

"It always does," Harvey considered. "There's comfort in that. And it'll be a pleasant morning."

"It will be," she noted, "once the clouds part."

Harvey pursed his lips as he eyed the overcast sky. "Another hour." He handed her a mug.

"Oh," she said. "I can't have—"

"It's not coffee," he replied. "I made you some herbal tea."

She stared at the mug in surprise. Cupping her hands around it, she brought it to her nose. Notes of ginger and peach curled up her nostrils. "Thank you," she murmured.

"Morning sickness?" When she only gaped at him over the lip of the mug, he nodded. "My Mabel had it. Just the first trimester with Hoyt. Then for the full course with Boyd. She swore after she'd never put herself through another. And it was never just the mornings. I can't understand why they call it morning sickness."

She tested the tea, sipping delicately. The honey soothed her throat. He'd added just enough cream, too. "This is good."

He gave a nod. "How do you like our island so far?"

"It's lovely," she admitted. The seclusion lured her. And she'd always preferred nature as a focal point. "I can see why you've lived here so long."

"There were times life called me elsewhere," he pointed out. "There were times I thought I wanted to be elsewhere. But the island won out. It's not an easy life. It's lonely. But it's my calling." He canted his head curiously. "Do you believe in such things?"

Looking out across the frothing channel, she said, "The sea calls me."

"Does it now?"

"I didn't understand—not fully—until I went scuba diving for the first time. The silence of the water. The pulse of it. The hidden world underneath this one and the biodiversity that exists there. I remember it felt like home more than any house ever did for me."

A smile bloomed on his hard face. "Sam's found a kindred spirit, then. We couldn't any of us adults get him out of the water once he went in. It nearly took him from us altogether."

"He told me." She frowned. "Did it happen on this side?"

"It did," Harvey confirmed. "God knows how long he was in the channel before the other boys got my attention. I knew we'd lost him once I saw his face."

He'd lost his child to the Gulf. It was unimaginably sad that he could snatch Sam from its grasp and lose his youngest son to it less than a decade later. "You saved him."

"When his chest rose on its own and he rolled over and spit up half the Gulf…" He laughed, disbelieving. "He might as well have stood up on the waves and walked from here to Escatawpa Island for all the shock it gave me."

Pia narrowed her eyes on the beach in the distance, just visible as the morning light strengthened. "That's Escatawpa?"

"It is," Harvey confirmed.

"Do people visit there like they do here?"

"It's wilderness. Nobody's lived there since Jean Lafitte and Nez Coupé ruled these waters. Word is they used it as a hideaway. Nowadays, boats come up and fish alongside it, but nobody's inclined to go to shore for more than a pit stop. Not when they can come here. Smuggler's Island's got its own public restrooms, picnic areas and swimming holes free of alligators and snakes. Plus, there are the footbridges that crisscross the nature preserve, the old weather station on the east end and the fort."

"A working lighthouse, too," she noted.

"It's a draw, for sure. I open it up for tours a few weeks out of the year."

She pointed to the lighthouse on the distant beach. "Sam told me that one's no longer operational."

"It was decommissioned when I was a kid and abandoned shortly after because of structural concerns. It was built on solid ground, but years of storms have cut the land away by the channel. Smuggler's and Escatawpa used to be a lot closer. But once the land and the sand dunes disappeared, it didn't have a chance. It leans about thirty degrees one way, and at high tide, it's wet up to its first set of windows. One day, she'll tumble into the water."

Pia frowned at the decommissioned lighthouse dome. "How sad." He was fond of the old lighthouse. It would be his misfortune to witness its fall. "Thank you for pulling Sam out of the channel," she said. "If you hadn't…"

Harvey's smile came back, quiet this time. "The world would be a lot less bright, wouldn't it?"

She nodded. "My world would be."

"He'll make a good father."

He already is. Pia took another sip of tea, let the heat of it wash through her.

"You've seen it with your little one. Babette."

"She's not so little anymore," she said mutedly.

"They grow up quick," he said. "It's a cliché for a reason. He tells me you're not the traditional sort. But if there's a wedding in the future, I wouldn't turn my nose up at an invitation."

"Oh," she said with some trepidation. She glanced down at her hand before remembering she'd lost the ring back at the beach house.

Harvey's shoulder bumped playfully against hers. "I can't

think of a better reason for a salty old seabird like me to fly back to the mainland."

She found she could smile back at him, even if she was unsure of what to say.

When Harvey pivoted on his heel and left her to her thoughts, Pia marveled at how fast she'd grown to like him. He reminded her of Sam in that way. Unavoidably likeable and warm.

"Here."

Metal chair legs sank into the sand. She stared at the lawn chair Harvey had brought her and the blanket he offered. "You didn't have to—"

"We used to do this," he said, ushering her into the seat. He unfolded the blanket and laid it across her lap. "Mabel and me. Every afternoon. There weren't a whole lot of sunsets we missed once we decided to make a life here."

Moved, Pia gathered the edges of the blanket around her and felt the dregs of last night's flashbacks cool. "You're too kind."

"No such thing. Enjoy your tea. I'll see to it the little one has a hearty breakfast."

Stunned, Pia let him get several steps away before she called him. "I was wondering…"

"Yes?" Harvey asked, turning back.

"What communications do you have on the island?" she asked.

"I'm proud to say we have Wi-Fi," he said. "There's a computer in the office. There's a radio there and a telephone. Use it as you wish."

"Are you sure?" she asked, reluctant to reach for the openness of the offer.

"Sure."

Pia thought of Sloane. After the flashback last night, she wished she could speak to her, if only for a moment.

"Babette won't enjoy the fact that we don't have television here."

Pia shook her head. "Babette doesn't watch a lot of TV."

"No?"

"She likes the outdoors," Pia admitted. "She reads a lot. And she paints. I'd like to take her fishing. Tomorrow, I think. Once we've settled in."

"You'll need a boat," he considered. "I got one tied at the marina. I'll see to it you have the keys tomorrow morning."

Yes, Harvey's innate kindness was so like Sam. It made her blink. "Is there anything you would deny us?" she asked experimentally.

He pursed his lips in a thoughtful expression. "Not a whole lot, truthfully. But then, Sam already knows that."

Once the sun's rays split the clouds, Harvey gave them what he called the red carpet treatment and Sam, Pia and Babette enjoyed a full morning's walk around Smuggler's Island.

"The island's an eighth of a mile wide," Harvey announced. "Normally, the tide only rises and falls twelve to fourteen inches, so we don't have to worry about flooding unless there's a major weather event. Containment booms circled the entire island to protect it from the Deepwater Horizon oil spill in 2010. The island's open to day-trippers from March to October. They come by ferry or personal boat. We bring out lifeguards for the summer months. Since the nature preserve was established, there's no camping. One accident with a campfire, and with the winds, the whole island burns to the ground."

There were signs posted with historical markers, including the one that marked the split that Katrina had left. When questioned by Babette, Harvey offered a long and technical explanation of the engineering involved in bridging the gap.

The island was the same in some ways, Sam found. The waves along the south beaches were huge. They pounded the shoreline, roaring like thunder. The sand dunes weren't as high as they had been pre-Katrina, but they'd come back as certainly as the vegetation. The family of raccoons that had been there since Spanish explorers had landed on the island long ago had survived though their population had expanded more on Escatawpa Island across the channel. The scientific weather station was half-gone and roped off with signs warning not to climb the remaining structure. Old Fort Kimball had been dug out since the last hurricane. It had survived several wars and had had Spanish, French, British, Confederate and Union flags flying over it before its casements were abandoned.

Sam showed Babette the hiding places that had once thrilled and terrified him. "Alek and Hoyt threatened to lock Boyd and me in here when we annoyed them," he remembered, pointing out what was left of the sunken armory. "I had dreams about the tide coming in and being trapped inside."

"Sounds awful," Babette said with a shiver. "What was the fort used for?"

"Fort Kimball was built by the Army Corps of Engineers over the remains of other strongholds left by the Spanish and the French. Then the British," Harvey explained, the consummate tour guide very much in his element. "Once these walls were four feet thick and twenty feet high. It was completed before the Battle of New Orleans, which our friend Jean Lafitte played a hand in to great advantage to the country that eventually ousted him from these waters. The Confederates used it during the Civil War and were forced to abandon it. The Union claimed it, but it was never manned again."

"Sea turtle!" Babette said, pointing toward the lapping waves.

Pia and Sam followed her to the water's edge where she crouched, watching the shadow of the turtle's shell.

"That's a big one," Sam observed.

"Bigger than a dinner plate," Pia calculated.

"I miss Slider," Babette moaned.

Pia crouched, too, by Babette's side. She looked at Sam. *We'll get another turtle.* It was what he wished he could say and perhaps what Babette needed to hear. But he couldn't make the words come any more than he could make that happen until Jaime was gone.

If we go home again, if we return to Flamingo Bay, we will get another turtle, he thought to himself.

The sea turtle went with the current, its shape fading to shadow before blending in with the foamy green.

As they continued the hike, Babette reached for his hand. She held it as they traced the paths of the nature reserve and found the cove where the ill-fated spearfishing trip had taken place. It, too, had changed. The beach had eroded completely, and the waves licked the exposed roots of the surrounding timbers.

Pia leaned toward him as the four of them made their way back to the lighthouse. "There's a radio, phone and computer in Harvey's office."

"You want to contact Sloane."

"I do," she admitted. "But I don't know if I should."

"The Solaros can't tamper with her phone," he pointed out. "She's a Fed."

"I think they have more power than we think," Pia muttered. "Why else haven't they been caught?"

"Maybe they have," he said. "News comes slow to the island."

"As of two days ago, Jaime was still free. You saw the news bulletin at the gas station."

"If the last few days have taught me anything, it's that two days is a long time for someone on the run," he noted. "I'll check the news on Harvey's computer. Maybe we can send Sloane an email through his handle. We'll code it, just in case."

Pia thought about it. "We'll need to be ready. If the Solaros are monitoring Sloane's communications, if they've hacked her inbox, they could break that code. It won't be difficult to trace Harvey's family to yours."

They wouldn't be safe here forever, he understood. But it wouldn't take forever for Jaime Solaro to be captured and detained. He had faith in that. Taking Pia's hand, he threaded his fingers through hers. He felt the space at the base of her ring finger. There was a rough spot there, a small one.

A ring callous. His heart lifted. "Pia?"

"Hmm?" she mumbled, distracted.

He worried the rough spot on her finger, his heart rate picking up. *Have you been wearing my ring?*

Would you wear it now—for me?

He saw her again as he had on Christmas night, after asking her to be his wife. Her face had turned as white as the sheet pooled at her waist, the impact of the question playing out like a slow-motion train wreck in her huge dark eyes.

His free hand balled into a fist. He loved her, goddammit. It hadn't stopped. When the hurt was fresh, when he'd gone away, he'd wished it would. He'd wished he didn't need her like he did and had put an ocean between them—continents. And he'd realized that he was never not hers. The ultimatum he'd left with her, all or nothing, wasn't true. He would take any part of Pia she chose to give. She could break his heart a thousand times. It wouldn't change the fact that she and Babette were his home.

I'm hers. Whatever part of him she needed, however much, it was unequivocally hers. All she had to do was say so.

He wondered how long he would have to wait for her to say something. She'd given him the words once, quietly and unbidden—*I love you.*

Would she be wearing his ring right now if Jaime hadn't poked his head above ground?

He pushed the questions down. He buried them.

When this was all over…when the time was right…he would do it again. Get down on one knee. Ask her to be his. He would risk his heart. And no matter her answer, he wouldn't leave. He would accept whatever version of a life and family she could offer him.

He hoped she would know it wasn't because of the baby. The child she carried was every bit as much a part of the picture of family life he wanted as Babette was.

Ahead of them on the boardwalk, Harvey's head bent low over Babette's, eager for her questions.

Sam found he could smile. Watching Babette explore the island was like watching her come to life again. Pia drew her strength from the sea. Babette found hers in all aspects of nature. Being cooped up in the truck or the hunting cabin had dimmed her light.

It shone now as she turned her face up to Harvey's, angling it as she did when seeking knowledge.

"Babette likes it here," Sam said.

Pia stared at her daughter's back and the stooped line of the lightkeeper's. "She likes him, too."

"I wish I'd brought her here before," he lamented, "when things were easy."

"She thinks we're staying," Pia said. "She feels safe and thinks the running's over."

"Let her, if it helps."

Pia nodded silently, the color high on her cheeks. The sun was bright, and the breeze was brisk. It tossed the sea oats, making them whisper incessantly about how winter wasn't done.

He wanted to draw her against his side. There were many ways he could think to warm her. He thought of the marina yesterday, the kiss, and the heat cleaved into him.

He skimmed his fingers up the inside of her forearm and heard her catch her breath. "Harvey likes you."

"He hardly knows me."

"Whatever you said at the beach this morning..." Sam trailed off, wondering if she'd tell him what her conversation with Harvey had been about. "It made an impression."

"He loves you like a son."

"I have two father figures," he acknowledged. "Most people only get one."

"Some don't get any."

He recalled Pia's father, who had disappeared before she had grown to know him. Then she'd had to raise a mother who couldn't be bothered to raise her. It was where some of it came from, he knew—her hesitancy to accept him in her life as a husband. Outside of the brief time she'd spent with her uncle, Giovanni Russo, in New Orleans while attending Catholic school, she'd never experienced traditional home life, or even a supportive one.

He wished he knew other reasons she could have for rejecting him. Was it the hacienda? Somehow, after all this time, were her memories of Mexico and Jaime's abuse holding her back?

Or did she just not want him enough—love him enough?

He dismissed that before pain or frustration could seep in. "There's no high point."

He frowned. "What?"

"The island," she said as her head swiveled to look back the way they had come. "It doesn't have any high ground."

"Most barrier islands don't," he reminded her.

"Yes. The lighthouse is surrounded by trees. It's not the lookout point it was when it was built."

"The island hasn't been used for defense since the 1860s," he pointed out.

"What about the lighthouse on the other side?"

"What about it?" he asked cautiously.

"Harvey said it's fallen into disrepair," she said. "But there're no trees around it. It's taller than the one on Smuggler's Island. I imagine, from the top, you can see for miles."

"Yes," he acknowledged. "But it's prohibited. When I was a kid, there were signs posted warning people not to climb it."

"Did you, Alek or the Dunagan boys climb it, anyway?"

He swallowed the answer. "It's dangerous. Now more than ever." He saw the intent in her eyes. "Don't go there."

Her frown deepened. "Is that an order?"

He pulled her to a stop. Turning her to face him, he took her other hand, so he had both of hers in his. "Look at me."

When her eyes met his, he fought to speak through the knot forming in his throat. "I'm asking you not to approach the Escatawpa lighthouse. Please."

She blinked, then stared blankly at his Adam's apple before returning her gaze to his. Her chin bobbed.

Relieved, he squeezed her hands again. Then he lifted them.

His lips skimmed across her knuckles. They felt like blocks of ice against the heat of his mouth.

He heard her sigh. "Sam."

"You're not sleeping again." He rubbed his thumbs across the inside of her wrists. "Tell me what to do to help you feel safe."

Her gaze steadied on his. "I feel safe right now."

She said it in a whisper. His feelings beat against the walls inside him in response.

"Mom!" Babette called.

Sam looked up as Pia did. Babette had stopped at the edge of the boardwalk. She pointed, beaming, to three white-freckled red tubes sprouting out of the sand. "Pitcher plants!" she exclaimed.

"They are," Pia said, and she moved forward to join her and Harvey.

Sam didn't miss how the sun glinted off the clean, thick basket weave of her braid or how her hand slid from his slowly, reluctantly. The smell of the almond bar soap from the lighthouse shower trailed her.

His attention strayed slowly to Harvey, who was watching him. The smile had faded from his face and a frown rode it.

"Is everything all right?" Harvey asked.

Sam had a feeling that a storm was building. He wished he knew from which direction it would come and how much time they had. Shrugging his shoulders back, he tried to ease the tight feeling between his shoulder blades. "Yes," he said.

Harvey's brow furrowed. "It's not like you to lie, Sam."

Right. Because Harvey knew Sam, Pia and Babette were in trouble. Guilt filled him with uneasiness. He shifted his feet under Harvey's unbroken stare. "The wind's picking up. Should we head back for lunch?"

"We'll do that. Then I may find something for you and me to do. Together."

Alone. So Harvey could pick his brain and find out what

had brought them to Smuggler's Island. "I told you," Sam said, "I'd help you with the work."

Harvey made a rumbly noise of acknowledgment before moving along. He raised his voice to the girls. "There was once a whole bog of pitcher plants here. I've got pictures at the house. Why don't we head in for lunch and I'll show you?"

They explored what was left of the bog, then Harvey extended the tour to the lighthouse itself.

"What's it like being a lightkeeper?" Babette asked him.

"Well, you have to be self-sufficient, as we're so far from the mainland," he explained. "You have to be ready for anything, really. It's the only way to survive."

"You don't actually light the lantern, do you?" Babette asked.

Harvey chuckled. "No. All lighthouses in the US are automated, save the Boston Light in Boston Harbor."

"Then why do you need to stay here?" she wondered.

"Light stations require maintenance," he answered. "Somebody's got to keep it going. These are shallow, dark waters, treacherous for navigation, particularly between Mobile and New Orleans. Shoals shift, too, and storms lead to chaos. The government's required to keep navigational aids in place along channels and beaches. Smuggler's Island Lighthouse is forty-five feet from base to lantern, with walls three feet wide to withstand the elements. There was considerable damage done during Katrina, of course, but with public support and funding, we made it livable again. Did you know that lighthouses have played an important maritime role for over two millennia?"

"Sam said you retired before Katrina," Babette pointed out.

Harvey nodded. "I did. Yes."

"But you came back?"

Over Babette's head, Harvey and Sam exchanged looks. "The island needed help. I didn't want to see it abandoned entirely like Escatawpa. That didn't seem right. My family's been seeing to Smuggler's Island care and maintenance for a hundred years or more. We have to do our duty, Babette, even when it's hard."

Harvey moved up the stairs to the cupola, and Pia followed. Babette tugged Sam's hand before he could join them. "Like you did with Alek," she breathed, regarding him solemnly.

The admiration he saw in her expression hurt. He'd thought a lot about Alek on the walk around Smuggler's.

How did Harvey live with the loss of his son every day? It took strength Sam couldn't fathom. Sam had returned to the place where Alek had disappeared time and again, but he didn't live there. He didn't work there. And now that he knew what had happened to his brother, he didn't plan on going back.

Harvey's duty, as he called it, sounded like purgatory. But then, life after the death of a loved one could be just that if you refused to move on.

Sam watched Babette head up the stairs. The pit in his stomach complained like a sore tooth, as it always did when he thought of the condition of his brother's body and the intense agony he must have suffered leading up to his death.

She turned, eyes bright. "Are you coming? The beacon's at the top. Don't you want to see it again?"

She was a beacon. She and Pia were the beacons that had always led him back from the desert, the terrible things he'd left there as a soldier and the disappointing realities he'd encountered in the long search for Alek.

Purgatory wasn't something he had to face when he had them to come home to. He was determined to live the life he wanted—the life he'd envisioned with them. His duty to his family and his brother had prevented him from seizing that before. But Alek was home. And however much failure he may feel over the fact that he couldn't bring him home alive, he couldn't let that keep him from Pia and Babette any longer.

"Lead the way," he told her, and followed after her.

Chapter 13

Harvey kept Sam busy throughout the afternoon. Pia didn't see him until dinnertime.

Clem was surprisingly adept in the kitchen. He prepared a meal of shrimp, okra and sausage kebabs.

"It's like jambalaya on a stick," Babette complimented as she polished off a second helping.

Clem said nothing in response, but Pia saw the skin above the line of his bushy beard turn a fair shade of pink.

Pia offered to do the dishes. Harvey joined her, drying each and putting them away. "I'm sorry I kept Sam away from you this afternoon," he rumbled in a quiet baritone.

She handed him a dripping plate. "It's okay," she assured him when she noticed the exhaustion folded between the ever-present lines around his eyes. "I wish there was something I could do to help as well."

"This is enough."

She owed this man something more than washing. "I'd like to cook tomorrow night." Before he could shake his head, she quickly added, "Please. It's the least I can do."

Harvey's eyes narrowed on hers. "Because you're doing more than just visiting?"

Pia pressed her lips together. "I don't understand."

He shut off the faucet and dried the plate with a faded hand towel. "I'll tell you why I kept Sam out with me all afternoon. I thought I could talk him into revealing your secrets."

"My secrets?" Pia repeated carefully.

Harvey grunted. "I know you've got trouble. I know that's what brought you here. He's loyal to you. Protective. I questioned him. Interrogated him, to tell the truth. He revealed nothing."

Pia's lips parted. She closed them before taking the towel he offered to dry her hands. "I…"

"Just tell me one thing," Harvey said. "Are you running from the law?"

"No."

"But you are running from someone."

She hesitated. "Yes."

"And neither of you can tell me who."

"If neither of us tells you, will you ask us to leave?"

"Sam's family," Harvey replied. "Which makes you and the little one family." He dropped a glance down at the bump underneath her shirt. "Both of them. I'm not in the habit of turning family away. Particularly a pregnant woman and her ten-year-old daughter."

Pia closed her eyes briefly as Harvey turned away from her. She'd only just met him. But she knew he was worthy of her trust. "Sam wants to tell you why we're here," she murmured. "It's not in his nature—to lie to those he loves."

"He told me about Alek."

She nodded. "The more he talks about it, the more it'll ease his mind. There's a big part of him that thinks it should have been him in Alek's place. He believes he knew the realities of capture more than Alek did."

"Survivor's guilt," Harvey said, clutching the counter. "I've had my share. But it's more than that. Sam feels he failed his parents for not bringing him back alive."

"No one could have expected Alek to still be alive."

"No," Harvey acknowledged. "And the sting of that failure will fade with time. But part of it will always be there. I
was a soldier, too. You know on some level when you deploy
that there's a fair chance you won't come back alive. Your
family prepares for that, too, in their own way. Nobody—
including Sam—was prepared that it would be Alek who
never returned from war. His parents won't see it that way
and neither do the rest of us, but a part of Sam will always
believe it should have been him instead."

His fingers bit into the counter for a second longer before he met her gaze again. "He'll move on, though, after
the memorial. He has you, Babette and a future. He told me
you always pulled him back from the edge. It was why, after
Lyudmyla died, he never went back to Minnesota. He knew
his place was at your side."

Pia struggled for the right words as her heart took a tumble.

"He loves Babette like his own," Harvey said. "And he
loves you."

Does he love me, still? After Christmas, was Sam still
every bit in love with her as he had been before she refused
him? Or had some of that dimmed? Would he move on with
her now because of what she carried—this link to him? She
cupped a hand over her womb.

Harvey patted her on the shoulder. "If you're taking the
boat out tomorrow with Babette, you'll need your rest. I'll
finish up here."

Pia would have refused, but she didn't think she could
take any more of his curiosity or questions. "Thank you,
Harvey," she said, and turned for the stairs.

"Good night."

She found the lamplight spilling from the door to Babette's

room. As she moved closer, she heard the rumble of Sam's voice and peered around the jamb.

Babette lay under the covers. She'd turned toward Sam's seat at her bedside. Her eyes were closed, one hand fisted in the sheet, as it once had around the slip of a blanket she'd carried around as a lovey forever ago.

Sam's shoulders were slumped low, both hands underneath an open paperback. *Island of the Blue Dolphins*, Pia realized as she listened.

He or Babette must have found it on Harvey's shelves downstairs. Sam had read it to Babette twice before. She'd read it on her own a dozen times after.

Sam's voice faltered a bit as he neared the part where Karana's brother, Ramo, met with a pack of wild dogs. Babette dozed, unawares.

He knew she was asleep. Why was he still reading? As he kept on, Pia pushed off the jamb.

He jumped when she touched his shoulder. He fell silent.

She reached down, taking the book from his hands. Closing it, she set it on the bedside table and switched off the lamp. "Come to bed," she whispered.

He didn't argue. In the room next door to Babette's, he pulled the long-sleeved shirt over his head.

He'd lost weight, she realized. The ladder of his ribs pressed against the skin. His shoulders were still breathtakingly solid. With his back to her, he unbuttoned his pants and pushed the waistband down.

His waist was smaller, and she could all but see the burdens he carried.

He carried far too much.

He set the pants on a chair carefully when he discarded them, then he folded the shirt and did the same.

She zeroed in on the bandage on his hip and moved forward. Without saying a word, she laid her hand across his back. He stilled. She kept her head down as she carefully peeled away the bandage.

His chest rose on an inhale, but he said nothing as he braced a hand against the wall, angling toward the light so she could see the gauze pad beneath.

It was dry. The wound had healed over. It wasn't pretty, but as it wasn't red around the edges or warm to her touch, she couldn't find fault in it. Looking around, she found the first aid kit on the dresser where she'd left it.

He moved first to retrieve it. As he did, the lamplight shifted over his torso. She could see ribs pressing against the wall of his abdomen. Had this happened in the desert? Or was it what had happened since he'd come home? Some combination of the two?

Or had she done this? Had her refusal to marry him eaten at him so much that she could see it on the outside?

I'm sorry. The words knelled, loud as church bells inside her head. *I'm so sorry.*

The vision of him blurred. She turned away to escape into the bathroom where she disposed of the old bandage in the trash, then wet a clean towel with soap and water. Returning to the bedroom, she made sure her eyes were dry before she folded to the edge of the bed.

If she was responsible for the protrusion of those ribs, she didn't deserve the comfort of his arms.

He handed her the kit silently. Opening it, she selected a fresh gauze pad and the roll of medical tape and laid them out. First, she washed his wound and dried it. Then she covered it with clean gauze and taped it in place. Satisfied with her work, she closed the kit.

"Thanks," he mumbled.

She wanted to ask him if the wound still hurt, but she

couldn't get the words out. He'd already laid out a fresh T-shirt and black boxer briefs on the bed, his usual sleep clothes. She gathered them in her hands and lifted them to him.

He took them, moving to the chair where he'd laid his other clothes.

She didn't look away as he removed his socks or the boxer briefs he wore. The uninterrupted line of his vertebra followed his long, firm ass and the ranks of strong thighs made her lungs seize.

Everything about him was real and strong. She wanted to trace the triad of freckles on his lower back. Need gripped her, a vise. She pushed off the bed.

He stopped moving when she laid her lips across his ribs.

She let her hand rest against his hip and turned her ear against his skin.

The sound of his heart was fast-clipped.

"Do you still love me?" she asked.

He turned to her. "What did you say?"

She didn't lift her face for him to see. "I know I hurt you. I know there's a part of you that can't forgive me."

"What is this?"

"But I need to know," she said. "Does a part of you still love me like you did before?"

His hands took her face and raised it.

His eyes were summer blue. She wanted to swim in that blue.

His mouth dropped to hers.

The kiss brought her up to her toes. When his tongue found hers, her body bowed against the naked line of his.

She felt the wall at her back. His breath came fast, and her heart tripped as his mouth found all the sensitive places he knew underneath her jaw, along the column of her throat.

His hands glided across her back, down, over the curves of her rear to her thighs in an encompassing sweep.

She nipped the lobe of his ear. He groaned, then lowered his head, yanking the neckline of her camisole to uncover the globe of her breast.

"Blue," he said, surprised, tracing the veins underneath the surface.

She jerked her chin in a fast nod. "From the baby."

She felt the teasing note of his breath across her sensitized flesh. Then his mouth closed over her nipple.

She arced like a current, crying out as the pleasure-pain bolted to the vee between her legs. He sucked and she writhed.

She hissed when his stubble scraped across her skin and he loosened the straps of the camisole, uncovering her left breast so he could treat the other nipple to the same sweet torment.

"You're so sensitive right now," he groaned.

Need pulsed between her legs. She was on fire. His breath across her skin was enough to bring gooseflesh to the surface. The hand she still had locked in his hair fisted.

His knuckles followed the curve of her belly. He loosened the catch of her pants. Spreading, they lowered beneath her waistband.

When he plucked her, she keened. She watched his eyes fire and his jaw tighten as understanding gleaned.

He could make her break, just touching her like this.

He used fine strokes that made her hiss and moan. Her head tipped back to the wall, and she ground her teeth together to make herself quiet.

He pressed his mouth to hers, catching her gasp as he inserted one finger and felt how aroused she was. "Sweet Christ, Pia."

"Please," she begged. Just… "Please."

She heard the catch of his breath. "One question."

She wanted to move around him, squirm. She wanted the friction.

His gaze held, direct. "Do you love me?"

His thumb flicked against her. Her mouth dropped.

He did it again, making her bite her lip and breathe roughly in and out through her nose. "Do you love me, Pia?" he said again, slower this time.

The air was too hot, too thick. And her heart wept. "Yes," she cried.

He stroked now in the same fine, measured motion he had before. His cheek pressed to hers. His lips touched her ear. "Say it then. Say it so I know."

"I love you."

His moan didn't escape her attention. Hers followed in protest when he removed his hand.

He pushed her waistband over her hips, letting it slump to her ankles. He stepped back, took her hand and helped her step out. Then he lifted her against the wall. "Wrap around me," he said.

She crossed her ankles at the small of his back. His erection was thick, pulsing.

His lips brushed across her cheek, loving, as she took him in.

Her nails bit into his shoulder blades. She opened her mouth wide, but no sound came. It was too fine…too tight… too wonderful. She was so full, she felt every space inside her burn with light.

He began to move and she could have wept in relief.

"You're squeezing me so good, baby," he breathed as his hips fell into rhythm. "I missed this. Missed you."

She couldn't speak. Couldn't breathe. His pace quickened ever so slightly, and it was enough.

She unlocked, unspooled. The orgasm shot through her like a jet breaking the sound barrier. It shook the walls of her consciousness.

His mouth opened against her throat. "You love me."

She was levitating somewhere in the contrail. "I love you."

"Say it again. Please."

It was him begging now. So she said it for him again. He slowed, deepening his glide so that she felt every inch of him sliding home.

She clung as he brought her up toward another jet trail. "Don't leave," she heard herself say. Disturbed, she felt her cheeks wet with tears.

He stopped. His throat moved in a swallow, and beacons of emotions surfaced in his eyes. "You...you've never said that. You've never asked me to stay."

As he lifted his hand to wipe her tears, she pressed her lips together. "Would you have?"

"If you'd asked once, just once," he told her, "wild horses couldn't have dragged me away."

"Alek—"

"I belong to you," he swore. "This is my place. I've known that. Since that first walk on the beach with you."

She was going to ruin this if she didn't stop crying. "I hurt you."

"What I feel for you isn't sand," he told her. "You're going to have to learn it won't wash away—storm or no storm."

"You said *was*." She let the words fall like an axe swing. The sob that followed made her want to turn her face away. "When you left. You said you *were* mine. You said it in past tense and it's lived inside my head since."

"There's nothing past tense about it," he assured her. He kissed her to seal it, caressing her hair. He moved inside

her again, a long, sinuous caress that made her body hum.
"Nothing."

He brought her to completion slowly, drawing out her
pleasure so that it was a living thing inside her. He let her ride
it out and watched until his muscles seized and he planted
his hands against the wall to stop his knees from buckling.

She would've stayed there, letting the aftershock of or-
gasms take root. He summoned enough wherewithal to re-
arrange their feet so that her back was no longer to the wall.
In a series of shuffling steps, he directed her backward until
her thighs met the bed.

Instead of letting her tumble to the mattress, he swept her
up, one hand under her shoulders, the other under her knees.
Dipping one knee in the bed, he laid her across the pillows
gingerly before falling face-first into the comforter.

She felt a smile tug at her lips at the sound of his groan.
Feeling sparkly and replete, she lifted her hand to his back.
She stroked him, from shoulders to the base of his spine,
until his breathing evened out.

The smile faded as she charted every one of those ribs
with the tips of her fingers.

He shivered.

She paused.

"Don't stop," he whispered. He pillowed his head on his
arms, crossing them underneath his cheek and turning his
head to look at her. "Just tickles."

She went back to her tracing. When she reached the bottom of his rib cage, she shifted, laying her cheek across the
base of his spine.

They lay in companionable silence for a while before he
murmured, "I should get you a towel."

She closed her eyes, absorbing him—the smell of his skin,

the soft texture of his back, the strong shape of it. "Not yet," she whispered.

He subsided into the quiet but rolled carefully, stretching out on his back. He waited until she resettled her head on the flat plane of his stomach, angling one arm underneath his head. Then he brushed the hair from her face, tucking it behind her ear. He followed the strands, rolling their velvet ends between the pads of his thumb and first finger before repeating the motion.

It lulled her, so much so she caught herself dozing when he said, "I missed this the most."

She lifted her cheek as she blinked, trying to look alert. "Hmm?"

"When I went away," he added. He tilted his head so his gaze could circle her face. "This is the part I missed the most."

She didn't want to think about missing him. For once, she didn't want to contemplate who she was without him.

A small vee appeared on his brow. "I won't let anything come between me and you again."

She wrestled with all the things she wanted. From him, she wanted too much. She'd always wanted too much.

"Do you believe me?" he asked.

She swallowed. Her voice was lost, so she nodded in answer.

"You won't have to wonder anymore," he told her. "Where I am. Whether I'm coming back for you. Okay?"

Her eyes closed. Because she was tired. And because she didn't want him to see the storm behind them. The emotions swelled, and she had to swallow several more times to choke them back down.

For now, this was enough.

Chapter 14

Pia woke the next morning as Sam kissed her. She opened her eyes and noticed he was dressed, jacket buttoned to his chin. "I'm going to help Harvey," he whispered. "Sleep a while longer."

"Maybe I will," she contemplated, then grabbed his collar. He'd shaved. He smelled like soap and—just enough—of her. A smile curved her lips, lazy. "I'll see you?"

"You will," he promised, and kissed her more firmly.

She let him go before her body could wake up, too.

She allowed herself to stay in bed for another half hour. When light hit the windows, she rose.

She dressed warmly and found Babette stirring, too. "Are we going fishing?" she asked eagerly.

Pia smiled. Her baby was ready for an adventure of their own making. "Coat and boots."

"Yes!" Babette said, scrambling for day clothes.

The rest of the house was silent and empty. She found a carton of eggs, peppers and spinach in the refrigerator. She set about making omelets. By the time Babette jogged down the stairs and into the room, Pia had plated them and arranged them on the rough-hewn table. "Eat up," she said. "I'm packing lunch. We should find a picnic spot."

"There're lots of places to eat on the island," Babette said.

"Harvey showed me where the picnic tables are on the north side."

Pia rounded the table as Babette sat and dug into her meal. Pulling the band from her wrist, she finger-combed Babette's hair, then twined it into a fishtail braid. "Are you up for more exploration today?" she asked carefully.

Babette chewed, then took a swig of orange juice. "I thought we were going fishing."

"We are," Pia said. "But I thought we'd motor around, learn the area…"

"Harvey gave me a notebook and pencil for sketching. Can I bring them?"

"Of course," Pia said, finishing the braid. She banded the elastic around the tail before sitting down to eat, too.

"Does Sam know where we're going?" Babette asked.

"He knows we're going out."

"Is it a secret?"

"Not at all," Pia said. "We won't go far. I found a bottle of sunscreen in the bathroom vanity upstairs. You'll need some before we go."

Harvey had left the keys to his boat on the sideboard. When Pia drove the truck to the marina where the ferryboat was moored, she studied the '90s model Pursuit bobbing on the waves. Its white coat had yellowed slightly with age and the windscreen tinting was peeling in places, but it looked shipshape and ready for action.

When she and Babette came aboard, she located the life vests, flare, whistle and fishing gear. As Babette untied the bowline from the dock cleats, Pia cranked the outboard engine. It caught right away. The gauge showed a full tank of gas. "We're ready," she called.

Babette bent over to untie the bow line. Clem beat her to

it. "Thank you!" she chirped before toeing the gap from dock to boat.

Pia grabbed her hand to guide her over. When her feet were safely on deck, Pia sent Clem a wave. "Heading back to the mainland?"

Clem shoved his hands into his pockets. Under his beard, he scowled at the pair of them. "Nah. Just seein' to repairs."

He jerked his thumb over his shoulder at the ferryboat. Pia's hand hovered over the throttle.

Something in his manner set her ill at ease. He kept hold of the bowline, tethering the Pursuit to the dock.

Babette's back buffered against Pia's front. Pia laid a knowing hand on her shoulder as Clem continued to glower. She raised her voice. "Harvey left us the keys. He knows we're taking her out."

"On your own?" he asked, one thick brow disappearing underneath his ski cap.

"Why not?" Pia asked. "We've got gear. Harvey mentioned yesterday the fish are running between the islands."

"In the channel," he clarified.

"Yes," she said.

"Those are rough waters."

"I work on a boat," she told him. "I know how to handle one."

"Don't be going to Escatawpa."

She narrowed her eyes and said nothing to the warning.

"If the tide doesn't get you," he said knowingly, "the gators will. They eat everything."

"I thought Harvey said there were goats on the other island," Babette piped up.

"Sure, there are goats," he grunted.

"And raccoons."

He shifted his long rubber boats on the treads of the dock. "Yeah…"

"And a seabird sanctuary."

"Uh-huh."

"So the alligators don't eat everything," Babette theorized.

He pursed his lips so that the shape of them was distinguishable from his scruffy beard. "If the gators don't get you, then Escatawpa's secrets will. Pirates used it back in the day. Lafitte and his ilk left booby traps. Might find some old sailor's toes sticking out of the sand. Erosion uncovers the victims as time wears on."

"O…kay," Babette said speculatively.

"And that lighthouse. It's bound to fall any day now," Clem added.

"We aren't going to the other island," Pia assured him. "If we're lucky, we'll be hauling in our catch before the afternoon. Would you mind casting us off, please?"

He looked down at the rope in his hands. Then he seemed to give in, tossing it aboard. "You know how to radio for help?"

"We do," Pia called as she shifted the throttle into Reverse to put distance between them.

Babette waved. "Be back later!"

As Pia turned the boat and hit the throttle, the engine purred, the wind snapped, and the boat hopped over white caps.

Babette cleared her throat. "We're going to Escatawpa. Aren't we?"

"Yes," Pia answered readily and set a course.

The approach from the channel was indeed treacherous. It was almost impossible, running the boat up to the shrinking beach at the foot of the old light tower.

Pia avoided the salt marsh on the north shore that was indeed likely full of gators and other reptiles. On the south side, she found a pretty white beach to anchor the boat to. She tied it off to the trunk of a low, twisty tree.

It was clear Escatawpa Island was abandoned. None of it looked developed. There wasn't a hint of chimney bricks or the footprint of a home's foundation in the sand. There were no boardwalks, footpaths, picnic tables and certainly no restrooms. Babette pried an old beer can from the sand. Pia saw others, older, littered along the beach. "Fishers," she guessed. "They come here to avoid the crowds on Smuggler's."

"Campfire?" Babette asked, pointing to a circle of stones.

Pia nodded. She took the pack from the boat, shaking the water from her boots. "Got your sketchbook?"

Babette patted the lump under her jacket.

"Let's go inland," Pia suggested. "See what we can see."

Babette was nothing short of delighted when she saw the first goat, a kid who maaa-ed in alarm at their approach and took off through the trees. She stared in open wonder at the hole in a timber Pia uncovered. "It's a pirate post office," Pia told her. "A safe place to leave messages or weapons." She fumbled inside the hole, trusting there were no crustaceans to grab her fingers. "Not that there's anything left."

Again, they steered clear of the marsh, trekking east.

The lighthouse jutted up over the shrub trees, a once-proud fist that had gone jagged and rusty around the edges.

"High tide," Babette said.

"Yes," Pia said, disappointed when she saw the waves seeping through the open entrance. The sand was piled up along the sides, making the door level with the ground an easy access point for the tide.

"It's kind of creepy," Babette observed, raising her hand over her eyes to shade them. "And cool."

Pia heard something and looked around. She smiled at the raccoon. "We're not alone."

Babette spun. She crouched quickly, holding out her hand. "Can I feed him?"

Pia pulled the pack off her back. She took out a bag of unsalted nuts. "Not from your hand," she said as she dumped a variety into Babette's palm. "Toss a few and see if he takes them. Then walk away so he knows it's safe."

Pia stood back to watch Babette work. She did exactly as she was told, cooing to the raccoon. It looked self-sufficient, large and round. A wild thing, though it didn't bare its teeth and there was no hint of foam around its muzzle.

Babette stepped back, allowing the raccoon to pick the nuts from the sand and stash them in its mouth before it scurried back into the trees. When she turned to Pia, she was smiling hugely. "It left little baby footprints everywhere."

"They do that," Pia noted. "Walk with me?"

They found a mermaid's purse in a tangle of sun-dried seaweed. It was slit on one side. Pia pointed the opening out to Babette.

"It hatched," she breathed. When she held out her hand, Pia set the egg case in it. "Can I keep it?"

"I don't see why not," Pia said.

"Are there more?" Babette asked, looking around at the trail of seaweed that followed the tide line. "I've always wanted to find one with babies inside."

Pia let her search while she combed the shoreline for her own purposes. Smuggler's Island was visible across the channel. She wondered if the men could see her and Babette's figures wandering the forbidden beach.

After an hour more of exploration, she and Babette found a nice, flat area to spread the picnic blanket. They split a few leftover shrimp kebabs and an apple. Babette finished eating quickly, took out her sketchbook and pencil, and began to draw, belly down and comfortable, on the blanket.

The tide was now at its highest as it churned around the first set of porthole windows.

She could swim it, Pia wagered. Not today. After the hike, it would tire her out too much. She studied its design. The stairs were on the inside, not outside—just like Harvey's lighthouse. The small windows went all the way around and there was a set on every level.

Five stories up, a broken glass enclosure stood underneath a tarnished roof. The railing was in place. Pia sliced a chunk from her apple with her pocketknife and brought it up to her mouth, considering.

"No gators," Babette said after they had packed up and were making their way back to the south beach.

"Mmm," Pia said with amusement. "Not on this side."

"No bodies."

Pia almost smiled at that. "No toes, anyway."

"No booby traps either."

"Clem would be disappointed."

"If he knew," Babette added.

"If he knew," Pia said with a nod.

"Can I tell Sam we came here?"

Pia thought about it. "Best not, I think."

"He wouldn't care."

"He would," Pia asserted. "He drowned trying to swim here from the other island when he was a boy."

Babette halted. "What?"

"Harvey had to revive him."

"Why would he swim across the channel?" Babette asked. "There's a rip current."

Pia was pleased Babette had recognized the fact. "He said it was a dare."

"Stupid thing to die for."

"He didn't mean to drown."

"Still…" Babette heaved a sigh. "I can't believe anyone would try, least of all him."

Pia saw she was shaken by the truth of Sam's near-death experience and reached out to soothe the line of her shoulders. She kept her arm around Babette as they moved past the pirate post office.

Pia memorized its position, counting their paces from it to the beach.

They spent the afternoon fishing, reapplying sunscreen as needed. Babette reeled in a black drum. As thrilled as she was by the size, Pia couldn't let her keep it. "The large ones have too many parasites," she reminded her as she repaired the line.

They found a sandbar on the north side of Escatawpa Island where the birds winged and clustered and the dolphins hit the top of the water, chasing a school. Pia reeled in a bonito and Babette surprised them both with two bright red vermillion snapper.

The sun was sinking fast, and Pia's fatigue showed its face as Babette caught the last fish of the day, a triggerfish. "Look at its teeth," she marveled when it calmed enough for her to pull its gums back. "Like a really big, really ugly parrotfish."

Pia heard herself laugh. "Ready to call it a day?"

"Yes," Babette said with a contented sigh as she settled against the gunwale and hugged her knees. The orange light of the setting sun spilled across her face, and she closed her eyes. "It's been a good day."

"It has," Pia said. Unable to help herself, she combed the loose strands of Babette's braid away from her face where they'd caught on her lips.

"Just like home."

Pia tilted her head. "We'll go home again," she assured her.

"You think so?"

Pia nodded. "Yes." And she smiled to make it true.

Babette considered. "I was starting to wonder what it would be like for you."

"What?" Pia asked.

"Giving birth on an island with two people on it," Babette said.

Pia laughed again. "I doubt Clem's adept at catching babies."

"Like Grace caught me."

"Yes."

Babette snorted. "He'd run when your water broke. I miss Grace and Sloane."

Pia traced the line of her cheek. "We'll see them again. I'm glad we took the day. Just the two of us. Good medicine for both of us."

Babette sobered quickly. "But it won't just be the two of us anymore, right? Sam's staying."

Pia found, for the first time, she could answer freely. "Yes," she said.

"So, you'll marry him?"

Pia sighed, taking a moment to lean against the gunwale, too, and look up at the thin blanket of high, icy clouds. "Let this be enough for now. Can you do that for me?"

Babette paused only briefly. "Okay."

Babette napped on the way back to Smuggler's Island. Pia tied up at the marina and transferred the pack and their catch to the truck before rousing her for the drive to the lighthouse.

She felt exhaustion creeping in, but she cleaned the fish and left the fillets to soak in a bowl of icy water before discarding the remains in a hole outside, covering it, and heading upstairs to shower.

Like yesterday, the men didn't join them until dark. Harvey and Sam went to clean up. Babette helped prepare a salad, tearing lettuce, shredding carrots and slicing cucumbers while Pia pan-fried the fillets in butter and lemon. She served them over a bed of angel-hair pasta, letting the juices soak through.

"May I say," Harvey said as he and the others pulled their chairs up to the table, "this looks excellent, ladies."

"The triggerfish was my catch," Babette boasted. "Mom caught the bonito."

"You were out later than you said," Clem said without looking up as he sliced the fish with the edge of his fork.

He'd still been at the marina when she'd brought the Pursuit in. "It's hard to call an end to the day when the weather's fair," Pia said.

"Hear, hear," Harvey agreed heartily, spooning greens into his mouth.

Beside her, Sam cast his eyes up to hers. "It's very good," he murmured.

She softened. "I had a good teacher."

His eyes warmed into a smile before he went back to eating.

"Where'd you go?" Clem asked.

Pia exchanged a quick glance with Babette before nodding for her to answer. "Just off the south beach. We trolled back and forth for the better part of the day."

Clem grunted. "I noticed you headed west when you left this morning."

Harvey's fork clinked against the plate lightly as he raised his napkin to his face and patted his mouth. "You crossed the channel."

"Just from north to south," Pia claimed.

"We had a picnic," Babette chimed in. "I fed a raccoon and found a mermaid's purse. I'm going upstairs to sketch it after dinner. Oh, and there was a baby goat, too!"

Clem paused. "A goat?"

Harvey narrowed his eyes. "There aren't any goats here on Smuggler's. Not that I've seen in thirty years."

Pia felt Sam stiffen beside her.

It was Clem who said it. "You went to that other island. Didn't you?"

She didn't miss the accusation in his voice. Still, she looked him dead in the eye. "I told you this morning there was no need to worry about us. We stayed well away from the marsh. Though Babette and I appreciate your concern."

"And the light tower?" Sam asked.

She shook her head. "We didn't go near it."

Clem scoffed. "I knew you were lying," he muttered as he raised his glass of sweet tea to his folded mouth. "You both had that look about you."

"Clem," Harvey said in a low warning. "Pia and Babette can handle themselves."

"Oh, yeah?" Clem asked. "Then what have they got to say about them weapons I found in the back of their truck?"

Pia stilled and felt Sam do the same.

Harvey's frown deepened. "What kind of weapons?"

"Guns, mostly. Though I saw a mean spear."

"Gig," Pia muttered.

"What was that?" Clem barked.

She threw his hard stare back at him. "It's not a spear. It's a gig. My gig."

"Are the guns yours, too? Or did you steal them?"

"That's enough," Sam said low.

He was quiet, so quiet Clem didn't question them further.

Harvey leaned back in his chair, considering. "I take it this has something to do with that trouble you won't tell me about," he surmised.

Sam set down his fork.

Harvey considered. "I won't begrudge a man—or a woman, for that matter," he added quickly with a glance at Pia, "his or her weapons. But a truck full of them—"

"And ammo," Clem inserted handily.

Harvey spared him a quick glance before he continued. "—does warrant something of an explanation. Wouldn't you say?"

Sam let the question lie. As the silence thickened and the tension between him and Harvey tautened, Pia could stand it no longer. "It does," she admitted, and continued. "You have a right to know why we brought them. If trouble follows us here, you'll need to know what kind and how we plan to meet it."

"Pia," Sam said.

"He's right, Sam," she said. "If we plan to stay, we can't keep this secret."

He searched her face.

Pia turned her attention to what was left on her plate. "If you'll excuse me, I think I'll head up to bed." As she placed her napkin on the table, she met Harvey's eyes. "If you can wait until morning for an explanation."

He nodded. "Get some rest."

Not likely, Pia thought as she dropped a kiss to the crown of Babette's head. "Let me know when you'd like me to tuck you in."

"I'm sorry, Mom," Babette muttered.

Pia folded Babette's face between her palms. "You've done nothing wrong. I put your sketch pad on your bed." She kissed her temple before heading for the stairs.

* * *

Sam found Babette on her bed, sketching, when he went up to check on her. When she folded the cover over it carefully at his approach, he shook his head. "I'm not mad."

"You're sure?" she asked, peering at him with eyes deeper than shadows.

"Yes," he said, and lowered to the bed's edge. "Show me, please."

She opened the sketch pad hesitantly and nudged it toward him.

He flipped through the pages. There was a tree with a large hole in it. Then a beach littered with seaweed. A raccoon digging in the sand and another, a close-up of its face.

"The raccoon made quite the impression," he noticed.

She said nothing, banding her arms over her middle.

He found the baby goat, its small goatee and smaller mouth etched endearingly. Then, on the next page, the light tower.

He felt his brow furrow. "You got close."

"Mom didn't lie to you," Babette said. "We didn't go inside. We couldn't go near it at all because of the—"

"Tide," he finished. On the next page, he saw the sketch she had done of Pia at the helm of the Pursuit. And on the last page, the mermaid's purse.

Sam closed the sketch pad.

"Please don't be mad at Mom."

"I couldn't." He cleared his throat when his voice cracked. "I couldn't be. Not for long."

Babette's cheek nestled against his shoulder. "You don't have to read to me."

"Don't you like *Island of the Blue Dolphins*?" he asked. "Or are you reading Woolf, Hemingway and Tolstoy now?"

"I like *Island of the Blue Dolphins* just fine," she said,

missing the joke. "It's just that it makes you sad. Especially the part when Karana's brother dies."

How astute she was. More than he'd given her credit for. "I thought you slept through that."

"I pretended to, so you wouldn't have to read that part. But you kept going. And you sounded so upset."

"We can skip that part tonight."

"I think I'd just like to sketch a little longer."

He nodded. "Want me to tuck you in?"

"Mom said she would, remember?"

"I'll send her in," he agreed. "Ten minutes?"

"Twenty," she said.

"Agreed." He touched a kiss to the top of her head. "Good night, Babette."

"Good night, Sam."

He left the light on and the door open.

Pia wasn't in bed. She wasn't in the bedroom at all.

He wandered through the lighthouse before he wound his way up the spiral staircase to the cupola.

At the top, the Fresnel lens rotated and beamed. After the dark of the stairwell, it took Sam's eyes a moment to adjust.

Pia's figure coalesced on the far side of the dome, her attention fixed through the glass. Beyond her, he could see blinking lights along the mainland.

He moved around the lens to stand beside her.

Her chin sliced up, and her eyes found his. She didn't offer him a greeting.

The silence between them wasn't comfortable. He felt it pricking along his skin. Trying to drain the tension from dinner, he broke it. "You said you were tired."

"We both know I can't sleep," she muttered.

He wanted to curse. "We don't have to tell Harvey."

"Yes, we do," she said. "He's worried about you. He

thinks you're mixed up in something you can't control. And Clem—"

"I don't give a damn what Clem thinks," he told her.

"He lives here, too," she reminded him. "This is their home. Not ours."

"Why did you say that at dinner?" he asked.

"What?"

"'If trouble follows us here, you'll need to know how we plan to meet it.'" He studied her closely. "Not run from it. Meet it."

She hesitated. Then, "Yes."

"Is this why you tried to go to the other lighthouse?"

"I didn't go there."

"Pia," he said.

She subsided. "I tried," she admitted. "I did. But the timing was wrong."

He whispered an oath.

"Do you think I'd take Babette anywhere she wasn't safe?"

"No," he said, and meant it.

"There aren't a lot of easy ways out if Jaime finds us here," she told him. "It's head for open sea or…"

He turned to face her. "Or?"

"Or we stand our ground."

His lips parted. "Do you know what you're saying?"

"I do," she replied. "I've tried running on the water. I've tried running on land. Neither lasted for long. If we head for open water, who's to say how long the fuel will last or our provisions? Our ammunition?"

"Do you understand that standing our ground means meeting Jaime Solaro and his men face-to-face?"

She tipped her chin. "Yes. The light tower has defensive positions on all sides. There are windows all the way around every level. The only other option is the fort. But it's vulnerable at several points. There's not a lot of cover in those places. It's penetrable. The light tower on the other side isn't." She noted the look of incredulity on his face. "I know it seems crazy. But it's—"

"Falling down," he told her. "In disrepair. You'd need to time Jaime's arrival at low tide. That's asking for luck, something we haven't had a lot of."

"I'm a strong swimmer."

"*I* was a strong swimmer," he countered.

"You got caught in the current between the islands," she said. "Not on either side of it. A boat could get us past the rip current. From there…"

"We stand our ground?" he repeated. "Against God knows how many men and how many weapons with our backs against the wall and no one to back us up? No Sloane. No Feds or police or coast guard for miles? We're not an army, Pia. And this isn't war. This is your life. This is Babette's life…"

"I can't think of anything more worth fighting for," she murmured. "Can you?"

He winced. "You *know* I'd fight for you."

"But you'd rather run," she guessed.

"It's safer for both of you."

"And what if Jaime never stops coming?" she challenged. "What if this never ends? Are we going to spend the rest of our lives in the wind? Where am I going to have this baby, Sam? On the deck of Harvey's Pursuit? On a deserted island somewhere south of here we don't know the name of? Are *you* going to deliver it?"

He took a steadying breath. "You're scared. Fear makes it hard to think objectively."

Her face hardened. "I'm thinking more clearly now than I ever have. I'll take my chances here. If Jaime brings the fight to us, I won't run again. I'm going to defend myself, Babette and this child with everything I have."

Apprehension bit down on him. He could see the girl from the hacienda with a lighted match between her fingers. "What if it's not enough?"

She must've heard the waver in his voice because she blinked several times. She closed the space between them and raised her lips to his.

His hands wrapped around her wrists as she brought her hands up to meet his jaw. When she lingered, he made an involuntary noise in his throat as his heart kicked up a pace.

She broke off but didn't shift away, her arms twining around his waist. "Then I'll have to be stronger. I'll have to be more."

"You're everything," he told her in a whispered rush.

She smiled, and there was a hint of sadness in it. "Are you with me, Sam?"

She'd do this with or without him. She'd done so much on her own. Her eyes shone with tears. She kept them at bay, and the strength of that alone was tremendous.

"I'm with you," he told her. "You know I'm always with you."

A breath cascaded out of her in relief.

He wrapped her up and held her as the rotating light passed over them once, then twice again.

"You were wearing my ring." It left him in an involuntary rush. "The night Jaime's men tried to take you from the beach house. I found it above the kitchen sink."

Her eyes went round.

He nodded as silence took her. "You would have put it back on, wouldn't you, when you were done cleaning the flounder?"

"I..." She trailed off, fumbling.

His hands slid over hers, then under them before he took them both in his. "I'm going to ask you once more. Just once and never again, I swear. And if your answer is the same as it was before, I'll live with it. But I need to know…would you marry me?"

Her face crumpled. "Sam."

He tried not to hold his breath. And failed. "I need to know."

She shook her head. "That's not… That's not how you asked me the last time."

He frowned. "I asked you to marry me."

"Yes, but…"

"I'm pretty sure there're only a handful of ways to do that," he considered.

"You asked me," she said carefully, "to be your wife."

"It equates to the same thing, doesn't it?"

"It hit differently," she told him.

"Why?" he asked, perplexed.

She closed her eyes. Her brow knit. "Because that's what he called me. At the hacienda. He called me his wife."

He went cold. "Jaime."

She nodded. "And after hearing that word…even after all these years… It *paralyzed* me."

He looked back. Three months back. And saw her as he had then—pale, tight-lipped. Silent as the grave.

She hadn't refused him, he thought. She'd been rendered speechless.

"Why didn't you tell me?" he asked. "If I'd known, I could have phrased it differently."

"Because I thought he ruined me," she said, and her voice shook. "I saw his face in that moment. I heard his voice when I only should have heard yours. And I was afraid every time you said those words to me…those sweet, sweet words…*my wife*…that I would see and hear *him*. You deserve more than that. You deserve somebody who can give herself freely— who hears you, only you."

"He didn't ruin you," he said fervently.

"Sam…" Her lips trembled. She pressed them together, making them still. "Sometimes…when I dream of the hacienda, I'm back in that bed…with Jaime's hands around my throat."

Sam heard the groan work its way up his throat. He reached for her.

Her grimace made him stop. Even more so when she held up her hands. "But in these dreams, he doesn't stay Jaime. Sometimes…" She swallowed and made herself continue. "Sometimes he turns into…"

When she trailed off again, unable to finish, it became clear to him. It made Sam hurt. "Me."

She didn't meet his eyes now. It took her a minute to gather herself. "You're wrong, see? He did ruin me. He warped some part of my mind. You need someone whole and untwisted. I'm not that person."

He had to curl his hands in on themselves to stop himself from touching her. "Pia, do you *want* to marry me?"

"You're not hearing me," she argued, her voice strained.

He dug in his pocket and pulled out what he'd carried there for days. "When I showed this to you the first time, there was a moment before I asked you. You knew what it was. Before you heard the words 'my wife,' what were your mind and your heart saying?"

She thought about it. Then she shook her head. "That's not the point."

"That's exactly the point," he insisted. "When I was gone, and you put my ring on your finger and wore it, was it because you didn't want me?"

"Of course not."

"Why, then?" he asked.

"I…" She licked her lips. "I wanted to know…what it would be like."

"What?"

She released a breath. "To…give myself freely. To belong to you."

"Is that what you want now?" When she didn't answer, he asked, "In these dreams, do you believe I'd actually hurt you?"

"No!" she blurted. "Of course not!"

"Okay," he replied. "Then wear it again. Please. You don't have to marry me. I'd just like to see my ring on your finger, the same way you wanted to."

His heart pounded between them as she considered, the lines in her brow refusing to go away. Finally, she lifted her chin in acceptance.

The breath left him. He made his hand steady as he took hers and slid the ring into place on her fourth finger.

The Fresnel lens caught the diamond on its next rotation. The facets flashed, blinding.

They stared at it together. Then he murmured, "I will stand beside you. I will fight for you. For ours. And I will love you, no matter what comes."

"You want something more," she groaned. "You always will."

"I'm yours," he said. "With or without an exchange of names."

Her eyes shone when she turned them up to his.

"Keep it," he breathed, tracing the band. "Don't look at it as a promise of marriage. Look at it as a promise for forever. *That's* what I should've said at Christmas."

She bit her lip, then cast her dark eyes back up to his. "I will," she whispered.

Emotions filled him to bursting. He touched his brow to hers. "Thank you."

"I do love you, Sam."

"I know," he said. "And I'm keeping that with me."

"I like wearing it," she revealed shyly. "Before, it made me feel close to you."

"Get used to that feeling. It's you and me, Babette, and this—" he cupped a hand over her womb "—against the world. This is my place. This is where I stand."

She lifted her arms around him and kissed him like her life hung in the balance. And it was more than enough.

Chapter 15

Harvey released a heavy breath. "That's a hell of a plan."

Pia watched him. None of this would work without his consent. "We were hoping you'd have some input."

"As a former marine?" he asked.

"As a friend," Sam put in. "As a father. A husband. An islander. And yes, a soldier. We can't move forward with this without your say-so. This is your home. We'll scrap everything and move on to the next plan if this isn't something you want."

"I want all of you safe."

"When Jaime Solaro is back behind bars or, better yet, dead," Sam said grimly, "that'll be the case. But not before then."

Harvey thought about it. "Based on what you've told me, a truck bed of weapons makes perfect sense."

"I just hope it'll be enough," Pia said.

"How many men does this Solaro fella have?"

"We're not sure," Sam weighed. "Our contact in the FBI estimates anywhere from eight to twelve. One or two may have been wounded in a shoot-out a little over a week ago when they went after Pia's friend, Grace Lacroix, and the man traveling with her who has past ties to the Solaro crime family, Javier Rivera. There might've been a few disabled, too, during the shoot-out at Alek's hunting cabin."

Harvey tapped a finger on his chin as he stared at the printout of Jaime's face. Sam had copied it from a news bulletin off the computer in Harvey's office. "Every law enforcement official in the South has joined in the manhunt for this guy and he's stayed hidden for well over a week?" He shook his head. "That's not luck. Neither is a dangerous criminal escaping from maximum-security prison and getting across the border from Mexico to the United States scot-free."

"We've considered that."

"Then you've considered the fact that Solaro's likely got a private jet on standby somewhere," Harvey ventured, "and the means to escape once he has what he wants."

She ignored the acidic taste in her mouth. "Yes."

Harvey eased back against his chair. "Knowing the resources he has at his disposal, you still think you can best him?"

"I have to," Pia told him. "If we follow the plan, I think we have a chance."

"You ever been in a firefight, sweetheart?"

Pia felt her jaw tighten. "No. But I was taught marksmanship. I can hold my own."

"She can," Sam confirmed. He reached for her under the table.

Grateful, she took his hand and held it.

Harvey tapped the tip of his pencil on Jaime's face. "Tell me more about this man and the claim he thinks he has over you."

Pia took the lead on that. "His father, Pablo Solaro, was the head of the Solaro crime family. They ran guns and drugs, but their specialty was human trafficking, which Grace, Sloane, and I unfortunately fell into during our Mexico vacation twelve years ago. Pablo had several sons. The first, Jaime, was illegitimate. When his second son, Alejandro, came of age, it was clear he would be Pablo's successor. No matter what Jaime did within the organization—and he did many terrible things in the name of his father—he could never be seen as Alejandro's equal. By the time he kidnapped me and took me to the hacienda, he'd started to unravel."

Sam continued the story. "Pablo saw Pia and the girls as valuable property. By taking one of them, Jaime was stealing from the organization. The Solaro men were trained not to touch their captives or call them by name. Jaime calling Pia his wife was all the insult Pablo needed to cut him off at the knees."

"Jaime's behavior at the hacienda escalated," Pia said. "He started to hurt me and the maid who lived there. When Sloane came to get me out and he caught her..."

Sam lowered his eyes to the table. "He broke her leg and left her without medical attention until she was rescued by Javier and Grace shortly after."

"Jesus," Harvey muttered.

"They were nearly too late to save me, too," Pia noted. She could still feel the licks of heat, the way the smoke had burned her airways... She could remember exactly how Bianca's blood had felt on her hands.

She shuddered, closing her eyes to stop the flashback.

"These men who follow him now," Harvey said cautiously, "is he paying them?"

"The FBI doesn't think so," Sam explained. "Pablo died in prison after the Solaros' reign in crime went belly-up thanks to Pia, Sloane and Grace's testimony. A few of the lower-level thugs escaped justice. These men likely had a hand in Jaime's escape. It was no secret that Jaime was Pablo's son. With Alejandro dead and Javier branded a traitor, they now see Jaime as Pablo's heir."

"Pablo inspired a great deal of loyalty among his foot

soldiers," Pia said. "They'll want retribution for him and Alejandro."

"Is that what Jaime wants?" Harvey asked. "Retribution for the man who never gave him his due?"

"There's a price on Javier Rivera's head," Sam told him. "Which is why, with the help of Sloane and the FBI, he and Grace have disappeared. Jaime won't mind seeing Sloane wiped off the map because she did some damage of her own when he caught her inside the hacienda. The scar on his face. But he wants Pia alive."

"He's still under the delusion that you belong to him," Harvey guessed.

She nodded. "He wasn't stable when I knew him. I can only imagine what twelve years of prison has done to his psychosis."

"He's obsessed with her," Sam put in. "With finding her. He's made it clear there's not much he won't do to make that happen."

Harvey shook his head. "He won't find her. Not if we have anything to do with it."

A slow smile spread across Sam's face. "So you'll help us fight it out?"

"If Jaime Solaro or any of his lackeys step foot on this island," Harvey said, "I'll put a bullet in him myself."

Pia's breath hitched. "Sam and I would ask—if Jaime does come—that you get Babette to safety."

"You think he's coming for her, too?"

Pia trod carefully here. "She's a piece of me."

"You're afraid he'll use her to convince you to cooperate?" he asked.

"I wouldn't put anything past him," Sam replied.

Harvey nodded. "It'd be my honor to protect that little girl."

Pia breathed a sigh of relief. "Thank you."

Sam leaned forward. "You know the island better than anyone. Where would you hide her?"

Harvey's attention strayed to the map spread across the wall. There, an overhead shot of the island had been framed in driftwood. "Did I ever tell you we have a dungeon here on Smuggler's Island?"

Babette groaned. "It's like something out of my nightmares."

"We found it after Boyd died," Harvey explained as he slipped into the underground bunker. His feet hit the floor with a splash. Shining his flashlight down, he said, "Don't worry. Outside of storm season, the water never gets higher." He pointed to the door overhead. "Katrina didn't just split Smuggler's Island in half. She cracked the foundation. Hoyt and I found this chamber when we returned to survey what remained."

Sam squinted into the distance where sunlight glinted off the surface of the Gulf. "It's far enough away from the Gulf to stay dry."

"This is dry?" Babette drawled.

"In a manner of speaking. You see these cleats?" Harvey called, gripping a metal bar on the wall. "We think they were used to string prisoners up by their wrists. A few days underground with no light would straighten a man out."

"Or make him go crazy," Sam added.

Harvey nodded. "It's an expansion of the brig."

"You said you give tours of the fort during tourist season," Pia remembered. "Is this known to the public?"

Harvey planted his hands on his hips. "We figured people would try to lock themselves in here, get trapped, and we'd have a lawsuit on our hands. Other than the historians we invited out, we've kept it a secret."

"What's that?" Babette asked. She, too, had a flashlight and was shining it on the wall near one cleat. "'HJK.'"

"Initials," Harvey said. "Another reason we asked historians to come. We thought it'd be interesting to find out who HJK was. He likely didn't enjoy his tenure on Smuggler's Island, but he left a piece of himself here."

Sam caught Babette's involuntary shiver. He draped a hand across her shoulders. "Do you want me to go first?"

"Do I *have* to go down there?"

"We'll need this chamber to keep you safe, if necessary." Sam watched her bite her lip, eyes a cloud of trepidation. "I can try it out first."

"Will you?" she asked.

Sam didn't need to be asked twice. He stripped off his jacket and handed it to Pia. Then he bent down to unlace each of his boots. Toeing them off, he left them at the mouth of the chamber, rolled up the cuffs of his jeans before dropping over the edge.

He hissed when the water covered him to the ankles. "That's bracing."

"If the waves can't make it this far," Babette called after him, "then why is it wet down there?"

"You dig deep enough anywhere on the island, you'll hit water," Harvey said good-naturedly. "It's not so bad. We'll leave a flashlight. A radio, to communicate with your mother and Sam. And you'll have me."

"The whole time?" Babette asked.

"The whole time." He stretched his arms out to her.

Babette took one look at Pia, who nodded encouragement. Harvey had set Babette up with a pair of child-size waders—something he'd bought for Hoyt's children when they visited—so she didn't get her clothes wet. She crouched down and shimmied into the drop.

Harvey caught her and set her to her feet, unharmed. "See? Nothing to be scared of."

"Will we have to close the hatch?" she asked.

Sam heard the nerves underneath the question, but it came out clear and she held her small chin steady.

Just like Pia, he thought, and shook his head at how brave his girls were.

"We will," Harvey said. "But not tonight. We'll come out tomorrow and test it out again. And the day after that. I'll let you decide when to practice closing the hatch and adjusting to the dark."

Babette looked relieved.

A shout echoed into the chamber. Sam looked up and saw Pia's attention fixed on the beach. She lifted a hand to shade her eyes.

"What is it?" Harvey called.

"It's Clem," she said. "He says there's someone coming ashore."

Sam cursed. He grabbed one cleat and hoisted himself up. Placing his foot on the wall, he could grab the lip of the opening. Pia took him by the shoulders to pull him the rest of the way out.

"Stay here," he told her when he spotted Clem at the beach, arms milling. "If you hear shouting or gunshots, close the hatch."

She gave a single nod as she watched him unclip his side-arm from the holster on his belt.

Sam sprinted to Clem. "Is it a boat?"

"No," Clem said, holding on to the top of his ski cap. "It don't make no sense. Why would anyone swim? The water's colder than a witch's you-know-what."

Sam had found the man's position some fifty yards down the beach. He tore off before Clem could finish.

The unwanted visitor stood up. He was wearing a dive suit but no mask or hood. He tossed the hair out of his eyes as he staggered out of the waves.

Sam placed the grip of his Beretta in a two-handed hold. "Don't move!" he shouted.

The man's hands went up, but he pivoted to face Sam.

"I said don't move!" Sam said again, advancing.

"Sam Filipek," the man said, eyes narrowed. "Right?"

He seemed far too comfortable or accustomed to being in the crosshairs. He stood tall and straight with plenty of muscle and a solid fifty pounds on Sam. "Smuggler's Island is closed. Diving's out of season. State your business here or—"

"Remy?"

Pia moved past Sam. "Stay behind me," he instructed.

She ventured forward, anyway. "It's Remy, isn't it?" she said, staring at the man. "Remy Fontenot."

The man kept his hands up, but he smiled. "I'd hug you, but your man would drop me like a stone."

Pia waved a hand at Sam. "It's okay. It's Sloane's Remy! 'Thirst Trap' Remy!"

"Come again?" Sam said, confused.

Remy made a face. "She still calls me that?"

"No," Pia said. "But Gracie and I do."

Sam lowered the weapon as she crossed to Remy and threw her arms around his neck.

"I've had a hell of a time finding you." Remy placed his hands on her shoulders and moved her back a step so he could give her a long once-over. "Still in one piece, right? No broken bones?"

"No," she assured him. "Did you swim here?"

He pointed offshore, far into the distance. "My sloop's that way."

She shook her head. "I can barely make that out."

"Who are you exactly?" Sam wanted to know.

"Remy Fontenot," he said.

"I got that much," Sam drawled.

"Remy was Sloane's bodyguard when she came back from Mexico," Pia filled him in. "He took care of her."

"When she let me," Remy added.

"You were good for her," Pia pointed out.

"What are you doing here?" Sam asked, cutting to the point.

"Sloane charged me with finding you when it became clear the FBI couldn't," he said. "I'm a bounty hunter now. Finding people's my job."

"You tracked us here," Sam surmised.

"With difficulty," he admitted.

"Which means," Sam said, holstering his sidearm once more, "the Solaros can do the same."

"It may take them longer," Remy weighed. "But I wouldn't be surprised."

"No," Sam considered. "Especially when the FBI comes running."

When Remy frowned at that, Pia touched his arm. "We think the Solaros have someone on the inside."

Remy stared. He shook his head. "It can't be anyone on Sloane's team. She handpicked every person herself."

"We can't be too careful," she cautioned.

"She can put you in a safe house. There's WITSEC."

"We have a plan in place. We've been prepping."

"For the Solaros?" he asked, and sent Sam a speculative look.

"If you contact Sloane and tell her we're here," Sam told

him, "tell her to come alone. It's the only way to keep our location quiet."

Remy's stillness belied the readiness in his stance. Sam read *fellow soldier*, despite the absence of weapons on Remy's person.

"She'll take that deal," Remy wagered.

Pia took his hand. "Come and see Babette. She's grown so much since you last saw her."

Remy's grin returned with a flash of teeth. "Since last I saw her," he repeated, and held out his hands, measuring. "She was this big. I could hold her in the crook of one arm."

Sam searched for Remy's boat offshore. They'd have to bring it in before much longer.

He had a bad feeling that Remy was the first of many uninvited guests on Smuggler's Island.

Chapter 16

The next day, a vessel came ashore. Harvey, Sam, Pia, Remy and Babette met it at the marina.

When Pia saw Sloane at the wheel, her heart leaped. As Harvey and Sam fastened the cables to the cleats, Pia held out a hand for Sloane to take and helped her out of the boat. Her arms went around her instantly.

Sloane returned the embrace, hard. "I thought you were dead."

"Sorry," Pia said, squeezing her eyes shut. Emotions overwhelmed her. "It's what we needed Jaime to think."

"I'm just glad you're okay."

Babette raced forward. "Sloane!"

Sloane released Pia to scoop Babette off her feet. "There she is! How's our beach sprite?"

"Okay," Babette said. "They put me in a hole."

"They what?"

Sam cleared his throat. "It's not what it sounds like."

"It is," Pia said with some chagrin.

"Sam," Sloane greeted. "You found them."

"I did," he acknowledged.

"You never lost faith," Sloane said.

"I had my moments," he admitted. He pulled her in for a hug. "It's good to see you."

Sloane patted his back. "You, too."

As Pia linked arms with Sloane and followed Harvey toward the truck that would take them to the lighthouse, she glanced at Remy, who waited there. "You never lost faith, either. Not really."

"How do you know?" Sloane asked.

"You sent Remy to find us."

Sloane grinned at the man as they reached the small shell-lined parking area. "He volunteered."

Remy gave her a nod. "Sloane."

She raised a brow. "Looking good, Fontenot."

"Don't you mean 'Thirst Trap?'" he asked with a half smile.

Sloane rounded on Pia.

"It slipped," Pia claimed.

Sloane trudged the rest of the way to the truck. "I'm driving."

"You don't know where we're going," Sam pointed out.

Sloane closed the driver's door smartly, then rolled down the window. Lowering her aviator sunglasses, she leaned out and called, "I always drive. Get in or you can walk it."

Sam placed one hand on Pia's hip. He kissed the place beneath her ear. "We're going to need to buckle, aren't we?"

"If you want to live," she confirmed, thrilling in the little shiver he chased across her skin.

"You're wearing a ring."

Pia eyed the diamond on her left hand. She fought the urge to cover the sparkle with the other. "Oh."

"You thought I wouldn't notice?" Sloane asked as she sipped the beer Harvey had slipped her on his way out with the men, leaving Pia and Sloane to their after-dinner round of catch-up. "So, you're marrying him."

"It's complicated."

"There's nothing complicated about the way he looks at you. Or how you look at him. Especially if he still makes you happy."

"He does."

"Then tell me what the problem is."

"First, you and I need to have a conversation about this," Pia said, laying a hand on her belly.

Sloane's brow knitted. "Indigestion?"

Pia snorted. God, it felt good to sit down with her bestie again. "I'm expecting."

Sloane's face fell. "Since when?"

"I found out after Christmas."

"And I'm just now hearing about this?" Sloane asked incredulously.

"It's bad luck to mention anything before the first nine weeks," Pia said quickly.

"Gracie and I were the first to know about Babette. You told us weeks before you told your own mother."

"I wasn't scared to tell the two of you," Pia remembered. "Not like I was scared to tell her. And you're right. I'm making excuses." She exhaled carefully, deflating. "Sam and I fought before he left. Part of me didn't think he was coming back. And then I found out about this and…" She laid a hand on her stomach again. "I've spent the last two months trying to process everything. Trying to figure out what I would do if he didn't want to return."

"He's in love with you," Sloane pointed out. "The man's always been in love with you. There's nothing he wouldn't do for you."

"I know that now," Pia granted.

"Good. And I love you, too, but if your levee breaks anywhere near me, I will have the sense to flee this time."

Pia folded her lips together to curb a wide smile. She

toyed with the condensation building on the outside of her water glass. "I suppose I'll have to ask Gracie to deliver this one, too."

"She'll want to tell you herself," Sloane contemplated, "but as she's out of range until Jaime's been recovered…"

"Spill the tea," Pia said, bracing herself.

"She's engaged."

"To whom?" When Sloane only raised one fashionably thick eyebrow, it dawned. "Javier?"

"Yes."

Pia surveyed Sloane closely, black eyes perpetually narrowed in suspicion, thick black hair that always swung from a high ponytail, skin that trended toward brown even when the sun was at its farthest from the earth, and nails forever painted some shade of red even if she kept them short to maintain her certification as an expert marksman. Pia liked to think she knew Sloane better than anyone. After their return from Mexico, Sloane's lengthy physical recovery had come shortly before nearly a year of hard partying. If Pia hadn't begged Sloane to get help for her drinking, Sloane would never have turned her life around. She certainly wouldn't have joined the Bureau or the Crimes Against Children unit that hunted human traffickers in the States.

Pia heard the negativity tripping through the words and tilted her head. "Can you tell me more?" she asked carefully. "About him?"

Sloane thought about it. She took another sip of beer, crossing her legs. "I tried putting them both in a safe house since Javier is Jaime's half brother and Jaime tried to kill him. But Javier insisted he could take care of her."

"What does he do in the States?" Pia asked.

"Same thing he and his mother did in Mexico before Jaime

assassinated her," Sloane revealed. "He works horses and cattle."

Pia shook her head after a moment. "I can't see Gracie with a cowboy."

"She's wild about him."

"You don't like it," Pia pinpointed.

Sloane lowered the beer. "He's a Solaro."

"Yes," Pia granted. "But…" She glanced around, lowering her voice. "So is somebody else we know and love."

Sloane's eyes softened—truly softened for the first time since she had arrived. It was so rare to see her let her guard down… Babette coming into the world had changed her irrevocably, too. "You said you told her about Jaime. Does she know about that, too?"

"No," Pia answered. "And I don't plan on her finding out."

She waited for scrutiny. Questions. Sloane simply offered a nod.

Pia grabbed the solace of the silence. Babette had gone to bed. The men were outside…doing whatever men did when women needed the comfort of sisterhood. Then she said it out loud—what she'd never said before. "She's never asked me who her biological father is. She's so smart, I think on some level she already knows. But she finds such comfort in Sam's place in her life. He's all the father she needs. When she's older, she and I will no doubt have to have a hard conversation about how I became pregnant with her. But for now…"

Sloane finished for her. "This is enough."

"It is," Pia said heartily. "She's excited about the new baby. I was afraid after being an only child for so long, she'd resent another. But she can't wait to be a big sister."

Sloane set the bottle on the tabletop with a small thump. "Which brings us to this plan Remy tells me you and Sam have devised to get Jaime out of the picture."

"You won't like it," Pia warned.

"Try me."

Sam watched Sloane make her way from the house to the beach. As she neared the spot where he, Remy and Harvey stood around a small campfire, she stretched her hands out toward the heat. "You know you could've done your hemming and hawing indoors. Pia and I never said you had to retreat."

"You both needed the time," Sam said knowingly. "Did she tell you the plan?"

"Yes," she replied.

He read her well. "You think it's foolish?"

"Remy," Sloane said experimentally, "do I like men telling me what I think?"

Remy's smile was loud in the dark. "I imagine you've buried a fair few who've tried."

At Sloane's pointed look, Sam raised his hands. "Sorry. Why don't you tell me what you think?"

"I'd love to," she said with a false cheer that had Harvey chuckling into his beer. "First, you've got some balls thinking you can take on a psychopath and his homeboy devotees with a handful of guns and a fishing spear."

"Gig."

She frowned at him. "What?"

"It's a flounder gig."

"Is that supposed to make me feel better?" she challenged.

Sam weighed his options. He leaned toward Remy. "I take it she's killed men for telling her how she feels."

Remy raised his bottle in mock toast. "You learn fast for an army guy."

Sam knew by route of conversation that Remy had served as a Navy SEAL. He let the ribbing slide off his shoulders and turned back to Sloane. "Protective custody isn't an option. Neither is WITSEC."

"Why not?" she asked testily.

"Because Jaime's working with someone high up the chain of command," Sam explained. "Or someone with enough bureaucratic clout to pave the way for his entry at the border."

"How do you figure?"

"The same way you do," he said pointedly. "It's one thing for a son of a former crime boss to escape prison. It's another to trace phone calls and avoid capture when his face is featured in every nightly news bulletin from here to the Atlantic."

She studied him closely in the flickering orange glow of the fire. "Go on."

"You wouldn't have come alone or sent an outsider like Remy if you thought every person on your team could be trusted," he added.

She turned her head to look out over the channel. "Is that the other lighthouse?"

The moon was low and full. The tower's silhouette stood out in relief against the night. "Yeah."

"And you're comfortable with the idea of Pia fighting Jaime one on one?" she asked.

"Why wouldn't I be?"

"She's pregnant."

He felt his gut twist. For a moment, his lungs burned. But he pushed out a breath anyway. "I won't stop her."

"No?"

"I've spent the last five years pulling her out of flashbacks and nightmares. I know how many hours of sleep she's lost and how many times she's looked over her shoulder."

"It was barely a week ago when you told me in no uncertain terms you wanted the pleasure of killing Jaime yourself."

"I still want that." He could taste it. "But I won't begrudge Pia taking his life. Not if it helps that part of her rest."

She stared at him. Then, in a near whisper, she said, "That's big of you."

"It's justice," he contended. "You may have put the scar on Jaime's face, but it was Pia who burned down his whole goddamn house."

"I don't underestimate her," Sloane said. "But if I see an opportunity to end him, I will."

Remy spoke up again. "That's your right as well. You've had your fair share of nightmares."

"I won't ask how you know that."

"I know you," he answered anyway. His normally inscrutable expression turned grim. "I knew the part of you that was fresh off of Mexico."

"You've fantasized about killing Jaime every bit as much as I have," she charged.

"I have," Remy owned. "I told Grace I would. But I won't begrudge you or Pia your due, either, if you put him in the crosshairs first."

"So, you agree with their plan," Sloane surmised.

"If you don't like the odds, I can call in some old teammates," he offered.

"SEALs?"

"One of them's still active duty," he asserted. "The others, like me, have moved on."

"You still trust them?"

"With my life."

"What about Pia's?" Sam asked. "Sloane's? Babette's?"

"More than I trust anyone else," Remy certified.

Sloane considered. "When can they be here?"

"Forty-eight hours, max."

Sloane looked at Sam. "Are you comfortable with this?"

"I could be." Trusting Remy had grown easier after a few days at the man's side. Sam had learned how Remy had pulled Sloane out of her post-Mexico spiral. It took a skillful person to tail Sloane Escarra through the hard streets of New Orleans, much less have the wherewithal to save her. "Forty-eight hours gives us enough time to finish prepping. Could we get more weapons?"

"Give me a few hours to sleep on it," Sloane suggested. "We'll regroup in the morning. In the meantime, where's the ferryman? He's the only one I haven't laid eyes on since I got here."

"He's hunkered down in his living quarters," Harvey said.

"Does he know about the plan?"

"He's seen us prepping," Sam said.

"I'd like to question him."

"Why exactly?" Harvey barked.

"His rap sheet."

"So, the man's been in a few bar fights," Harvey dismissed. "Do you know what it's like to be an openly gay man in the state of Mississippi?"

"I imagine he hasn't had it easy," Sloane said with some empathy. "Nor did your son when he was alive."

Harvey's head dipped slightly. He took a long pull from his bottle.

"But there's a lot riding on this," she continued, "and if I'm going to let this operation go forward, I'm going to need to look every man in the eye and know he's got Pia's and Babette's backs."

"If you trusted him completely," Remy told Harvey, "you would have let him in on the plan already. You told me, and I'm a stranger."

"Pia trusts you," Harvey said.

"Do you trust Clem?" Remy pressed.

Harvey hesitated the barest hint of a moment. Enough to make Sam second-guess Clem himself. "Why not?" he asked.

Harvey stuffed his ham-sized fists in the pockets of his waders. "Since Boyd's disappearance, he's developed something of a drinking problem."

Sloane lifted her chin. "How bad?"

"He returns to the mainland once a week for supplies," Harvey explained. "I know he uses that time to stock up on Wild Turkey and frequent bars."

"Hence, the bar fights," Sloane finished.

"I told him after I bailed him out of jail the last time, no more," Harvey said grievously. "But I don't see it stopping. He's not the same man he was before we lost Boyd. Hell, neither am I. I'll die on this island, same as he did. But I'm afraid the man he loved will die in the bottle."

Unsure what to say, Sam reached out and placed a hand on Harvey's shoulder. He stepped closer to him.

"I'd like to speak with him," Sloane held. "As soon as possible."

At last, Harvey relented. "Go easy on him if you can. It's grief that's made him what he is."

Sloane inclined her head. She switched gears. "What's this about putting Babette in a hole?"

Remy tipped his head toward Sam. "She's going to love this."

An hour later, Sam hiked the stairs to the second floor. He checked in on Babette even though her light was out and found her sleeping soundly, clutching the sheet as she'd long done. He pulled the blanket to her chin, looked long out the window at the spit of beach spread out under the moon's glow, closed the curtains and left the door parted.

Next door, he found the light on, but Pia on the bed with

her eyes closed, the thin throw blanket normally folded at the foot of the bed half covering her.

Did she know she slept in the same way Babette did, curled on her side with her nose all but buried in the covers?

He took off his boots, decided a shower could wait for the morning before discarding his jacket, jeans and overshirt.

When he stretched out on the bed next to her, she stirred.

"Shh," he murmured when her eyes flew open. "It's just me."

He was accustomed to seeing the flash of relief, but knowing she still woke like this—startled, ready—didn't melt the ice inside him. As she relaxed, lashes fluttering over heavy-lidded eyes, he turned to her. He knew how cold his hands were, campfire notwithstanding, and kept them away from her skin. She was sleeping, as she always did, in her tank top, arms sleeveless, shoulders all but bare.

"You talked to Sloane," she mumbled.

"We did," he amended. "She's in."

Pia's eyes cleared. "Truly?"

"I think so," he confirmed.

"We can't do this without her."

"We could," he weighed. "It would just be harder."

"You talked her into it."

"She had questions."

"It's her nature."

He nodded. "She wanted to be sure we knew what we were doing. Remy sealed the deal by offering to bring in some SEAL operatives he trusts."

"That would even the odds."

"I expect they'll be here in the next day or two." Keeping his touch light, he feathered his fingers over the jewel-toned tentacles of the jellyfish beneath her ear. At her indrawn breath, he lifted them. "Sorry. My hands are cold."

"I could warm them," she suggested.

"You're tired."

"I'm awake enough to want your hands on me."

He groaned and sealed the jellyfish in an open-mouthed kiss. Awareness had already sunk deep. His blood siphoned fast, warming him. The smell of her skin was like the air before a storm. It was elemental.

The strap of her tank top slipped over the slope of her shoulder, leaving it free for him to navigate. He sipped at the hollow of her clavicle as her arm hooked around his head, her hand latching in his hair. He gathered the material of her tank at the base of her spine in his fists.

"Saints, Sam," she whispered. "Touch me."

He wanted to tell her how worried he was about her, how when Jaime arrived, she should hide with Babette. But he couldn't. He'd meant everything he'd said outside, and he was torn between how important justice was to her and how much he needed to protect her.

The only thing keeping him together was the knowledge that he'd stand beside her. He'd lay down his life for her.

Flipping their positions, he spaced his knees apart, digging them into the bed. He propped himself on the heels of his hands so that none of his weight collapsed on her tiny baby bump. As she undressed him and laid claim to every inch of him with her hands, he kept the pressure of his body off her.

She stopped mid-kiss and canted her head as she studied him, her face flushed with need, eyes kindling. "You're holding back."

He lifted his hand to her mouth and traced the bottom curve. When her lips parted, he let her suck the pad of his thumb. His body lit up with a thousand demands.

She could take him apart, piece by piece, and he'd lie back and ask for more.

He cupped her wrist and caught the flash of the diamond in the lamplight. "You're still wearing it."

"I told you I would." Her mouth folded into a contemplative frown. "Sloane said something."

"She usually has something to say."

Her smile came slowly. It burned bright inside him. "She said you make me happy."

"Do I?"

"Yes," she answered.

He made a noise and found a smile grappling with the corners of his mouth. He gave in to it.

"I'm not sure I knew what happiness was until Babette smiled at me for the first time," she revealed. "Or when she said your name that day on the beach. I looked up and saw you walking toward us—then running to meet her and something inside me healed."

"You didn't believe me," he mused, "when I said I'd come back that first time."

"No," she admitted. "But you did. A ring is a circle. Like faith and the ocean. They never end." Her eyes filled. "You're my ocean."

He touched her face. "You're mine, too."

She moved, pressing her hand to his shoulder so that as she rolled, she positioned him beneath her. Her hair fell to curtain both their faces. When he reached up to brush it back from hers, she caught his wrists. Pressing them back to the bed, she lowered her mouth a breath above his and whispered, "Let me."

He thought his heart would beat through his chest in answer. Her mouth took his, not softly, and his lust grew haphazard and frenzied.

It never failed to astound him how quickly Pia could go from her serious self to a seductress. He'd been there to watch her grow comfortable in her own skin. He'd been there to see her come into her own sensuality.

The first time she'd seduced him, he'd been helpless. She'd owned him, taking him down like a linebacker.

She still owned him, he found, as she slowly stripped out of her tank, then shimmied out of her panties. Then she took him in, slowly, and he watched her eyes go dark.

He panted. She was wet and hot and irresistible. "Pia."

She circled his wrists with her hands again and anchored them above his head, watching him as she took him in deeper.

His mouth opened. He emitted a lengthy moan and broke into a fast sweat. All the warm, fuzzy feelings had morphed into a hard-edged need that went on a tear inside him each time she lifted her hips.

She brought his hands to her waist. She leaned back, quickening on him, over him.

Like that night on the beach. The vision of Pia bathed in moonlight, every bit as caught up in the rhythm she'd set as he had been, wasn't lost on him. It did nothing to dull the edge of his need. If anything, it sharpened it.

Skillful, she knew when to bank his arousal, when to hold it and when to meet it, and he let her keep the pace because some gluttonous part of him liked being firmly reigned by her.

When she flattened against him, her body slid easily over his and she closed her eyes, chasing her own climax. The small of his back drew up taut at the promise of completion.

She sighed as he tilted his hips up toward hers, meeting her. He tightened his arm around the back of her hips and did it again when he felt her tremble around him.

She cried out, and when he felt her come apart, he followed blindly.

* * *

Much later, when he felt her twitching in her sleep, he helped bring her out of the dream. Cupping her face in his hands, he murmured and buoyed her until the shudders subsided. When her arms linked around him, he held her, wishing that this nightmare could be her last.

Chapter 17

"It's coming together again," Harvey said in wonder as he stood back with his hands on his hips and squinted up at the light tower on Escatawpa.

Pia watched him. Then she felt the fluttering at the edge of her belly and drew in a breath.

His hand came to her shoulder when hers pressed to her stomach. "All right?"

"Fine," she said. The concern on his face didn't ease, so she added, "The baby's kicking."

His smile was broad and bright. "That's a good sign."

"It is," she mulled.

"Have you told Sam?"

She nodded. "It happened at the hunting cabin. He couldn't feel it like I can."

"Not yet." Harvey squeezed her shoulder gently. "You'll have to come back to Smuggler's after the baby's born."

He could see through the coming storm to what came after. Emotions rose quickly, overwhelming her. "I'd love that," she murmured.

"It'll be late summer then," he said. "And warm. The four of you can stay in the lighthouse again."

"The baby will keep you awake all night," she warned.

He chuckled. "I like babies, even when they're screaming. It'll be like having another grandchild."

The thought brought on a smile. "We'll come back," she promised.

"That door'll hold," he assured her, nodding to the Escatawpa light tower entrance. "Sam and Remy did a fine job with it."

Pia's smile fell away as she measured the new entry. "They did." The men and Sloane had spent the entire day on Escatawpa's east beach shoring up the light tower's weaknesses. They'd removed debris and ensured the integrity of what remained within.

Sloane approached, her arms crossed, eyes hidden behind her shades.

"How's the pulley system coming along?" Harvey asked curiously, referring to the climbing ropes Sam and Remy were busy erecting between the second and third levels of the stairwell. That section had fallen into such disrepair that the two men had spent the previous day cutting it away and adding to the debris pile.

Sloane's wide mouth formed into a straight line. "Other than some debate over knots, they seem to know what they're doing. I think we're decided on stations, too."

"Let me hear it," Pia requested.

"Once the Solaros arrive at Smuggler's, whoever sights them first will sound the alarm. Then everyone will hit the west beach where Remy's skiff and Harvey's Pursuit will be anchored. This will transport us to Escatawpa. Since we're staying on Smuggler's and will be working there primarily on preparations until they come, they won't have any reason to assume our plan involves Escatawpa."

"All the while," Harvey added, "Remy's three SEAL buddies will be posted inside Escatawpa Light Station, waiting."

"That's right," Sloane said with a nod. "Bracken, Savitt and Pettelier should arrive tomorrow morning. From here, they can watch the channel and the sound. The railing on the top level's gone, but they'll still have three-sixty visuals. With the right equipment, they'll be able to spot a craft en route for Smuggler's. They'll radio Remy and he'll sound the alarm. Harvey, you'll take Babette to the fort. The rest of us will draw the Solaros here. Remy will be on level one with his weapons. If they breach the new entryway, he will be the first line of defense. Bracken will be the second on the next level with Savitt assisting both him and Remy as needed. I'll be on the third level with Sam assisting. Pettelier will be with you on level four."

Pia eyed the cupola far up above them. The fourth level was just below it. "You're giving me a bodyguard."

Sloane didn't deny it. "It's precautionary. The Solaros won't get that far."

Pia mulled over that. She wanted to be closer to the ground. From the fourth-floor windows, even with a choice weapon, there was little chance she'd be able to do any damage to the Solaros on the ground. And Sloane was right. Remy seemed unstoppable. Pia tried to imagine three more men like him, plus Sam and Sloane between her and the door to the light tower.

Jaime may not stand a chance unless he ran to escape justice, which was another possibility they had to consider. If he went into the wind again, he would never not be a threat to her family. "What if he runs?" she asked finally.

"Jaime?" Sloane confirmed. When Pia hiked her chin in answer, she said, "As soon as Bracken, Savitt and Pettelier see the Solaros coming, they'll run a call through the sheriff's office dispatch on the mainland. Once word gets out that Jaime Solaro and his men have been spotted on the islands, marine police and choppers will be put in place to intercept. Once the cavalry arrives, chances of him slipping away again are slim to none." Pia said nothing for several moments, so Sloane added, "He won't get away this time. You can count on it."

"It's a solid plan," Harvey opined. His hand was still on Pia's shoulder, supportive.

"I know," she said. "That doesn't stop my mind from trying to find the flaws."

Sloane stepped closer. "It won't be like before. There's no building you'll need to burn down to escape."

Pia stared at the light tower in answer and prayed it would hold.

"I didn't want to say this earlier with Harvey," Pia said quietly when she and Sloane and all the others were back on Smuggler's Island.

"We're alone now," Sloane pointed out. Pia needed a walk. Since Remy, Harvey, Clem and Sam were busy rigging the alarm system, Sloane had elected to go with her.

For protection, Pia knew. Just as she knew what former Petty Officer Pettelier's job would be once his boots touched down on Smuggler's the next morning. Still, Pia didn't mind Sloane's company. She knew Babette didn't either. "The dreams won't stop."

Sloane frowned as she walked down the beach at Pia's side. Ahead, Babette crouched with her sketchbook where the ground lay soggy and marsh periwinkle snails clung to bright green cordgrass. "Pregnancy made you have dreams before," she recalled.

"It did," Pia remembered. She hadn't understood it then and thought she was losing her mind.

"Is it the hacienda this time around, too?"

"Yes, and it's been coming in bits and pieces since we left Flamingo Bay."

"I've been having them, too," Sloane admitted.

Pia studied her friend. It was unlike Sloane to admit weakness or vulnerability. "What are yours about?" she asked quietly.

Sloane shrugged it off. "The usual."

Pia waited for her to say more, knowing not to push. She, Grace and Sloane had all handled their trauma differently, and still did. When Sloane said nothing more, Pia wished she could ease Sloane's troubles.

Sloane's nightmares more than likely stemmed from her failure to rescue Pia from the hacienda and how Jaime had punished her in the attempt.

She caught the purple shadow of a stingray winging underneath the peak of a wave. The tips of its disc pierced the water before the silent creature surrendered itself to its sub-aquatic cradle. Like a fetus, Pia thought, testing the margins of its mother's womb.

Something about that centered her. Some of the tension that had entrenched itself inside her before she'd woken this morning fell away and she found her voice again. "Is this too hard for you—hearing it again?"

Sloane shook her head. "Listening's easier than telling."

Pia wanted to ask if she was sure, but the stubborn bent of Sloane's mouth answered for her. "Last night's started after you tried to rescue me. He attacked you. You fought back, made him bleed. I didn't know he could bleed, or that he was vulnerable at all until you did that."

"I cut him with the fork I stole from my dinner tray. I'd spent days making it sharp enough to draw blood. It didn't make him weaker, though."

"I always knew he was an animal," Pia explained. "But when he broke your leg and dragged you out of the hacienda screaming, I knew he'd lost whatever he'd used to hide it."

Sloane made an assenting noise.

Pia paused. "I can stop if you want me to."

"If I can't handle it after all these years, how am I going to face him?"

Pia waited several moments, long enough to watch Babette spread her jacket over the ground so she could sit cross-legged and arrange her sketchbook over her lap. "He was gone for a long time. Bianca told me to pick a room and lock the door. But I knew if he couldn't find me, he'd just go after her again. She was so battered. She couldn't have withstood another attack. So I told her to find a window that could be loosened from the jamb, and I used the matches to light a fire in the fireplace."

"You tore his house apart," Sloane said with some pride.

"Chairs first," Pia admitted. "There was no firewood. So I used pieces of them to get the blaze going. Then… I don't know…watching him do that to you… Something must've snapped inside me, too. It escalated quickly from chairs to china. Then stemware. All his fine art—paintings, vases, pottery. There was an oil painting he'd commissioned of himself hanging on the second-story landing. I took it out of the frame and broke it over my knee."

Sloane's lips curled into something akin to a smirk. "You savage."

"Cushions followed. The sheets, too. The fire spread from the hearth to the rug and had caught the drapes when he came back."

"You'd think I would've stopped then," Pia considered. "You'd think I'd have cowered."

"You didn't."

"It might have been different if I had," she said. She couldn't close her eyes without seeing Bianca's blank stare, the pool of blood under her head spreading across the travertine tiles. "Maybe he'd have taken my life instead."

"He would've taken you both out," Sloane said with finite certainty.

"He shot her," Pia said numbly. "Just…shot her. Right between the eyes. I was the one wrecking his house and burning his precious possessions. Not her."

"He shot her because he knew it would take the fight out of you." The muscles along her friend's trim jaw were taut. "You said that you've spent a long time thinking Jaime ruined you. I want you to think about this instead. He punished Bianca when you wouldn't give yourself to him. He assumed it would pit her against you—and you against her. The hacienda was hell. But friendship was born in that house. Sisterhood lived there, just as you and Bianca did for weeks."

Sloane looked off to where Babette had broken her observation long enough to stroke the back of a periwinkle snail. "When we all found out your baby was going to be a girl, it felt right. I'm not superstitious or particularly spiritual, but I believe Bianca died in the hacienda so that Babette could live. Maybe there is a piece of her still alive in this world."

The part of Pia that was still broken was linked irrevocably to her fallen friend. Something about what Sloane said made the pain of that lessen slightly.

"Yes," Pia agreed.

Sloane frowned for a minute more before letting the subject rest. "If I've ever been strong, it's because you were."

"Sloane," Pia said, losing the grip she'd gained on her emotions.

"After we came back, I was willing to light myself on fire to forget. Then I watched you give birth and Grace help with the delivery and knew I had to step it up."

"Does that mean you've decided to be my birthing coach this time around?"

Sloane barked a laugh, startled by her own mirth. With a quick glance back toward the marina where they'd last seen the men, she stepped closer. "Not for all the 'Thirst Trap' Remys in the world."

Pia would have laughed. But the earth ruptured. She was thrown backward, and for a split second, she thought the ground beneath their feet had opened.

The landing jarred every bone in her body. For a moment, she was suspended in shock. Then the acrid tang of ozone assaulted her senses, and she raised her head to see Sloane lying several feet away.

She was still. Too still.

Pia coughed and pushed herself up on her hands and knees. Smoke burned her eyes, her throat, her airways…

"Mom?"

She scrambled to her feet. "Babette?" she called, fear pounding at her chest like a battering ram.

"Mommy!" came the answering cry.

She couldn't see through the smoke. *"Babette!"*

Another explosion rocked the ground. She went down on her knees again.

Farther away, she thought. Farther away this time. But close enough… She glanced at Sloane again, willing her friend to rise.

And saw Bianca dead in her place.

"No." She choked on it.

"Mom!"

Pia gained her feet again and didn't think.

She ran through the smoke.

Sam felt like he'd been hit with a brick.

The sound of a groan made him open his eyes. Something obscured his vision. He reached up to wipe it away and smelled blood over smoke before he saw the stain of it smeared across his fingers. His face was wet, and he realized why.

"Son of a bitch," he hissed as he rolled from his back to his front. His spine and hips protested. His left knee squalled.

He curled his hands into fists and felt sand sift through them. The ringing in his ears took him back to the 101st and the heat of battle.

Get up, soldier.

As he gained his hands and feet, the world blurred. He shook his head like a dog and watched clarity snap back.

It looked like a war zone.

The marina was gone, posts and decking scattered, splintered, everywhere. A black column of smoke funneled toward the fluffy white clouds.

It registered slowly. The ferry. Sam could see its white hull beneath tongues of sinister flames.

An explosion.

A bomb.

Where was Harvey, Remy, Clem? The first pair had been assessing the area with Sam, debating which approach the Solaros would take from the mainland. Clem had finished his repairs on *The Smuggler* minutes before the explosion ripped through the bridge.

Sam heard the groan again. He looked around and started moving toward the pair of waders ten feet to his right.

The man attached to them was as white as his hair. Harvey coughed and reached for Sam's hand.

Sam saw the long slice along his midsection and shook his head as Harvey's bloodied lips parted. "Don't talk. Just lie still."

Harvey laid his head back.

There was no fight in his eyes.

Sam tightened his grip on Harvey's hand. "You're all right."

"Harvey." Clem dropped next to him. He lifted his bloodied hand. "What… What can I do for him?"

Sam shook his head. He didn't know. He felt helpless. The feeling grew worse as Clem wrung his ski cap between his hands and tears rolled into his beard.

"Move."

Sam felt himself being shoved aside, and Remy was there with a nasty gash down the length of his arm, another across his cheek, and blood soaking the leg of his cargo pants. Despite this, he moved in sure measures. He parted Harvey's shirt to examine the wound. "Sloane's boat," he grunted.

"What?" Sam said. Did the bounty hunter know what he was saying, or was he as disoriented as the rest of them?

"Radio," Remy barked, and jerked his head toward the water.

Sam followed the gesture and saw, impossibly, Sloane's rented speedboat, ripped from its moorings. Other than a smoking hole in its stern, it looked unharmed as it bobbed toward the beach.

"I can administer triage," Remy said briskly. "But if he doesn't get to a hospital in the next twenty minutes…"

Clem moaned. Sam cursed. He sprinted toward the water. He waded the first few feet in before arcing his arms over his head and diving into the first wave that curled toward him.

"Mom!"

No sooner did Pia spot Babette's wavering silhouette through the heat of the smoke than she dived through it and scooped her up in her arms.

Sobs tore through Babette as her arms locked around Pia's neck. "Mom!"

Pia felt herself go to her knees as relief pierced her. "Are you hurt?" she asked, pulling back enough to catch Babette's smoke-scored face in her hands. "Are you bleeding?"

"My ears!" Babette cried, raising her hands to them.

Pia cupped her hands gingerly over Babette's ears. She turned her head, trying to see the damage.

Externally, there was none.

Internally…

Pia made Babette look at her before she spoke again, rounding out the words so Babette could read her lips. "We need to go to the fort."

Babette stared at her mouth. She shook her head. "What about Harvey? Where is he?" Panic took hold of her. *"Where's Sam?"*

I don't know. Pia had to bite the inside of her lip to bear down on the threat of losing her grip on calm. "They're coming," she said. "Can you run?"

Babette nodded fervently. Then her eyes locked on something beyond Pia. She opened her mouth and screamed.

Before Pia could react, hard hands tore her away.

The radio worked. Sam used it to put out a distress call on several frequencies. Then he located the boat's first aid kit and swam to shore.

Harvey was conscious, but it was clear from his tremors that shock had taken hold.

Is he going to make it? He didn't want to think it. Couldn't make himself ask. Remy's expression was a mask of foreboding as he went about his work, using the supplies Sam had found aboard the boat where he could.

"It's not good," Clem muttered, shaking his head listlessly. His palm repeatedly passed over the space between the man's forehead and his shrinking hairline while Harvey's eyes reached for the sky.

Sam's blood chilled. "He's the toughest man I know," he said. Hell, he'd take a leaf out of Captain Jean-Luc Picard's book and *make it so*, if it came to it. Harvey Dunagan, his hero, wouldn't die today. Then he said what had been beating at his chest. "Pia."

"I know," Remy bit off. He closed Harvey's shirt again, then tore open his own jacket, ripped it off, and laid it over him.

Clem spoke up. "I can watch over him. Until the rescue crew arrives."

Sam studied the few parts of Clem's face that weren't covered in bristly hair—windburned cheeks, watery eyes and the worry behind them.

"Are you sure?" Remy asked.

Clem nodded in a quick bob.

"Do you have a weapon?" Remy asked.

"I've been packing one," Clem admitted. "Since I saw what was in Sam's truck."

"In a few minutes, this island will be crawling with Jaime Solaro's men if it's not already," Remy informed him. "Can you defend Harvey if necessary?"

"I can," Clem said, "and I will."

"You'll need the flare from the boat," Sam said, offering it to him. "When you hear the chopper, light it. They'll know there's someone here who needs help."

"What are you going to do?" Clem asked.

"Find Pia and Babette," Sam answered. "Make sure they're safe. Then hold the Solaros off until backup arrives."

"Here." Clem took a long blade from the pocket of his torn waders.

Sam unsheathed it and scanned the black sawback blade.

"That's a fair sight more than a pig sticker," Remy observed.

Sam sheathed it. "Thank you."

"Just...keep the little one out of danger," Clem said. "She's something special."

"She is," Sam agreed. He touched Harvey's shoulder before he clasped Remy's offered hand and let him pull him to his feet.

"We can take Sloane's boat," Remy said, the words clipped.

"The prop's gone."

Remy swore. "Then we'll need to go on foot. Can you handle a jog?"

Sam ignored his knee. "Can you?" he asked, pointing to the blood on Remy's pant leg.

"Flea bite on a dog's ass," he dismissed as he checked his weapon, a P226 with a fifteen-round capacity. Standard issue for a Navy SEAL.

"Pia and Sloane would have heard the explosion and taken Babette to the fort," Sam said.

"Blowing the ferry was either supposed to disable us..."

Sam let it play out in his head. "...or it was a diversion."

"We'll need to move. Fast and ready."

Sam palmed his Beretta and put one in the chamber. "Then let's roll."

Chapter 18

Someone grabbed her by the hair. She clawed at the hands dragging her backward.

Babette had fallen. She scrambled away, toward the marsh grass.

Go, Pia thought wildly. *Run*.

The hold on her loosened and she dropped to the ground.

She didn't have a weapon. The pistol she'd carried had been lost in the chaos.

She swung up with her fist as a man bent over her. Her knuckles connected with his jaw.

Pain shot through the bones of her hand as the man's head arced back and he stumbled away from her. White-hot agony spidered across her knuckles. She cradled her fist.

Through the smoke, she could see another figure. She saw the sheen of silk rippling across his chest, his shaved head and the scar tracking across his face.

Paralysis gripped her, making everything stop except her heart. It threw itself against her ribs.

His eyes snared her. Smiling. Amid the smoke and wreckage, the son of a bitch smiled as he came ashore.

"Mom?"

Babette's voice was like a current. It surged through Pia. Suddenly, she felt intent coursing through the numbness.

The man she'd punched closed a hand over her arm. His fingers bit into her skin.

She struck out again.

This time, he was ready, batting her hand away. He slapped her.

Her head snapped sideways. Stars blinked in front of her eyes.

A shot rang out. Pia flattened herself against the ground. She wrapped her arms over her head as a volley of gunshots followed. Someone cried out. Shouts rent the air.

The first thing she saw when she opened her eyes was the assailant who had grabbed her on the ground, bleeding. Then, in the distance, Sloane—service weapon clenched between her hands—exchanging gunfire with the other men on the beach.

Her eyes met Pia's briefly. "Go!"

She didn't need to be told twice. Gaining her feet, she flew to the marsh grass. At first, she didn't see Babette. Then she spied a slash of blue behind a thick gnarl of driftwood. She grabbed her around the waist, pulled her to her feet. "This way!" she urged, leading her into the trees.

Sam's clothes were wet and heavy. The cold knifed through him. Like any good knife, it had teeth.

His head knocked, and his knee protested. But adrenaline was efficient, wolfish, familiar, and the noise of everything fell to a dim backdrop as he tore through reeds, palms and high grasses, dodged trees, and startled birds.

He didn't know if an hour passed, or minutes, before he cut across the island. He kept up with Remy, whose lengthier stride set him five paces ahead.

The old bones of the fort came into view. Something crept

up Sam's throat. The taste of it did nothing to assuage the ill feeling that they wouldn't find Pia and Babette here.

He climbed over a fall of stones, stumbled once, then righted himself as they loosened underfoot.

The hatch was closed. The hose Harvey had used to siphon water from the bottom of the hole lay curled nearby.

"We're clear," Remy said from the top of a casement where he could clearly watch the surrounding area.

Sam fit his fingers in the finger holes, barely discernible from the foundation. The iron hinges shrilled in protest as he tore the hatch open. He peered down into the dark.

A flashlight hung from one cleat below. It bobbed, and the light illuminated the bowed head at the base of the chamber.

"Babette?" he said, heart in his throat.

The head lifted from a pair of knees. The oval of Babette's tear-streaked face glowed in the flashlight, her dark eyes pleading. "Sam," she said, unfolding her arms from around her legs.

He held out a hand. "Stay."

She froze. "Where's Harvey? Is he with you?"

Ah, hell. "Where's your mother?" he asked.

"She left for the other island."

He took a steady breath. "Okay," he said. He caught sight of Remy and knew what had to be done. Kneeling on the edge of the hole, he said, "I have to go."

Distress winged across her face. "Is Harvey coming?"

He worked to swallow and failed. "No. But Remy's here. He'll stay with you."

That made Remy do a double take. "Come again?" he said.

Sam eyed the gun on Remy's hip, the ready set of his form, large and muscle-bound. No doubt he had extra clips on him.

He'd been a bodyguard. A SEAL.

"You're all I've got," Sam told him.

Remy stared. No emotion colored his face, and no argument came to the stern line of his mouth.

He would beg, Sam thought, if Remy refused. "Will you?" he asked.

Remy trained his eyes on some point in the distance. After several heavy seconds, he jerked his chin in affirmation.

Relief struck Sam like a blow. Again, he looked down at Babette. "Remy will be with you," he told her. "Is that all right?"

She nodded mutedly.

He wanted to hug her. He wanted to get her off this island. But Pia was somewhere out there alone against Jaime, and God knew how many of his men. It was the hardest thing he'd ever had to do, but he said, "I'll come back for you. Do you believe me?"

Her lower lip protruded. It trembled. She nodded once more.

"I love you," he said before making himself leave her.

Remy's frown was entrenched. "We don't know how many they have."

"I know."

"Could be six. Could be twenty."

"I know," Sam said again, without inflection.

After a heavy moment, Remy lifted his hand to Sam's shoulder. "There's a skiff. It's Clem's. He keeps it near his quarters, in the inlet from the channel."

Sam thought about it. "Does it run?"

"I never got around to asking," Remy said. "It's there, though, if you find yourself stranded on this side of the channel."

Sam lifted his chin. "Take care of her."

Remy's grin had nothing to do with mirth and everything to do with intent. "Consider your daughter untouchable."

* * *

Air scraped raw across her throat. The wind had shifted and the air around the lighthouse looked dingy from the smoke that had ridden there on pockets of air.

Pia had known she couldn't go to the marina. The second explosion had come from that direction. Even if it was still intact, the Solaros would bring their boats in there.

The sight of movement had her ducking behind Harvey's greenhouse.

Men roamed the grounds. Armed men. She thought she recognized the one near the door to Clem's living quarters from the hacienda.

Shoving the recognition aside, she crouched. She had weapons on the other side of the channel. Defenses. The plan was still in place to hold the men off, at least until help arrived.

Saints, please, let help arrive soon. Surely, the columns of smoke could be seen from the mainland. It was a clear day. Hadn't Harvey told Babette that on sunny days when the air quality was good, people on the mainland could sight trees on the island?

She heard them talking, speculating on where to find her and Babette. There was talk of the fort and Pia closed her eyes, praying Babette stayed hidden underneath the secret door.

As they veered off, her fear bobbed. She searched the grounds, wondering how to get their attention without falling prey to them.

Her eyes seized on flames.

The Solaros had found the boats tethered on the west beach, Harvey's Pursuit and Remy's skiff. They'd set fire to both.

As she watched, Harvey's Pursuit went up in a combustible fireball. She ducked at the noise and debris. The smoke turned black, curling away into the sky to join the haze.

She wrestled with panic. The Solaros had cut off the escape route to Escatawpa. Did they have men there, too? Had they somehow known the fight plan all along?

Pia saw the one remaining boat. It was a little thing. Shiny. Spiffy. Likely speedy. Something Jaime and his men had brought ashore.

She stepped out from her hiding place and broke into a run.

Shouts went up behind her. One of them called her by name.

She kept running hell-for-leather.

When she reached the boat, she ripped the anchor up from its sandy bed. Heaving it aboard, she let its weight carry her over the gunwale.

The first bullet caught the windscreen.

"Don't shoot her!" one of them shouted.

Pia rose. Her head was level with the windscreen, but she knew they wouldn't risk killing her.

Jaime wanted her alive.

She turned the key. The engine purred to life.

She threw the throttle into Reverse. The bow shied away from the point.

She reversed until waves slapped at her stern. Then she cut the wheel, shifted and throttled forward.

The sleek line of the boat sliced cleanly into the channel, leaving a trio of Jaime's men behind.

Once she knew she was no longer in shooting range, she set her course southwest and searched.

They'd left no weapons aboard.

She gnashed her teeth. Then she thought of the pirate post office she'd revisited days before.

As the sea breeze stung her cheeks, she felt the dampness

on her skin. Distressed, she lifted her hand to them, worried she was bleeding somewhere.

The dampness didn't come away red, but clear.

Using her sleeve, she scrubbed her face dry. Then she re-adjusted her course.

She wouldn't think about Sam. Or Babette. Sloane. Harvey, Remy or Clem.

If she thought about them, she'd lose sight of what she had to do.

Help would come. And when it did, Jaime would be the one trapped on an island, awaiting capture and custody.

She ran the boat aground, bracing herself against the gunwale. Then she shut off the engine, snatched the keys from the ignition and pocketed them. From the boat, she took the anchor, the flare, one life preserver and a rope.

The noise in her head was loud, but she counted her steps, focusing on the numbers, only the numbers.

When she reached the pirate post office tree, she reached deep inside the trunk.

She'd wrapped the Glock in one of the ragged hand towels from Harvey's kitchen to protect it from the weather. As she unrolled the cloth, she found the magazines she'd stored with it.

There was another cloth-bound weapon buried inside the tree. She debated whether to take the handgun and rounds Sam had placed there for himself.

She left it there and started running again.

By the time she reached the light tower, her lungs hurt. She could feel small fingers of fatigue weaving through muscle and bone. Encouraged by the sight of the low tide line marked by sea foam, she pushed herself the rest of the way, weapon up.

There were no signs of the Solaro men. The only footprints belonged to Pia, Sloane, Harvey, Sam and Remy. The five of them had left for Smuggler's only two hours before.

How had things gone so wrong so fast?

She was strong enough to face this. In the last twelve years, she'd knowingly or unknowingly transformed her body, as much as her mind, into something Jaime wouldn't recognize—lean, muscled, tattooed. She'd grown knowledgeable and capable. There was power in that. *She* was powerful, and she held on to that now.

There were cracks in the sand packed around the old light tower's footing, sure signs of weakness. The concrete foundation was perhaps the only thing that had anchored this spit of land from being washed out to sea already.

Before she veered inside, she checked the channel.

It was clear, but she identified two boats in the distance, similar to the one she'd run aground.

They're coming.

She put herself on the other side of the new door. The latching mechanism was made of sturdy wood. It would hold, she told herself as she dropped it in place.

The beacon of navigation no longer felt like a place of solace or efficiency. Its winding wrought iron staircase had collapsed in places, making the ascent treacherous. She heard the wind and sea moaning and whistling around the structure. The duet carried a haunted melody, made worse by the porthole windows that had been blown out to make it easier for their team to hold their position instead of struggling to force the panes open when the ambush came.

The first set of steps was still in place. She took the grated stairs two at a time to the landing, which was also grated. Her footsteps echoed loudly off everything, adding to the eeriness.

Ignoring it, she fell on the first cache of weapons.

None of them had caved when she asked to be somewhere

other than the fourth level, only one floor below the position of the missing Fresnel lens and the copper dome above it. It wasn't the height that had bothered her or the building's decay. It wasn't even the fact that the whole place shook with a strong gale...though that had given all of them pause.

It was the fact that every person who was supposed to be stationed below had been willing to die to keep her there. And while it was unlikely that anyone could get past the barricaded door and Remy frickin' Fontenot, the idea hadn't settled well.

If anyone took Jaime out, she'd wanted it to be her. Not because she'd earned it or for any sense of justice.

Because it felt right.

Him or me.

She dug through Remy's stash, loaded weapons, checked them twice, sighting down the barrel of a rifle through the window. She picked a spot in the distance and tried breathing to slow her heart. When that didn't work, she fell back on words.

Subdermatoglyphic.

She cocked the rifle and listened to the secure *chink-chink* of a round rolling into place.

S-U-B-D-E-R-M-A-T-O...

The diamond on her finger caught the light, and Sam's face wavered into her mind.

Her grip on the stock tightened.

She thought of Babette at the bottom of the hole, alone.

Screwing her eyes closed, she fought the tide of panic. Out loud, she tried picking up where she'd left off.

"... G-L-Y-P-H-I-C," she finished. She gulped several breaths, told herself she felt a mite calmer before taking the steps up to the second level—Sloane's position.

"Sesquipedalian," she stated, watching the distance rise between her feet and the lowest floor through the holes in the grating. "S-E-S-Q-U-I-P-E-D..."

The sound of shouting made her stop and listen.

Jaime's men were coming ashore.

She quickened her steps to the landing, eyed the supply box meant for Remy's teammate, Chief Petty Officer Kyle Bracken, then the window above it.

Peering out, she saw boats being anchored and men fanning out to search.

At their center, the white silk shirt flapped like a beacon.

The idiot wore expensive Italian loafers that were no doubt soaked.

Her focus narrowed on his figure. Her world spiraled around the target area of his wide chest.

She stuck the barrel of the rifle out the window. Took her time. Rested her cheek against the stock.

"E," she whispered. "D." She sighted. "A."

Steady, she thought, and willed every molecule inside herself to still. Sweat pebbled on her upper lip. She felt hot and cold, but… *Hold steady. Be still.*

"L," she breathed, not moving her jaw to keep that cross over Jaime's center mass.

She could count the buttons on his shirt front. She could see the hair on his chest through those he'd left undone near his collar.

"I." The lighthouse fell silent, as if holding its breath. She touched the trigger.

"A." She pulled a breath in. Then…let it out.

"N." She squeezed.

The gun kicked against her shoulder, the thunder drum of the report and its immediate echoes deafening. Even as chaos erupted on the ground below and the shell casing clattered to the grate at her feet, she kept her stance and her firm hold on the stock and took the second shot.

Chapter 19

Sam could hear the cacophony of gunshots clearly across the channel. From Harvey's lighthouse, he could see the men and boats on the far side.

Pia was there. It was impossible to see through the Escatawpa light tower windows from the distance.

But he knew she was there, alone.

She felt as far away as the moon.

"Goddammit," he spat.

Recalling what Remy had said about the skiff, he found the sliver of an inlet some twenty yards away. He followed it through cattails and palmettos. Either adrenaline was wearing off or his knee was getting worse. He had to gnash his teeth to stop a groan of pain from clawing its way up his throat.

The brush cleared, and the water pooled. A sad excuse for a floating dock listed to one side, half capsized.

But the skiff was there.

Seaworthy, Sam judged upon inspection.

Just barely.

He'd take his chances. Hooking his arms over the side, he hoisted his lower half out of the water, hooked his good leg over.

He rolled into the boat. There was one bench at the stern

where a gas-powered engine sat. The Evinrude's paint was flecked. It looked like it'd seen far better days.

Sam found the pull start. He yanked.

The engine gurgled and coughed. It died in a hiccup of fumes.

"Come on," he willed. He yanked again.

The Evinrude snarled at him before it coughed and died once more.

Sam took that as encouragement before he yanked the starter again.

The engine turned over. It sputtered, rattling.

Sam choked the throttle, just enough that the motor shivered and caught.

He didn't wait. He untethered the dock line and sped off.

Pia wished she, Sam, Remy or Sloane had thought of earplugs. Or eyewear. Twice a brass bullet casing caught the edge of her nose or cheekbone as they ejected from her weapon. The smell of gunpowder stung her nostrils.

She'd shot Jaime at least once. She'd flinched with the first shot, and he'd dodged the second, so he wasn't down.

From the porthole windows she rotated through on the second level, she counted three downed men. There hadn't been as many here as there had been on the beach with Sloane. Eight, she was sure of. Maybe she'd missed one. To be safe, she put it at ten.

Jaime hadn't crossed her sights since disembarking. Likely, he was directly below, up against the wall of the tower, where she couldn't get a clear shot without sticking her head out one window.

The slide clicked. The gun was out of rounds. Instead of taking time to reload, she set it aside, picked up the Glock, and took off the safety.

Instantly, she missed the long barrel of the rifle. She felt
more exposed with her arms extended into the Solaros' field
of view.

Focusing, she thought back to Sloane's marksmanship
teachings. Solid grip. Trigger control. She kept her draw
smooth and quick, grouped her shots, and aimed for center mass.

There were five remaining men and four windows on the
second level. As she rotated from one pane to the next, they
regrouped, separated, watched. There was no cover for them
on the beach. Their only choice was to retreat out of firing
range, but they didn't do that. Perhaps on Jaime's orders,
they kept up the ambush.

She clipped one of them in the leg. As he fell over sideways with a cry, she moved again from one window to another...

...and saw no one.

Ignoring the ringing in her ears from the barrage of gunfire, she sidestepped to the next window, flattened herself
against the wall before peering out cautiously.

The beach was a sandy white blank.

Before she made it to the fourth window, she thought she
caught the sound of shouting. Three figures sprinted across
her field of vision, and she lifted the gun, ready to fire.

They were running away. As she watched, they went down
in unison, bellies to the sand, and fit their hands over the
back of their heads.

She didn't have a moment to wonder at their behavior.

Thunder rocked the light tower. The grating seemed to
sway beneath her feet. Her shoulder hit the wall, sending a
shock wave through her clavicle. She swore the wall listed.
For a second, she thought the structure was going over, finally giving in to time and nature's demands.

The smell of smoke snapped her out of it. The tower was still intact. But the door had been breached.

They'd used explosives. Just like at the beach at Smuggler's. And the marina.

As her ears adjusted, she heard what remained of the door splinter as the Solaros forced their way inside.

She holstered the Glock. Heart pounding, she made a running leap for the system of ropes Sam and Remy had fashioned in place of the missing third set of stairs.

"Pia!"

She glanced down. She could see Jaime through the grate.

Forcing her arms to work faster, she pulled herself up the ropes. Her arms screamed. Sweat filmed her face, but her mind screamed *faster.*

She hooked her arms over the lip of the third level. Digging her fingers into the holes of the grate, she felt the metal bite into the skin of her forearms as she lifted herself over.

She didn't have time to think about how tired she was. How utterly drained the climb had made her. Rolling to all fours, she reached for the handle of the machete Sam had left close by. Using it, she hacked through the ropes.

A shot went through the grate, through the sole of her shoe. It pierced the bottom of her foot. The pain seemed to tear it in half. She went down on all fours again, screaming this time.

The Evinrude died on a cloud of purple smoke.

Sam was only halfway across the channel.

He worked the pull cord, yanking.

The motor didn't cough this time. It didn't gurgle or stir.

He yanked again and got the same result. And once more, when he tried yet again.

Turning to face the bow, he gripped the sides of the boat

as they heaved against the waves. Smoke stained the air. It poured from the mouth of the entry door.

Sam realized it had been breached, and his stomach hit the deck.

Jaime would be inside with her now. He wasn't one of the men lying on the beach.

Sam bit off a half dozen ill-chosen words. The skiff didn't have oars or a life preserver. Aside from hanging his arms over the sides and paddling like a Flintstone, he didn't see the vessel making it to shore.

Which left him with only one option.

He pushed himself up to standing, bracing his feet apart to prevent the skiff from rolling over with him in it.

Tearing off his jacket, he tossed it on the bench. He fisted the material of his shirt in both hands beneath the back collar and pulled it over his head. Balling the material, he deposited it onto the deck.

He crouched to untie one boot, then the other. He tugged them off and dropped them into the thin pool of water at the bottom of the boat, the result of a leak at one of the rivets.

Over the howl of the wind, he could hear the shots coming from inside the tower.

He pulled the holster off his belt. The gun likely wouldn't fire after being exposed to water.

Even as he set it aside, his mind argued. It bargained, turning away from the reality of the situation. He took up the knife Clem had given him and shoved the sheath into his waistband.

The wind and waves had turned the skiff perpendicular to shore. He did the same with his body, angling for the wounded white spire in the distance.

He took one breath, closing his eyes to stop memories from taking hold.

The current. Its invisible arms. How they'd wrapped around him—like an octopus. Tentacles gripping, tugging him away from the nimbus of sunlight above the shimmering surface.

Filling his lungs, he pushed all that away. He pushed away everything and propelled himself over the side.

Fire.

She felt like she was on fire, like before. She could remember flames curling toward her, the smoke feeding on the oxygen she pulled into her lungs, making her sputter and choke.

The heat had been enormous.

It had been easy to imagine what it would feel like wrapped around her.

Like this, she thought.

Sobs tore at her throat as blood pooled, warm and sticky, at the bottom of her shoe.

Up, she thought.

Sloane's weapons box was across the way, along the east-facing wall.

Too far. If she was going to go in any direction, it had to be up. She'd cut the ropes, but they could still shoot her.

The sound of shouting below didn't penetrate the noise inside her head. She gripped the railing and pulled herself up to stand. Sweat ran in rivulets down the sides of her face.

Something small inside her said to lie down. Lie down, curl up and wait for it to be over. The pain and the mountain of exhaustion followed the same litany, sending up a shrill chorus.

She whipped her head from side to side in refusal.

Up, she told herself sternly.

If the distance to the east wall seemed far, the view up the last set of stairs looked insurmountable.

Maybe she'd cracked, but her mind went to a book she'd read to Babette repeatedly. An Eric Carle story with clever foldouts and a ladder to the sky.

Papa, Please Get the Moon for Me.

She remembered the mountain and the impossibly long ladder at the top and how Papa had climbed it.

Let's do that someday, Babette had said, eyes half pleading, half wonder as she turned her face up to Pia's from her pillow.

Okay, Pia had said.

She tried to even out her breathing. Her hand was slippery on the railing, but she gripped it anyway.

Every other step was agony. She tried using her toes. Just her toes. The bullet was in her sole, close to the outside. *The medial plantar*, she remembered from biology. She hadn't thought that area of her encyclopedic brain would ever come in handy.

The medial and lateral plantar were home to the two largest nerves in the foot, which accounted for a person's balance. And why walking without shoes on hot sand in the summer was akin to torture.

That explains the pain, she thought humorlessly as she dragged herself up another step. She keened. Tears were rolling with the sweat now.

She wondered if the bullet had shattered a bone. *Bones.* The foot had thirty-six joints and twenty-six bones. Odds were more than one was fractured. Not to mention the hundreds of muscles. Tendons. Ligaments.

As she climbed, she tried focusing less on the pain and the sound of Jaime's voice calling. Calling endlessly.

"Pia. Chiquita. Come down from there. You've nowhere else to go."

To drown him out, she set herself to naming all the muscles of the foot she could remember.

The blood caught at the bottom of her shoe. Was it weighing her down? The effort to raise her foot was like lifting a dumbbell with her toes.

Her knees hit the landing first. She fell forward, catching herself.

She'd...*made it*?

The paint-chipped walls sharpened into focus. The lantern room was open to the air thanks to the three-hundred-sixty degrees of broken windows. Bird droppings littered the floor and small tufts of feathers were scattered across the concrete floor. The Fresnel lens was long gone, but its base remained to serve as a perch for seabirds.

The noise had made them all take flight. Except for one, a seagull that lay dead in a corner.

She inched toward the box that she had left close to where the lantern had once been to protect it from the weather. She riffled through the box's contents.

A handgun, like her Glock. Some spare cartridges. A bolt-action rifle, fully loaded.

She had the machete still in hand. The flare she'd taken from the stolen boat was jammed in her back pocket.

She eyed the last item she'd left in the lantern room.

Lying across the floor was her long-handled flounder gig, its three steel prongs lethal with backward-facing teeth.

A last resort, she'd thought. She hadn't thought she would need it.

If the plan had gone right, she wouldn't have.

"Pia?"

Was he closer now? Farther up?

Her stomach clenched with fear. She choked it back down. Propping her back against the base of the empty lantern, she put it between herself and the door. It was the only cover in the chamber. Then she laid out her weapons carefully, keeping them within easy reach. She counted the shots she had left in the Glock and laid it aside in favor of the other handgun.

"This can all end right now, chiquita. Come down. My men will lay down their weapons. They'll do as I tell them."

She took off the safety, listening for footsteps. How did he scale the third landing without ropes?

She closed her eyes. The grit behind them, the lull of sleep, made her force them open. She was worn down.

Again, she thought of Babette...safe inside the fort. Had rescue personnel reached Smuggler's Island by now?

Would Sam be alive when they got there? Sloane? Anyone?

She heard Jaime on the stairs, wise enough to be slow-footed. Watching, she saw his shadow cut across the wall. A smile bored through his words, almost teasing. "Hello, little wife."

Chapter 20

The guard posted outside the smoking door never saw the knife coming. He didn't cry out. The breath left him.

Sam caught him as he fell, lowering him to the ground without a sound. He extracted Clem's blade, leaving a bloody rose on the back of the man's shirt.

He took the man's gun, checked his shots...

Two in the chamber. One in the spout.

Hold on, Pia, he thought as he moved against the lighthouse wall near the broken jamb. Spider cracks weaved through the casing. He could hear noise from within. Voices, but no gunshots.

He tried not to think of what that might mean, but the possibilities raced through him.

Had Jaime captured her? Had she been caught in the crossfire?

Don't think. He'd buried the instincts that came with training and warfare. Still, he found them. They were every bit as much a part of him as his fingerprint.

There was a point in the action where the thinking stopped and instinct took hold—that sixth sense that had saved his life in battle.

Falling back on instinct now, he listened, collected footsteps, an exchange of words, the sound of brass casings bouncing across the concrete floor...

When the next man came through the door, Sam waited until the last second to seize him and slip the knife between his ribs.

An explosion of air left the man's mouth as he gaped, then slowly listed forward.

He sank at the knees. Sam lowered him down. He didn't have time to check his pockets. He pulled the knife as the next man came through the door quickly.

He brought his forearm up, dislodging the gun from his hold. It clattered to the ground as Sam grabbed the man's wrist in both hands, turned and flipped him over his shoulder.

He hit the slab hard.

As he coughed, Sam kicked the gun out of the way. When the man's mouth gaped, Sam pointed his gun at his head.

The man raised his palms.

Sam kept the gun trained on him as he patted the second man down. He disarmed him, pocketing a semiautomatic pistol. Then he patted down the third just to be sure.

"Where's Jaime?" he hissed.

"Fourth level," the man said.

Fourth. Sam resisted the urge to cast his eyes up to the railing. *Son of a bitch.* "And Pia?" He waited, barely breathing.

"He'll take her alive," the man told him.

"Like hell," Sam growled and brought the butt of the gun down on the man's temple.

The pistol jammed.

It took Jaime the split second between the click of the gun and her realization to cross the room. He knocked the pistol from her hand.

She reached for her Glock.

His wet Italian loafer came down on the back of her hand.

She cried out as his weight threatened to break the bones beneath it.

"Don't," he warned.

She looked up then into his eyes.

They were the same. Fathomless black with flashes of feeling. Anger. Relief.

She'd expected the animal to be painted plainly there for her to see. It wasn't. The scars across his face, faded with time, his shorn hair—not long and glossy like before—and the hollowness of his cheeks were the only things that separated him from the man he'd been at the hacienda.

It had been easy to dismiss perceived kindnesses, knowing in hindsight how they had groomed her. The sound of "little wife" had always been tender. He'd held out her chair for her at the table before seating himself and always made sure she ate, letting her take the first bite. He'd held her hand and stroked her cheek often.

So when he reached out, she froze. Her hand was still trapped under his shoe, but he feathered his fingers across her cheek. His lips parted, and she felt his breath stutter across her face.

When she saw the relief in his eyes triple, her stomach twisted so hard she wanted to retch. She turned her chin to the point of her shoulder, as far out of reach as she could manage.

"You're alive."

The statement struck her. Had he thought she'd died at the hacienda? He'd left her there to burn when she refused to move away from Bianca's body.

Out of the corner of her eye, she caught the black impression of the Glock on the floor. She made a dive for it.

The weight on her hand increased as he lifted his other foot to kick it away. He did the same to the rifle, leaving her to grasp at nothing.

She watched the Glock skitter over the railing of the gallery deck and out of sight.

His fingers latched over her chin, forcing her eyes back to his. His gaze burned into her. It was a brand. "I've counted the days until I could touch you again." Even as the other fingers tightened, his thumb traced the rim of her jaw. "Chiquita."

"Let go of me," she said through her teeth.

"Where's Babette?" When she flinched, a smile warped the contours of his thin face. "Si. I know about the child we made. The one you've hidden away all these years."

"We weren't hiding," she hissed. His grip on her chin hardened further, making her bite her tongue.

"Does she know?" he asked, the light of excitement making his dark gaze glitter. "Does my daughter know Papa's come to get her?"

Babette.

Had Pia been wrong this whole time? Had the chase been less about her and more about finding Babette? Did he want to take her child away from her?

Her heart twisted. "You can't have her," she told him.

"Does she know my name?" he asked, lowering his face to within inches of hers. "Does she know she's a Solaro? Or do I get to be the one who tells her about her legacy?"

Oh, Saints, no.

Legacy. Jaime had had many obsessions. Chief among them had been the Solaro legacy and his quest for legitimacy in his father's eyes. It was only when he thought he'd failed—when Pablo had cut him off from the organization and association with him and his half brother Alejandro—that Jaime had lost his grip on himself.

Now he wanted Babette. Why? So that he could pass Pablo's name on to her? So that he could teach her the family business?

Bianca had told her the rumor that Jaime had killed his own mother to wash away all physical traces of illegitimacy.

If he could do that to the woman who'd given birth to him—who'd nursed him and cared for him—what would he do to his own child? Where would he draw the line?

Jaime Solaro didn't have a line. He'd proven that—time and time again.

His hand lowered from her chin to her throat. Before she could lift her free hand to stop him, his fingers wreathed her windpipe. "Where is she?"

She tore at the back of his hand, her breath coming fast. The pressure on her windpipe wasn't much, but the flashbacks came back to her, vivid. His hands at her throat, his head thrown back as he pinned her to the bed.

Panic beat at her chest.

"You wear his ring," he observed. Jaime's smile stretched into a grin. "Did you tell him—before he died? That he couldn't have you? That you couldn't take a husband because you have me?"

Sam wasn't dead. He couldn't be… She sputtered when his grip tightened. She tried scooting back, not caring about the hand under his foot anymore.

The smile died. "Where is my daughter, Pia?" he asked, drawing each word out slowly as he shifted his weight forward, intending to lower her to the floor.

She fought to stay upright. She wouldn't die like this. *Not like this, please!*

Scattered dots of light appeared at the corners of her vision. They grew. One by one, she watched them pop.

At first, she thought the shadow on the edge of her vision was unconsciousness rearing up to get her.

It solidified into a familiar shape. Moving like a wraith, it reached for the rifle that had fallen near the stairs, lifted it.

At the last minute, Jaime ducked. His hold on her throat loosened. His weight lifted off her foot as he rolled out of range.

Pia grasped for the phantom fingers still at her throat. Air tore through her lungs. She coughed, her eyes watered, but as she scrambled away from the tangle of limbs, she willed them to stay open.

Sam. He was alive. Wet, his jeans, hair and the skin of his back and chest gritty with sand. But *alive*. He fought Jaime with wolfish intensity.

She'd thought she'd seen all there was of the soldier in him in the cabin. Now she realized there had been more. Underneath, there had been something grimmer. He hit Jaime over and over with his fist. Fury brimmed off of him, so he looked less like a man and more like something feral that had risen out of the waves.

The next punch sent Jaime back against the grate of the gallery deck. It clattered under his weight. She saw the railing shake. The wind grabbed at his shirt.

Sam picked up the rifle again, but before he could slam the bolt into place, Jaime wrapped both hands around the barrel. Using it, he yanked Sam forward. Like a ram, he butted his brow into Sam's.

Pia cried out as Sam went back on his heels.

Jaime ripped the rifle out of his hands, flipped it around.

Pia didn't think. She saw the flash of the gig prongs on

the floor and grabbed the handle. She gained her feet. Using momentum, she charged.

She drove the points deep into his midsection and watched Jaime flail like a flounder. His arms spread. His body jerked.

She absorbed his shock and awe as he gasped. Then she spoke to him, low, as she put pressure behind the gig, just as he'd put pressure on her throat. "You should have stayed in prison, because there was no way in hell you were ever going to get your hands on my daughter."

He made a noise, something terrible and garbled. She couldn't relieve the pressure, however, not until the light left his eyes.

As he sank to his knees, she felt Sam's hand on her hip. "It's okay," he said. His arm was wrapped around her waist. "It's okay. It's okay."

He chanted it. She fell back into him, the gig's handle sliding out of her grasp. As Sam drew her back from the gallery deck into the lantern chamber where their feet shuffled safely over concrete, she lifted her hand to her mouth. Turning blindly, she buried her face in his chest.

His arms came around her. They must have both loosened at the knees because the next thing she knew they were kneeling, and he was rocking her as sobs racked her bruised throat.

"It's okay," he said again. Maybe as much to assure himself as her. His lips pressed gently to her temple, then her cheek before he found her mouth with his.

He tasted of salt and earth and all things pure. It pulled her out of the grip of shock and back to him. She raised her hands to his face and felt the texture of facial hair gone soft with neglect. "He didn't come for me," she blurted. "He came for Babette. He came to take her."

"She'll never know him," Sam assured her.

She found she could close her eyes. It felt so good, just that.

"You're… You're bleeding."

"My foot," she said. "They shot me. I think the bone's shattered."

He laid her back on the floor so gently it was as if *she* were a child.

"Babette…" she began.

"She's safe in Remy's care."

As he untied her shoe, loosening the grip of the shoe, she tried not to whimper. "Remy's alive, too?"

"Yes. Harvey was hurt at the marina."

"Is he going to be okay?"

There was a pause. "We called in a rescue chopper. Clem's with him."

"And Sloane?"

"We'll find out," he promised. "Just as soon as I get you back to Smuggler's."

"I don't think I can walk," she said, crossing her arms over her face to keep from crying out. His ministrations were delicate, but the pain didn't let up. Not even a little.

"No," he agreed. "And I don't think I can take the shoe off. Not without something to cut it. I'm going to lift you, okay?"

"How're we going to get from the third to the second level?"

"Leave it to me."

His arm cradled the line of her shoulders and lifted her, easing her against his chest slowly.

Neither of them looked at the dead man on the gallery.

"I'm sorry I wasn't here."

"It's all right," she said. Her throat hurt. She could still feel Jaime's hands around it…

Sam's lips turned against her hair as he took the stairs one at a time. "You did so good, baby."

She tried holding on to the scent of his skin. It helped take the edge off the sickness welling up inside her.

"You're a hell of a fighter," he told her. "You always were."

"Sam?"

"Yeah?"

"Marry me?"

He stopped on the landing of the third level. His eyes went round. "What?"

She did her best to say it steady enough. "Will you marry me?"

"You said you couldn't be my wife."

"I didn't think I could be a lot of things. But I was wrong. And I want to be your wife."

"My wife," he repeated, and when she didn't turn away from the words, emotions bled through the blue of his stare. "You mean that."

"I do," she said. "And I love you. So much."

His eyes grew damp. "I love you, too. And I will gladly marry you."

She let out a breath. It tripped into a sob.

"First, let's get you to a hospital. Okay?"

"Okay."

"Anybody up there?" a voice called from below.

Sam crossed to what was left of the ropes Pia had cut away.

When she looked down, Sloane was moving a ladder into place, bridging the gap. There was a cut near her lip that had dried and another along her hairline still bleeding. When she saw them, she closed her eyes in relief. "Thank Christ."

"Hello to you, too," Sam offered back. "Where were you?"

"Getting Babette secure," Sloane said. "Jaime?"

"Dead," Sam replied, his voice flat.

Sloane nodded once. "Good."

"Babette's okay?" Pia asked.

"She didn't want to leave the island until we'd found you," Sloane admitted. "But she's unharmed."

"Harvey?" Sam asked. Pia heard the lilt of concern when he said it.

"Last I heard," Sloane said, "he was stable. If not for Remy and Clem, though…"

Sam nodded off the rest. "I may need help getting her down. She needs a hospital. Gunshot wound to the foot."

"Why didn't you say something?" Sloane snapped. She came the rest of the way up the ladder quickly. "Men."

No sooner was Sloane eye level than Pia blurted, "I'm sorry."

"Sorry?" Sloane asked. "Pia. For what?"

"You wanted to be the one who killed him."

Sloane looked from Pia to Sam, who nodded confirmation, then back to Pia. She softened. "He's gone and we'll all sleep better for it. Thanks to you. Now let's get you down from here."

Chapter 21

As always, when Babette's birthday rolled around, she, Pia and Sam made a pilgrimage back to where it all began.

Even so, Casaluna on the bayou was more crowded than usual. Sloane had joined them from the city with Remy in tow. They'd spent the better part of the journey sniping at each other. Remy grabbed the beer Sam offered him after their arrival like a lifeline. "Her driving hasn't improved," he muttered.

Grace had been released from protective custody. She arrived together with Javier Rivera and her kitten, Luis.

"What do you think about a double wedding?" she asked as they settled in.

"Uh…" Sam hedged. He pointed to the kitchen. "I'm needed in the kitchen."

Javier cleared his throat. "Me, too, I think."

"I stand by what I said about men," Sloane drawled as they retreated with Remy. "And a double wedding? Could you be any cheesier?"

Grace pursed her lips. "Talk Remy into marrying you. We could make it a triple."

"He wouldn't have me if I was naked and covered in whipped cream."

Pia met Grace's stare and watched her wiggle her eyebrows knowingly. "Yeah, somehow, we doubt that."

The door opened and Babette came in from her walk with Harvey. "Grace!" she shrieked when she saw her.

Grace caught her in a hug. "There's the birthday girl!"

"What am I, chopped liver?" Sloane said, arms out.

Babette laughed and hugged her, too. Pia watched Sloane's frown morph into a sentimental smile as she stroked a hand over Babette's hair. "Our beach sprite," she murmured. "I thought I ordered you to stop growing."

"Growing up's good when you do it well." Grace touched her nose to Babette's. "And you do it far more gracefully than any of the rest of us did."

"Ain't that the truth?" Sloane agreed heartily.

"Thanks." Babette tilted her head at Sloane. "So…since Grace delivered me, are you going to deliver my sister?"

Sloane blanched three different shades of white, making Pia and Grace choke on laughter. "That's not funny," she said, though her lips twitched when the light of mischief took hold of Babette.

Grace elbowed Sloane in the ribs. "She's turning out more like you every day. And *it's a girl*?"

As Grace laid a hand over the small mound beneath the belly of Pia's blouse, Pia placed her palm over hers. "We don't know the sex yet. I like not knowing. Though Babette's made it clear, she wants it to be a girl."

"Another girl," Grace said. "Wouldn't that be something?"

Pia pressed her lips closed. Later, after the party, she'd find a moment to sit with her friends on the porch and tell them all the quiet things her motherly intuition had whispered about the life growing inside her.

"Can I take Luis?" Babette asked.

"He'd love that," Grace said, handing the kitten off to her.

"He needs to run around a bit, stretch his legs. Maybe he'll let us sleep tonight."

"You realize that's a cat," Sloane told her. "Not a kid."

Pia smiled at them both. "I'm glad you made it. I needed this. All of us, here."

"How's your foot?" Sloane asked. "Should you be on your feet at all?"

"You and Sam," Pia said with a shake of her head. "Peas in a pod." She pointed to the boot on her foot. "And the doctor says I'm fine. I'll only need this for a little while longer."

"How's your pain level?" Grace asked, ever the doctor. "On a scale of one to ten."

"It's fine," Pia said again.

"And the baby's good?" Sloane probed.

"Sam went with me to my latest appointment with my ob-gyn. They did an ultrasound and everything's fine." Warmth flooded her, remembering. "He heard the heartbeat for the first time."

"Aw," Grace cooed.

Pia found Harvey standing at the back door, looking slightly ill at ease. "Excuse me," she said. She knew it was difficult leaving the island. Repairs to the marina and the used ferryboat the state had provided to replace *The Smuggler* were still under way. Day-trippers would be held off until mid-April. But Smuggler's Island would be open to the public soon. Although Harvey had left Clem in charge, Pia knew he was anxious to return. "Sam's parents should be here soon. Can I get you something to drink?"

"I'm fine," he said. "Babette gave me the grand tour."

"She didn't wear you out, did she?" Pia asked, only half teasing.

"She tried," Harvey said with a fond smile. "But I'm hale and hearty enough."

In truth, he'd recovered well from his shrapnel injury at the marina. "Remy arrived while you were out. I know you've been meaning to speak with him."

"I have. Thank you."

She laid her hand on his arm. "Thank *you*, Harvey. Babette's happy you're here."

"So am I," he told her before moving off to join the men in the kitchen.

The smell of burned birthday candles made reality sink in. Babette was officially another year older. It stayed with Pia long after the serving of cake, the opening of presents and the lively game of charades the birthday girl had called for everyone to join in. It ended only when Remy insisted Sloane had cheated in favor of the women's team.

"How does anybody cheat at charades?" Sloane was still muttering hours later.

Pia had finally gotten her quiet moment on the porch with Sloane and Grace. She reached for Sloane's hand to soothe her. "The longer you mutter about him, the more Grace is going to tease you about marrying him."

"That's right, chère," Grace said cheerily from the chair on Pia's left.

Sloane closed her mouth in studied restraint.

Pia looked at Grace. "You're coming back to New Orleans?"

"I am," Grace said. "Though I'll miss the desert."

Sloane stared at her as if she'd grown two heads. "You hate wide-open spaces."

"I do not," Grace pointed out. "Anymore."

"Did you ride horses while you were there?" Pia asked.

"I did," Grace said, grinning. "Though I much prefer taking care of them to being on the back of one."

"Is Javier going to live in New Orleans with you?" Pia asked, having a hard time picturing the cowboy in the city.

"Yes," Grace said. "I feel bad, taking him away from his lifestyle. But he insisted we come back. The hospital's offered me my job back, and my apartment above Russo's Pizzeria has been refurbished."

"Is he going to buy a mule and carry tourists around Jackson Square?"

"No," Grace said. "Dante's bayou tour business partner is leaving soon for Florida. He's asked Javier to step in."

"That was nice of him," Pia noted.

"It was," Grace agreed. She petted the sleepy kitten in her lap. "And I won't have to worry anymore about this one getting carried away by desert hawks. Though I'm not sure he'll like being confined to the apartment when he's had free roam over a cabin and barn for weeks." She made a disgusted noise. "I'm sorry, Pia. I didn't even ask. How was Alek's memorial service in Minnesota?"

Pia sobered quickly. "Sad. But there was something uplifting about it, too. It was like watching a circle close. He's home now."

"How's Sam taking it?"

"It's getting easier for him as the days pass," Pia said. "Figuring out what he wants to do professionally in the future will help. He's fixing the beach house up right now with his father. When that's done, he's tossing around the idea for a book."

"What kind?" Sloane asked.

"A memoir," Pia said, "about Alek. He wants him to be remembered. And he wants his sacrifice to mean something. He's thinking about mixing memories and narrative with his photographs."

"That sounds wonderful," Grace murmured.

"It does," Pia said with a nod. "It'll help him complete his own circle where Alek and the Middle East are concerned."

"You don't have a dive boat anymore," Sloane pointed out. "After the baby comes, do you want to go back to dive tours?"

"I do," Pia replied. "Salty Mermaid Tours will need a new boat, obviously. I'll miss a dive season, but with all the media attention from what happened, Sam thinks I'll be busier than ever when I open bookings next spring."

"And when is the wedding?" Grace asked.

"I thought you were going to have a double wedding," Sloane interjected.

"I was kidding," Grace countered.

"Mercy me."

"The baby's due in August," Pia considered. "We were thinking Thanksgiving or Christmas. Both are special." She thought of circles closing again and looked at Grace. "You?"

"June," Grace said readily. She smirked. "Javier and I aren't nearly as patient as you and Sam."

"Will he dress like a cowboy?" Sloane asked, sounding amused in spite of herself.

Grace's smile turned sly. "I wouldn't have it any other way."

They fell into a companionable silence. The sounds of the bayou awake with spring heightened as the afternoon wore on.

Pia had never felt completely comfortable at Casaluna after her mother's death. But she felt the past fall away and was gripped by contentment.

She reached for each of her friends' hands. "It's good to be here together."

Sloane made a sound of assent. "It helps. Knowing the Solaros are gone."

"Thanks to you," Grace said, squeezing Pia's hand.

"I didn't do it alone," Pia replied lowly.

"Give yourself some credit," Sloane demanded. "You took out an escaped convict. The same one who locked you up and tormented you. You did it with a bullet in your foot and a flounder gig. And I'm glad it was you."

"Really?"

Sloane met Pia's eyes with a level stare. "I would have preferred to be standing beside you when you did it. But yes. I'm glad."

"It's justice," Grace added. "At its finest."

"I still have dreams," Pia admitted.

"I watched Alejandro Solaro die at the end of Javier's scope twelve years ago," Grace explained, "and I still see him at night. But I'm different now. Stronger."

Sloane nodded. Pia still wondered what it was she dreamed about, but she knew better than to ask.

"You'll have to decide which of you will be my maid of honor, by the way," Grace said, effectively lightening the mood. "And you'll be wearing purple."

Sloane swore under her breath.

Pia shook her head even as her smile bloomed. "I'll be as big as a house in June."

"You'll have that nice pregnant glow about you," Grace pointed out.

"Summer in New Orleans," Pia considered. "That glow will be a glistening of sweat. I'll be there to stand beside you, regardless."

"I may spill something on this pink dress," Sloane chimed in, "but I'll be there, too. It's not every day one of your best friends ties the knot. Especially if you tell me there'll be a bull-riding machine."

"Not on your life."

"Is he going to lasso you? Are we going to throw grain instead of birdseed? And if you're going to ride off into the sunset together, I want pictures."

Pia laughed. She laughed until it hurt, and it felt perfect.

The first night she woke up again in the house on Flamingo Bay, she found the pillow and space next to her empty. She touched the sheets where Sam had lain and felt how cold they were.

Pulling the covers off, she slung both feet over the side of the bed, putting one on the floor. Gingerly, she tested the other by lowering it flat to the rug.

Tender, but bearable. She stood. Leaving the crutches where they lay near her bedside, she wandered into the bathroom.

Her body felt awkward enough with the rounding of her hips. She'd been happy to lose the boot so she could move around freely.

The nausea had faded, at last. She was eating everything. Wondering how on earth she was going to fit into Grace's maid of honor dress by summer, she swung her robe around her shoulders and pushed her arms through the sleeves before belting it and heading for the stairs.

She heard a slight rapping sound, smelled new paint and fresh coffee. When she'd made it to the bottom, she found Sam clad in shorts and a tool belt with his back to her on the other side of the room.

Her heart and stomach gave twin warm wobbles. She'd been hungry for a lot of things lately—him chief of all.

Last night they'd slept in their sleigh bed together for the first time since Christmas.

As she watched, he lifted a picture frame to the wall and hung it on a nail. Looking around, she found the others. He'd salvaged most of the photos from the Solaros' wreckage and hung several of Babette's paintings, too. They'd brought some from Casaluna to replace those they hadn't been able to salvage from the destruction.

Slowly, their lives were coming together again.

"You're up early," she said.

Sam turned, hammer in hand. When his gaze collided with hers, the hammer lowered. A slow smile wove its way across his lips.

She narrowed her eyes. "What is it?"

"Nothing," he said, dropping the hammer into its clip on his belt. "Mornings bring out the sea goddess in you."

Pia resisted the urge to roll her eyes when her body lit up and an answering smile touched her mouth.

A groan lifted from the direction of the kitchen. Pia looked around and found Babette seated at the table behind a cereal bowl and a half-emptied glass of orange juice. Her hair was braided back from her brow into two weaves that tumbled back from the high fall of a ponytail. "As much as I love us all being together forever, you two could do that less."

"What are we doing?" Sam asked, amused.

She used her spoon to gesture from him to Pia. "Kissing with your eyes."

Pia raised a brow. "That's a thing?"

"It is with you two," Babette said. She shook her head and scooped another bite up to her mouth. "And it's *all the time.*"

"I'd tamp down on the eye-kissing," Sam said, consideringly. His eyes touched Pia again. "But I'm not sure I can help it."

Pia felt those eyes everywhere. She crossed her arms over her chest to temper her own reaction. Looking away carefully, she walked to the teakettle on the stove. "I thought we'd go for a walk this morning."

"Where?" Babette asked.

"The beach."

"But you haven't walked on the beach since…"

Pia turned, lifted her foot, wiggling her bare toes. "My cast is gone now. There's hardly any pain when I walk anymore. I'd like to walk on the beach. With both of you."

After a slight pause, Sam nodded. "Then that's what we'll do."

An hour later, the three of them left the beach house. They crossed the narrow road to the sand dunes and the boardwalk growing rough with age. The air was briny with a touch of spring warmth that made Pia grin. The drone of waves filled the morning.

As they came over the rise, Babette broke into a run, kicking off her shoes. Birds winged off, startled, as she hooted and raced into the sand.

Sam's hand found Pia's as the sunlight flashed across the surface of the water, blinding. Pia's breath caught. "This never gets old."

"No," he agreed. They stopped to toe off their shoes.

The sand underneath their feet gave slightly. It was cool to the touch.

"Any pain?" he asked as she took her first steps across it.

"It's perfect," she said with a sigh and led the way to the tide line.

Babette was already wet up to her calves as she mirrored the restless running of sandpipers in their ceaseless foray into the wet sand and then out. The smile on her face was broad.

A tiny prodding in Pia's side made her reach for her belly. She held her breath, pressing slightly.

Something—a hand, a foot maybe—pressed back.

"What is it?" Sam asked.

"Here," she said, pressing his hand to the space. "Right there. Do you feel that?"

His brows came together. Then, slowly, the lines in his brow eased, his eyes cleared, and wonder struck his face.

"You feel it," she said, grinning.

"I do." Wonder broadened into happiness, and he swept her against him, holding her in the golden glow of the morning.

She felt so many things at once—joy, relief and a certainty that went deeper than her bones. Closing her eyes, she savored it.

Sam shook his head slightly. His lips turned in to her cheek, and he kissed her there, the brush of his lips roughened by the stubble around his mouth. "I have everything."

She beamed, holding him tighter. "So do I."

He rocked her over their feet in a dance all their own.

"Hey!"

Pia glanced up. Babette waved her arms. "Are we walking or not?"

"Coming!" she called back. Grasping Sam's hand in hers, she asked, "Shall we?"

Together, they made their way down the beach, following the trail of footprints Babette left and adding their own.

Epilogue

Typically, Mardi Gras weddings took place in February or March, but no one dared mention that to the bride. Grace wore a gold tiara with purple and green stones. Guests masqueraded in face coverings decked in beads and feathers.

The hall where the ceremony took place was swathed in purple, gold, and green. The parade from the hall to the reception covered two blocks. It was led by a jazz band with Grace and Javier close behind. The bride and groom carried black and white feathered umbrellas while their guests marched behind them. Spectators danced. The catering at the reception did not disappoint: Chicken Creole, Cajun mac-and-cheese, and jambalaya. The daiquiris flowed. King cakes were served in lieu of wedding cake.

Pia took a break from the dancing. She sat in the corner, stretching her back. Underneath the table, she toed off her heels. Someone had set up a fan nearby. She turned her face to it and let it cool the mist of perspiration on her skin. Her face hurt from smiling and laughing.

"Snagged some cake," Sloane announced, claiming the chair next to her. She set one of two plates in front of Pia then leaned over her own and dug in.

Pia sat forward. She breathed in the smell of glazed sugar. Yes, she would have some cake, she thought, brandishing a gold fork from the place setting on her right. "I'm a terrible maid of honor."

"Why?" Sloane asked, already halfway through her piece. Her brow, too, was beaded with sweat. A button on the back of her green gown had come undone from spinning and whirling on the dance floor. Neither Pia nor Grace danced with near as much skill or enthusiasm as Sloane.

Pia dropped her fork and motioned for Sloane to turn so she could fix the button. "Because I lost track of the bride half an hour ago."

"Okay, first of all," Sloane drawled, "it was my job to keep up with Gracie. You're pregnant, your feet hurt and you have every right to sit down."

"I'm fine," Pia dismissed though her hands did cross over her baby bump. The baby had kept her awake most of the night kicking. She would've liked to sleep before the wedding, but she loved the feeling of life inside her so much she'd lain awake, thrilling when the baby had responded to her touch.

"Second," Sloane continued, "Gracie disappeared with Javy. I'd wager that right now the two of them are getting it on in a coat closet somewhere."

Pia nearly choked on the next bite of cake. "Oh, saints," she said, amused.

Sloane handed her a water glass. "Third, she's damn near impossible to keep up with. She's talked to every single guest, she's danced with most of them, too, and she's managed to make time for a speech, a toast, and to mash cake in Javier's face. I'm glad she's taking a break because, frankly, I'm exhausted just watching her."

"You should have been the maid of honor," Pia pointed out.

"No dice," Sloane said, shaking her head and shoveling

the last of the king cake into her mouth. "The maid of honor doesn't pick up the hottest single male at the reception and take him back to her place. That's my job."

Pia spotted a familiar face in the crowd. "So you're taking Remy home then?"

She had the immense pleasure of seeing Sloane balk. "Why would you say that?"

"Well, he's single, I assume. He's male. And besides my fiancé, he's the hottest man under this roof."

"We've been through this," Sloane said, avoiding her gaze. She did dart a look at the man in question, however, and her cheeks flushed. "That's not going to happen."

"Why again exactly?" Pia asked.

"He put me in the friend zone a long time ago," Sloane explained. "Trust me, there's no getting out of it."

"He watched you dance," Pia revealed, giving in to a smug smile.

Sloane's expression blanked. "Did he?"

"Mmm-hmm." Pia leaned toward her. "I thought he was going to throttle that one guy whose hands went south of your waist for a second."

"I might've enjoyed that," Sloane weighed.

"There you are!" Grace all but collapsed into the chair next to Pia's. She pushed the curls back from her face, resplendent in her white mermaid-style gown. "Mon Dieu. I think this party's gone off its rocker."

"I think you love it," Sloane countered.

Grace aimed a coy glance at them both. "I don't mind it. Hey, isn't that Remy over there?"

"Hey, isn't that a hickey on your neck?" Sloane said without looking up this time.

Grace placed her hand over the guilty blemish. "I'm a

newlywed. I'm entitled to ravish my sexy Latin husband when he's amenable to it."

"Something tells me he's always amenable," Sloane muttered. "You two couldn't keep your hands off each other during rehearsal. Pia and I thought the priest was going to have a stroke."

"Poor Father Mathias," Pia said. She smiled when she spotted Babette in the crowd. She'd found a dance partner in one of Grace's young cousins.

They'd located an art school closer than the one in Georgia. It would be a drive every morning from Flamingo Bay, but Pia and Sam wanted her to go wherever Babette wished to further her artistic dreams. They'd toured the school just over the Alabama state line and Babette had liked it. She was looking forward to starting her first semester in the fall.

Pia could let her go. She wanted her daughter to live as she wished, without fear. She wanted her to achieve her goals and not let anyone take that from her.

A great many things would change soon and not just the school in Alabama. Pia felt the baby kick beneath her right ribs. She rubbed the spot. It was getting stronger. She and Sam had chosen to wait until the delivery to find out the sex. The due date was at the tail end of August. He and Maks had built the crib already. Sam had bought her a rocker and bassinet to go beside their bed.

Grace and Sloane had both agreed to be godmothers, and all was right with the world.

Except her feet. She grimaced as she curled her toes, trying to ease the strain in her ligaments. The bullet wound didn't plague her if she wasn't on her feet for long hours. While Grace had chosen a low profile heel for her to wear with her purple maid of honor gown, the wound was playing up a bit nonetheless.

"Ladies?" They looked around to find Sam approaching from the area of the stage. Sloane waved him over. "Cop a squat," she invited, sliding over to the next chair so he could take the one next to Pia.

"I actually came to steal Pia away," he revealed.

"Where are we going?" she asked curiously.

"Upstairs to our suite," he told her.

She sighed over him. "I don't need to rest, Sam."

"But you do," Grace said, covering Pia's hand with her own. "Everything's fine here. More than fine. Javy and I are having the time of our lives, but I know you're getting tired."

"Go with him," Sloane told her. "I'll handle this one. If I need help, I'll tag Remy."

Pia began to protest when someone began to slide her chair out.

Javier grasped her hand, helping her to her feet. He was a man, but he looked nothing short of stunning in his Western tuxedo with his dark hair slicked back from his all-too-handsome face. "Pia," he said, taking her hands. "You've taken good care of my Grace. Now it's Sam's turn to take care of you."

"You're ganging up on me," she observed. Still, she leaned forward and planted a kiss on his sun-bronzed cheek. "Is there more cake?" she added discreetly.

Javier winked. "We'll send some up for you."

"And Babette?" she asked, looking around until she found Babette chattering animatedly in a circle of young people.

"I'm still on duty," Remy said, appearing out of nowhere. He grinned at her, lifting his glass in salute. "She's safe on my watch."

Pia sighed over him. "I don't doubt it." Looking to Sam, she raised her arms. "Whisk me away, then."

"Don't mind if I do." He lifted her into his arms, reminding her of how he'd done the same thing after the standoff in the lighthouse had ended months ago. Her heart thumped wildly as the other cheered. She threw her head back and laughed.

Once they were out of earshot of the others, her arms circled his neck. "What are we going to do upstairs all by our lonesome?"

"I saw you eyeing the jet tub this morning," he noted, eyes glittering with promise. "I thought I'd draw you a bath, order some strawberries and sparkling cider from room service…"

"And?" she asked, anticipation sparkling through her.

"And then," he said, ducking out of the reception hall. He toted her to the elevator. "I give you the foot massage of your life."

She laid her head against his shoulder and beamed. "That sounds divine."

"After, you can take a long nap, undisturbed. Or…"

"Or?" she prompted when he trailed off, raising her brow.

"Or we can practice whatever it was Grace and Javy were doing in that closet."

She chuckled. "As long as we move the exercises to the bed, I'm willing."

He didn't let her down as they waited for the elevator. Instead, he tipped his mouth to hers and drank her mouth. "You taste like cake," he murmured, his lips bending into a smile over hers.

"You can feed me some more when Javy sends it up," she said, adding it to the list.

"Yes, ma'am."

"Sam?" she asked, twining his tie around her hand.

"Yes, Pia?"

"After the bath, the massage, exercise and cake…will you lay with me in the quiet and hold me? Just hold me?"

His expression turned soft. An ardent fold appeared in the space between his eyes. "I plan to do that tonight," he vowed, "and every night after."

The relief of that filled her to bursting. As the elevator doors rolled back, she tightened her hold around him, embracing him fully.

She'd found solace and hope, and everything in between, and she would hold onto it forever.

* * * * *